The Embezzler

The
Embezzler

by
Louis Auchincloss

Houghton Mifflin Company · Boston
The Riverside Press · Cambridge
1966

For two Blakes:

My son Blake Leay and
his grandfather, Blake Lawrence

Contents

Part I

Guy

1.

I HAVE THE distinction of having become a legend in my lifetime, but not a very nice one. In this year 1960, perhaps not
every schoolchild (for what do they know of America's past?)
but surely every college man who has taken even a casual course
in current history knows of Guy Prime. I am a symbol of financial iniquity, of betrayal of trust, of the rot in old Wall Street
before the cleansing hose of the New Deal. If I had not existed,
Franklin Roosevelt (who had a far more devious soul than
mine) would have had to create me. The Jews were not more
useful to Hitler than was my petty embezzlement to the Squire
of the Hudson. And the legend it has made of me has almost
destroyed my poor self. To my old friends and business acquaintances, such as still survive, even to Angelica and our two
children, I long ago ceased to have any real existence.

Of course, there must be occasional unpleasant things that recall the man as well as the legend. "Oh, yes, he *is* still alive," I
can hear them telling the persistent inquirer. "He lives down in
Panama, if you call that living. No, he's not so old. Seventy-
four, perhaps. Seventy-five? He was always strong as a horse.
We hear he has a nice little export business and a young Panamanian wife. He probably leads the life of Riley. Why not? He
always had the skin of a rhinoceros."

It is just as well that I should be remote, from mind as well as
eye. My grandchildren may have a better chance of being disas-
sociated with my deed. Evadne's children, of course, are Geers,

not Primes, and in American society, a maternal grandfather is too distant a connection to be much of a liability. The danger, if any, would be for Percy's boys, but happily for them, particularly if I am not around to force myself on the public attention, the fluffy abundance of Prime wool may almost suffice to cover that one dark hide. For the wool *is* fluffy. Considering the small civic contribution of the many descendants of Lewis Prime, that smug eighteenth-century Manhattan diarist and auctioneer, it is curious that the name should have developed so high and so aristocratic a flavor. I suppose a family is only the predominance of male issue, and certainly the male Primes, except for my own father, married well. As in the portrait gallery of a European castle where one's host, serene in his knowledge that a grand lineage swallows all, points out with equal complacency the ancestor who was a pirate and the grandfather who was a prime minister, so my descendants may take a collector's pride in bracketing, for the delectation of less exotic folk, the nefariousness of my peculations with the unctuosity of Bishop Prime's sermons.

Why then remind them? Why then this memoir? Because I have enough of my old egotism to think they may be interested. One may be interested, even if one does not care enough to be ashamed. Besides, I will let Evadne be the judge of who is to see these pages and when. If she thinks that my revelations will be painful to her children or to her nephews, or if she thinks that history has already done ample justice to my side of the story, then she need only consign this memoir to the flames. I trust her judgment better than I do my own. Portia has always been her natural role.

What I trust her to do, however, and what I *want* her to do may be two very different things. I passionately hope that my descendants may hear my case. I am convinced that I have been treated with the greatest injustice, not as to my prison term, which was perfectly in order, for I pleaded guilty, but as to the general opprobrium which followed it. What I did, however jailworthy, was not nearly so wicked as the world tried to make out, and in testing this I suggest that my grandchildren use either the moral standards of 1936 or of their own day, whichever they choose. If I have been made a pariah, it has been for the convenience of a great many people.

What it all boils down to is simple enough. Roosevelt in 1936 had already decided to regulate the New York Stock Exchange, but he still lacked an excuse that the greater public could understand. I came along providentially, and my example was howled to the nation. If a man in *my* position was a crook, what more had to be said? But Wall Street never understood this. Wall Street, the perennial ostrich, had no idea that regulation was already inevitable. Consequently it seemed to all those good burghers that I had let them down, that I had opened the gates, poisoned the reservoir, contaminated the air. I took my place in history as a financial Benedict Arnold.

I could laugh, I suppose, today, if I were not nearer tears. I have lived to see morals become frankly a game and businessmen treated by government as schoolboys are treated by strict masters. Prominent men now go to jail for evading taxes, or fixing prices, or forming monopolies, but nobody thinks the worse of them. In public life there may be rules of conduct, but they are purely formal ones. A presidential adviser may not accept the gift of a wristwatch from an old friend, but the senator who denounces him may make millions in office. So completely is it taken for granted that a man will prefer his own interest to that of his nation that our cabinet officers, men of the highest responsibility in the land, are advised to invest their private fortunes in government bonds. Compared to us the Panamanians are idealists.

But if I returned to New York today, would *I* benefit from this greater candor? Would it help me to point out that I served my term and paid my penalty and that the only persons who were out of pocket by my crime (in which I do not include my bankruptcy) were my wife, who had received from me far more than I ever took, and Rex Geer, a millionaire for whose financial start in life I was solely responsible? Certainly not. The late Mrs. Edith Wharton, who was a childhood friend of my mother's, wrote a very apt little story on this subject called "Autres Temps." It deals with a wife who is cast out of New York society for eloping with her lover and who comes back, a generation later, to find that the doors of her erstwhile friends, who have accepted the same conduct in her own daughter, are still closed to her. The world is too busy to revise old judgments.

Yes, they would all cut me dead in the street today, my old friends. Rex Geer, who might be a haberdasher in Vermont but for our Harvard friendship, would turn away his stony countenance and splash me with the wheels of his Rolls-Royce. Alphonse de Grasse, his partner, and one of my old golf foursome, might furtively nod as he hurried by, but only if he was sure that Rex's glassy eye was not upon him. Angelica's brothers, with their high harsh voices, might even insult me. And I remember them all, gathering about the long table in the sea-green dining room of "Meadowview," under Angelica's great Monet lily-pads, to organize, over the brandies and crême-de-menthes, a pool to push Oglivy Motors. Oh, yes, even the holiest of them went in for pools in those days, driving the stock up to dizzy heights before they dumped it and left the public to pick up the tab. Yes, even you, Rex, reading this memorandum over the shoulders of our common grandchildren! It may not have been quite "the thing," like the middle-aged husbands of Park Avenue who slipped off to stylish cat houses in West Side brownstones, but they did it!

The drama for which I could never be forgiven was not the drama of my trial, which was only a sentencing, but the drama of the federal investigation which followed. A hearing was held in New York in Foley Square, in one of those big bare varnished courtrooms that fail so oddly to capture either the spaciousness or the nobility of their eighteenth-century counterparts. Congress wanted to know all about the failure of Prime King Dawson & King and the extent of the involvement of de Grasse Brothers. Summoned from the penitentiary to testify, I sat with a police guard, watching the averted faces of my erstwhile associates. All of Wall Street, all its counsel, all the press were there. It was the Götterdämmerung of an era.

When old Marcellus de Grasse rose to testify, I thought his partners were going to rise with him, like a congregation following its priest. There was a tremor in his section, then a surge, then a subsiding as, coming to their senses, they restrained the impulse. The old dean of the banking world made his unsteady way to the stand, smiling with the timid graciousness of royalty, as if to fend off the assistance which even the humblest subject might presume to offer. In point of fact, this snowy-haired, pink-cheeked old gentleman, son of the founder of the firm whose name he bore and not founder himself, as the public believed, had lived largely in France for years and knew little of business affairs. I recall his gift to the *Alliance Française* of the busts of twelve figures famous in the history of Anglo-French relations. They began with Lafayette and ended with Marcellus de Grasse! Yet the Stuart adherents were not more scandalized by the spectacle of Charles I on trial in Whitehall than were the partners of de Grasse Brothers at the sight of their senior under the examination of Harry Cohen.

"When your partner, Mr. Geer, borrowed six hundred thousand dollars from the firm last September, did he consult you about it?"

"He did. It was a rule, when I was in New York, that I should be consulted about all advances in amounts over a hundred thousand. In my absence, my nephew would be consulted."

"Did it strike you as odd that Mr. Geer should need so large a sum?"

The pale blue eyes that Mr. de Grasse now fixed on his interlocutor suggested, despite the patrician benevolence of his manner, that he was quite aware of the other's antagonism. "Not in the least. He might have been low in cash and reluctant to market his own securities."

"Did he, in fact, tell you why he needed the money?"

"In fact he did, Mr. Cohen. But as the loan has since been paid in full, I fail to see its relevance."

"It is relevant to this investigation, Mr. de Grasse. In fact, I may say, it is of the essence."

"Very well. He told me that he needed the money for Guy Prime."

"Did he tell you why Mr. Prime had to have that much money?"

"He did not."

"What did you suppose?"

"I did not suppose, Mr. Cohen."

"Well, did you think it was for some unmentionable purpose?"

"Oh, good heavens, no. It was much too large a sum." Here the courtroom tittered, and Mr. de Grasse looked up to envelop it in his gaze of innocent surprise. "I knew Mr. Prime, and I knew that Mr. Geer was one of his closest friends. I assumed that there was some good reason for the loan. But that is not the point. The point is that Reginald Geer asked for the money. I would have given it to him had he vouchsafed no reason at all."

"So great was your faith in him?"

"So great, Mr. Cohen, is my faith in *all* my partners."

There was a stir of admiration in the room, but Mr. Cohen never flinched. As counsel for the Congressional Committee, he knew that he would have the last word. Balding, pale, with a lean feral face, blue cheeks, a fine strong nose and melancholy eyes, he might have been an ascetic monk by El Greco, but for an aridity about the thin lips, a twitch of the brow, a mannerism of scratching his chin that suggested our own more nervous era.

I remember contemplating how apt it must have seemed to the de Grasse partners that the Mephistopheles of the New Deal should be represented by a Jew.

"Three months later, I believe, Mr. de Grasse, Mr. Geer came to you once more for a loan," Mr. Cohen proceeded. "It was again a case of helping Mr. Prime?"

"Not 'again' Mr. Cohen," the old man replied patiently. "It was the *first* case of helping Mr. Prime. The other loan had been to Mr. Geer. The emergency was now beyond the scope of Mr. Geer's personal fortune. He came to me to recommend that de Grasse make a substantial loan to Prime King Dawson & King to save them from failure. That loan was not made."

"Why not, Mr. de Grasse?"

"On advice of counsel. It appeared that Mr. Prime had been guilty of irregularities."

"What irregularities?"

"The irregularities for which he was subsequently tried and convicted, Mr. Cohen!" Mr. de Grasse exclaimed testily at last. "The irregularities for which he is now serving a sentence in the state penitentiary! Surely, you don't wish me to recapitulate them for you. I suggest you call the District Attorney."

"I only wish to know who called them to *your* attention, Mr. de Grasse. Was it your counsel?"

"Of course not. It was because I had learned of these irregularities that *I* consulted counsel. Mr. Geer informed me of them. Before he could allow his partners to make the loan, he naturally had to give us the facts."

"But he did not do so in the case of the first loan."

"I keep telling you, Mr. Cohen, that first loan was to Geer personally!"

"I see. What I see less clearly is why you needed advice of counsel in such a matter."

"Counsel? My dear young man, I consult counsel in everything."

"I suggest that Mr. Geer wanted you to buy a respite for Guy

Prime so that Prime could cover up his embezzlements. Did a firm of your standing need the advice of counsel before rejecting such a proposition out of hand?"

There was a gasp of indignation from the bankers' seats, but Mr. de Grasse seemed quite unruffled. He took the high position of his years. "When you have lived a little longer, young man, you will learn that these problems are never quite so simple as they appear. I had known Guy Prime since he was a boy. He had once worked for me, and his firm handled our brokerage. I knew all of his partners, who were innocent of any irregularity, and who were bound to go down in his ruin. Several of his customers had accounts with me. They too would be affected. I was certainly not going to consign Guy Prime to perdition on any sudden impulse of righteousness. The matter had to be thoroughly explored. When counsel had done this, they concluded that we could have no further dealings with Prime. That we ran the danger of becoming accessories after the fact." Here de Grasse raised his hands and let them drop. "So there we were. We had to let him go."

"You mean if you could have saved him without criminal liability, you *would* have?"

"Isn't that question a bit hypothetical, Mr. Cohen? If it wouldn't have been a crime to save him, would it have been a crime that he had committed?"

I remember that I was as surprised as the rest of the courtroom that the old boy had it in him. The laughter that followed turned the El Greco friar into a grand inquisitor.

"Very well, Mr. de Grasse. Let me put you one more question. Did you ever consider that it might have been your duty to inform the governors of the Stock Exchange of what you had learned about Guy Prime?"

"Never."

"Yet your firm was a member, was it not?"

"Oh, yes. We have two seats. But I have never considered

that they put me under the obligation to be an informer. Perhaps if I had had the benefit of *your* counsel, Mr. Cohen, I might have felt otherwise. But I was not so fortunate."

"Thank you, Mr. de Grasse. No more questions."

I am not without a conscience, be it said at once. I know what I did and why I did it, and I believe that I have paid the penalty and should be quits with society. Yet I confess to a lingering remorse that I should have contributed to Mr. Cohen's little game. Like so many of the early New Dealers, he was a bit of a fanatic. Perhaps in the ideal society men will betray their friends and relations to the state, but I hope I shall not live to see it. When loyalty becomes the slave of patriotism, it is no longer loyalty.

The climax of the hearing came when Rex Geer was called. Rex at fifty-two was at the zenith of his banking career, which but for me might not have been the zenith. His appearance announced that his success was not superficial; it was as innate a part of him as his measured tread and his stocky build. Face to, his square regular face and small pronounced features, his high forehead and stiff waved graying hair made up too granite a wall to be quite handsome, but in profile and when talking, always with perfect articulation, the narrowed eyes, the raised chin, the slight hook of the nose, gave an impression of lively sensibility and intelligence. There was always a Lord Byron lurking behind Rex's Daniel Webster. In his youth, when he had been paler and thinner, and his eyes had been sadder and darker, girls had even found him romantic. Certainly my cousin Alix Prime did. But he was not romantic that day, in his costly black suit, the fingers of one thick hand clutching the Phi Beta Kappa key at his waist, his wide-apart gray-green eyes staring at Mr. Cohen with an unblinking balefulness. Rex would never admit it, but he was deeply anti-Semitic.

Certainly nothing about the examination was designed to alleviate this prejudice. Mr. Cohen spared Rex none of the details of his loan to me or the second attempted loan, underlining remorselessly his full knowledge of my depredations. At the end their two philosophies were summed up in pointed contrast:

Cohen: Tell me, Mr. Geer, as the partner of a member firm and as yourself a former governor of the Exchange, did you never feel that it was your duty to disclose to the Business Conduct Committee what you had discovered about Guy Prime?

Geer: You mean, did I feel it my duty to take the confidences of my friend and use them as the basis for his prosecution? It did not. I am not so Roman, Mr. Cohen.

Cohen: It is not only a Roman custom, Mr. Geer. In many American schools and colleges the honor system is practiced. It will only work, I am told, if the students are willing to report offenders.

Geer: Perhaps so. But the honor system is not practiced in the business world.

Cohen: The honor system, Mr. Geer, or honor?

Geer: I resent that, Mr. Cohen. It was quite uncalled for.

Unfortunately, the committee did not agree. Its findings spelled out the end of the age of the gentleman in all the complacent jargon of the new panacea:

> It is manifest from the testimony of the witnesses who loaned money to Guy Prime, all of whom were members of the Stock Exchange, and in particular from the testimony of Reginald Geer, that these men regarded the Exchange more in the light of a private club than a public institution. If a member erred, he had to be handled in such a way that the matter would not cause a scandal. This kind of code is hardly a policing adequate to protect the interests of today's investing public. The purchaser of a bond or stock is entitled at least to the protection accorded the purchaser of a patent medicine.

The legislation that followed the hearing had been drafted long before my arrest. Like the flight to Varennes and the fall of the French monarchy, my folly affected only the timing of things. But Rex and the others chose to see me as the traitor who delivered them to the Roosevelts and the Cohens of the New Deal. This was more dramatic than to face the fact that they were mere pebbles under the juggernaut of the socialist state.

Before I proceed to how it all happened I should offer a brief description of myself, as none of my grandchildren has ever seen me, nor does it now look as if any would. I have always been sturdy, but I am past the biblical life span, and the humid climate of Panama does not agree with me as did the cold dirty air of New York. My hair is as thick and curly as ever, but it is white as the snow I never see, and if I can still boast the broad shoulders and the straight build that made me the champion hockey player of St. Andrew's School, I must confess to a sizable pot. Still there are few wrinkles in my face, and my blue eyes are not yet gummy. When I slap my hand on the table at the Rivoli bar every afternoon at four and thunder at George for my first gin and tonic, people jump. Oh, yes, I am still what they call a "fine figure of a man."

Yet in my youth I was briefly beautiful. There is no other word for it. My grandsons may squirm, but let them look at the charcoal sketch that my adoring father commissioned Sargent to do of me (he could not afford an oil) when I was on my "grand tour" after Harvard. Maybe the features are banal in their regularity; maybe the curly hair, the straight nose, the manly eyes suggest a magazine cover hero, but show it to any girl in her teens and watch her reaction! In parlor comedy the heroine may turn down the blond athlete for the poet, the man "with a soul," but how often does it happen in life? Don't believe, my boys, all the claptrap you hear about women not caring about looks in a man. They know that beauty is rarer than "soul," and they grab it when they can. Ask your grandmother.

As early as my mid-twenties my face had filled out, and my shining quality was gone. I made the most of what was left of the Sargent youth by dressing immaculately and holding myself erect, but I fear that the word "beefy" was used behind my back, and Angelica in an ugly mood once likened me to an "Irish cop." When I was young I sought to charm; in my long middle age I sought to impress. Now, with dotage around the corner, I have returned to the earlier and safer tactic.

My life is very regular. Carmela and I have a small white stucco house with a red roof and a screened veranda from which we can see the Pacific. The dining alcove is set off from the living room area by a raised level and a partition of grilled iron-work. We have wicker furniture with gaily colored chintz, a mosaic cocktail table and a large watercolor of a clipper ship in full sail on a white-capped sea. How Angelica and Percy would sneer! But Carmela thinks it all very beautiful; she is per-fectly content with her old Yankee husband of the inexplicable (and to her uninteresting) Yankee past, who has raised her from a lower-middle-class status to one that is at least unclassifiable. She keeps a tidy house and leaves me alone. We never go out or entertain. She has her girlfriends for lunch, while I am in the city, and I have my precious two hours, from four to six, at the men's bar of the Rivoli Hotel. Only if I have one too many gins and fall asleep at supper does Carmel show her Latin tempera-ment.

At the Rivoli I live again. I sit every afternoon at the same table on the big white porch overlooking the palm tree garden and let any join me who care to. For some years few did, but I have now become a local character, even an institution, and the Rivoli management regards me as a drawing card. Not only do I drink free there, I receive cases of whiskey on my birthday and at Christmas. Panamanian officials of high rank, American army and navy officers, the Governor of the Canal Zone himself, join my table to discuss politics and personalities, wars and women. I think I get a greater kick out of having established the "round table" of the Rivoli than I ever did from being founder and president of the Glenville Golf and Tennis Club. But now I must be sure to limit my drinks even below the number that Carmela stipulates, for I plan to write this memoir in the evenings, and my head must be clear. A moment of truth, pure truth, may be my compensation. Surely it might be as intoxicating as gin!

2.

WHEN I THINK back on my days of glory, which reached their climax with their finale in 1936, they seem to merge with the glory of the Glenville Club. We both survived, but we survived as shells. We belonged too entirely to the era that made us.

Sometimes I think that, with the exception of Evadne, Glenville is the only part of my old life that I still miss. In the devitalizing humidity of the Isthmus, especially on those occasional Saturday afternoons when Carmela and I drive to Colon on a straight white bandage of a road through the wet, cluttered jungle alive with its glittering birds, I feel, like a damp cloth across my burning forehead, the memory of that softer, dryer green and of the high, serene porch front of the club house, a bigger Mount Vernon, overlording the rolling acres of its golf course, the neat copses of its woods, the polo field, the shimmering grass courts with their white-clad players. A country club? my grandsons may ask. What was so wonderful about a Long Island country club? Well, you see, my boys, there were clubs and clubs, but only one Glenville.

I was once offered a hundred thousand dollars to propose a dry goods tycoon for membership. Just to propose him, mind you, not even to guarantee his election. It may surprise you to learn that I indignantly rejected the offer and black-balled the would-be member when he had the audacity to have his name put up by another. Glenville, like all institutions that wish to survive, had to take its share of parvenus, but only when they had learned, if not altogether to be gentlemen, at least to recognize what gentlemen were.

To make it the first club of the Eastern Seaboard was my hobby. Don't think it was an easy matter. Young people never recognize the toil that goes into such things. I had the most efficient manager, the best golf and tennis pros, the quickest bartenders and the least rude waiters that money could hire, but these are all nothing without a vigilant master's eye. I checked every yard of the golf course myself, as I played it, and made periodic inspections of the kitchen, like an admiral, with white gloves. I met each candidate for membership and spoke to every delinquent dues payer. It was a working hobby.

You have probably already guessed that my real motive was to make Glenville my home. There I could be master; at Meadowview I was more like a guest. The latter was all Angelica's; she had copied it from a Georgian Irish house and blown her entire inheritance into it. Its moody romanticism, its big windows open on a field of black angus, its cool, high-ceilinged rooms and dusky canvases may have been as beautiful as her arty friends said, but it was a beauty that ruled me out. I was not so obtuse as to miss the point that Meadowview had been designed to enshrine everything that Angelica thought of me as threatening. We had long reached the point in our marriage where no questions were asked. I had my club, and she her Irish dream.

My happiest weekly moment was on Sunday when, after eighteen holes of golf with my usual foursome: Bill Dawson, my partner, Alphonse de Grasse and Bertie Armstrong, president of Merchants' Trust, and after a shower and an alcohol rubdown by the miracle-fingered Luigi, I would proceed, gorgeous in one

of my many sport coats, made for me in Glasgow, and a Charvet
tie, new each Sunday, to the submarine coolness of the men's bar
for the first gin of the day.

I would take my stand at the far end from the door. If another
was so ignorant or so presumptuous as to take my place, he
would receive a discreet whispered warning from Pierre, the
bartender. Conversation was general; those who wished to be
private went to tables. If there was a guest, I would address him
first, with my best "old New York" manners. Formality is not a
pitfall to one brought up to use it. With fellow members I was
louder and more blunt and with friends I might open with the
stentorian insult, delivered without hint of humor. "Well,
Judge, what decisions have you sold this week?" or "Good morning, Commissioner, who wrote that last speech of yours?" I was
a specialist in the seemingly filthy story that turned out innocently—and in its opposite. But I never repeated myself. I even
kept a notebook to be sure.

Oh, yes, the old ham, you will say. How he loved the deference, the prompt explosion of laughter, the exchanged glances
that implied: "Guy Prime is in rare form today." So long as
they laughed, did it matter if they were amused? Did I care if
they muttered in their teeth, "Look at the old fart!" so long as
they acknowledged the authority that limited their protest to a
mutter? I have always known what people thought of me. My
son Percy, who shrilly took his mother's side in everything, long
regarded me as the monarch of Philistia. How many times at
table, when I had expressed my fondness for the novels of Galsworthy or the art of Rodin or the music of Mascagni, had I
caught the exchange of visual sneers between him and Angelica!
Really, they seemed to be asking each other, how Babbitt could
Babbitt be? No doubt they still feel that way.

But they have never been to jail. They have never learned
the fundamental secret that one man is very like the next, that
our poor old shoddy human material is pretty much the same

beneath its surface manifestations. Consider how little flesh you have to cut off two faces to make them look alike. Guy Prime was a mask; we all wear masks. Thank heaven for them: they are what give us our individuality. Behind the mask my love of Galsworthy was the same palpitation as Percy's preference for Henry James. I cared as much as he for high thoughts and passions. As a young man I was even rather an aesthete, as he today, no doubt, is already rather a Philistine. But to my story.

My first hint of disaster, as ominous as the first dull throb of a fatal growth, came on a brilliant spring Sunday in 1936. As I proceeded, after my golf, from the locker room to the bar down the Audubon corridor, noisy with its prints, I saw Mr. Elkins, the club cashier, waiting to intercept me at the door of his office. He was a small, dry, tousled graying creature, a symbol of fidelity to duty in minor posts, with dandruff on the worn shoulders of his blue suit and eyes that looked like beetles behind the thick lenses of his spectacles. I nodded, a bit impatiently, for he was always waylaying me about trifles.

"Please, Mr. Prime, could I have a word with you?"

"What is it, Elkins? Don't you even take Sunday off?"

"I just came in to clear off my desk, sir. It makes Monday less rushed. Could I ask you about those America City bonds? The ones that were sent to your office to be sold and that the board then decided not to sell? They're still there, of course?"

"Where else would they be?"

"Oh, nowhere else, sir, of course. But it's been six months now, and Mr. Beal says it's most irregular for securities to be left that long in a broker's office."

"Even when the 'broker' happens to be president of the club?"

"It's not that anyone's worried, sir . . ."

"I should hope not, Elkins!"

Poor Elkins at this seemed about to weep. "It's the merger with Dellwood Beach, sir. The auditor has to see those bonds."

"Merger? Auditor?" I had arranged for Glenville to take

over a small near-bankrupt beach club on the Sound so that our
members could have the benefit of salt-water swimming. The
operation was only technically a merger. "Do you mean to tell
me, Elkins, that Dellwood has the presumption to look into our
books?"

"It's the agreement, sir, that the lawyers drew up. It calls for
each club to submit a statement. The auditor has to check our
securities. Mr. Beal wants me to make an appointment for him
to come to your office."

"You may tell Mr. Beal, Elkins," I retorted, "that when the
treasurer of the Club wants something of the president he can
come to me himself. It is not your function to discuss with him
my duties as bailee of club property. May I remind you again
that it's the Lord's Day?"

And I proceeded ineluctably on my way to the bar.

The America City bonds with which Mr. Elkins was so unhappily obsessed that morning represented the bulk of a million
dollar fund that I had raised from the membership for the construction of a stately pleasure dome that was to contain, among
other amenities, a vast swimming pool and two indoor tennis
courts. Remember that we were still in 1936 when the dollar
could buy something. The reason that the bonds had not been
returned was that a portion of them (a small one, as I then believed) was sitting in the vault of de Grasse Brothers as security
for one of my personal loans.

Wicked? Certainly, by all the ancient laws. But those laws
were passed when little children were hanged for stealing
spoons. The first thing that a fiduciary of our era requests is that
he be given the broadest possible powers. And he is promptly
given them. Fluidity is what people seek. My customers show-
ered me with powers of attorney. They did not want a bailee or
a trustee out of some dry volume of Blackstone. They wanted
Guy Prime, and the reason they wanted Guy Prime was that he
knew his market. Had I not been adviser to Herbert Hoover in

the first days of panic and the voice of de Grasse Brothers on the big board? Was not my firm known to the wags on the floor of the exchange as "Jesus Christ, Tom, Dick and Harry"? I had trained my own ship, picked my own crew and set my own course. In the roughest financial seas of our century I had kept her off the shoals, and I would have continued to do so had people only let me. Why should I weep for the money they lost in my wreck? It was the price they paid for the luxury of sending me to jail.

The group at the bar now opened to greet me. My opinion was sought about Karl Vender, a rough-and-tumble character who had made a killing in the Insull collapse and who had recently purchased one of the old estates in the neighborhood. Would he make a proper member? I thought so. It was one of my functions to pass on the new people.

"My father as a young bachelor in the 'seventies used to call on Commodore Vanderbilt," I told the attentively listening group, when Pierre had handed me the white brimming glass of my first Martini. "Of course, the ladies of the family did not accompany him. The Vanderbilts were not then what they are today, and the old boy's house was full of clairvoyants and charlatans and even worse. But Father always said that a bachelor could go anywhere, except, of course, to a fag party." Here I paused, raised my glass for a sniff and then drank off half the contents at a gulp. "He told me an interesting thing about Vanderbilt. The old pirate was not naturally coarse. He only pretended to have come from a low social milieu to magnify his success and to irritate his children. He made a tableau for history, and history bought it. I suggest that Vender may be doing the same."

George Geer had joined the group and was watching me with the respectful look of a prospective son-in-law. He was then twenty-six, a smaller, slighter, handsomer version of his father, under whose exacting supervision he toiled at de Grasse. He was informally engaged to my daughter Evadne, and everybody took for granted that I was delighted. Perhaps I should have been. He was honorable and industrious, and would probably one day be as big a man as his father. Yet at the moment he was an unpleasant reminder of the bonds sitting in that same father's vault. Rex had always condescended to me, and now his boy had to have my girl.

I left the bar, carrying my drink, and, putting my free hand on George's elbow, propelled him to a table. "Tell me something, fella. I know you have your father's memory. Do you happen to recall how many America City bonds I put up for my loan at your shop?"

"I think it was three hundred and fifty thousand, sir. I can check it for you right away. There's always someone in the office."

"No, no, don't bother." As I stared at George's face and made out the gathering mist of surprise in his bright eyes, I realized that an astonishing thing had happened. I had momentarily lost control. I was paralyzed, and in my paralysis I was perfectly aware that I could not afford it, that I had to smile, to cough, to whistle, to do anything to check that young man's growing astonishment. I even had a sudden shocking glimpse of a future in which such dissimulation might always be necessary, a future that was separated from all my past by the scarlet band of this very moment.

"Is there something wrong, Mr. Prime?"

"Nothing, George, nothing at all. Only I think I'll go back to the bar. Sometimes, when I look at you and think that here's the man who's actually going to take away my Evadne, I have a kind of shock. But don't worry. I'll come around. God bless you, my boy."

I talked with the men at the bar, but I could talk to them and think of the other thing. I could talk to them and speculate that I might at last be losing my mind. Three hundred and fifty thousand! My stock of Georgia Phosphates, the principal security for my loan, had been dropping badly all winter, and I had been tossing everything I could lay my hands on, including some of the America City bonds, on the pile at de Grasse to prevent a sale, but I had not dreamed that it had reached even a fraction of such a total. If what George said were true—and could one doubt it?—more than half the Club's bonds were hypothecated for my loan.

"Coming to lunch, Guy? It's nearly two."

"No, go ahead, fellows. I'll join you later."

I would go to Karl Vender in the morning. He would give me the money quickly enough. But I would have to watch myself in the future. I was alone now in the bar, for Pierre had gone to the pantry, and I surveyed the desolate pink face that loomed over the sport coat in the mirror facing me. Was *that* Guy Prime? That scared rabbit? That fat phony? Slowly, carefully, almost solemnly, I raised my empty glass until it was high above my head and then hurled it with all my force at that fatuously staring image. The shocking smash brought instant ease to my troubled soul as it brought Pierre, unblinking, back to the bar.

"There's been an accident, Pierre," I said impassively. "I seem to have broken my glass."

"Yes, sir. Shall I fix you another drink, Mr. Prime?"

"No, that will be quite enough. I'm going in to lunch now."

If the rest of the world would only be as sensible as Pierre, I reflected, I might still come out all right. But Pierre was part of the club I had created. I had not created the world that I faced each Monday.

3.

WHAT WAS the background? Well, what is a family? Is it anything more, as I have already suggested, than the predominance of male issue over female? We speak of families "dying out," simply because the direct male line from father to son has been snapped. The hundreds of descendants of Lewis Prime, who came from Liverpool to New York in 1740 to establish an auction business, include some of the most distinguished merchants and lawyers of Manhattan's history, but few of them were Primes. All of our renown, such as it is, rests on the simple fact that my grandfather, the Reverend Chauncey Prime, Rector of Trinity Church and later Bishop of the Episcopal Diocese of New York, had seven sons who made almost as many famous matches. *Puck's Weekly* in 1881 ran a cartoon that showed railroad and steel magnates desperately piling up their bags of gold before a group of tall, indolent, blond young men in sports clothes, with tennis rackets under their arms, who barely condescend to glance at the bait thrust under their languid eyes. It was entitled: "What Your Money Will Buy, or The Quest of the Primes." A decade later, in the 'nineties, the same bait was sent over the Atlantic in search of coronets, but by that time my uncles were all comfortably settled.

How did they do it? What did they have? Certainly not brains, nor business acumen, nor imagination, nor wit, nor even great looks. They were tall, slim and very straight, and had long, rather wooden, oblong faces that bore age well. Their resemblance to each other, which was of great assistance to the younger ones, was almost comic, for the father of an heiress, seeing that his neighbor in Newport had done well with one Prime, was pleased to find another available. The new rich always copy each other, and once the Prime fashion had started my uncles had only to bow to it. They had only, in short, to believe in themselves and in the world that constituted their immediate environment.

That may have been the answer, that they never questioned anything. They were too serene ever to suffer from the acidulous suspicion that is the bane of the conservative; they smiled with a sniff at the future, just as they smiled with a shrug at the mention of a name that they did not know socially. They did everything one had to do well but not too well; excessive expertise in the saddle, at the card table, even on the golf course, might have seemed "showy." Only in clothes did they really let themselves go, as if from some deep consciousness that their true function was to decorate the stage of society and persuade the observer that it was real. When I think of them now, I think of grays and whites and blacks, of striped trousers never wrinkled, of maroon gleaming shoe leather, of pearl studs and gray spats and gloves, of canes and tall gray hats, of gray against emerald garden parties, of gray against the glittering blue of a Newport sea and under a bright sun. My uncles at least made measured sense out of a life that was notoriously a source of discontent to the many who lead it.

Oh, they were bargains, all right, cheap for the relatively little they cost. They were faithful husbands, unlike the peers who followed them, and conscientious stewards of the money they had married. Like figures in Saint-Simon, they had implicit confidence in the validity of the social game as it was played from day to day. They grasped it by instinct, which was the only way to grasp a game without logic or even a set of rules, sensing intuitively which parvenu would make the grade and which divorcée would be forgiven, covering up the inconsistencies, like good priests of Mammon, with a mellifluous roll of generalities in which they at times almost believed. It is not surprising that their descendants should have totally lacked their style, for the later Primes inherited caution and thick skins with the maternal wealth, and concentrated more on the keeping of dollars than the making of friends. Indeed, by the time I grew up, the money of Fisks and Goulds and Villards had become so associated with my relatives that people began to believe there must have been a great Prime fortune. It was this legend, perpetuated in the social columns of a thousand evening journals, that created the particular problem of my youth.

For my father, Percy Prime, had married for love. He was the brightest and the most attractive of the brothers and had been expected to make the greatest match. There was even, uniquely among Primes, something of the artist in his make-up, for he saw the world of parties as something that could be made as beautiful as one aspired. To him the organization of a cotillion or picnic, the seating of a dinner table, the selection of wines and music, were matters quite as important as the making or merger of corporations. There could be no point to the latter without the former, he always insisted, as there could be no point to splendid moneymaking without splendid expenditure. What saved him, as it saved his brothers, from the ridicule of his male contemporaries, was that in the role of social arbiter and adviser to hostesses, a role usually associated with the effeminate, or at least the epicene, he was uncompromisingly strict and masculine. Father was just as happy among the gentlemen after dinner as with the ladies at lunch. I see him now, with his chair pushed back, his long legs carefully crossed, leaning forward to place his brandy glass on the edge of the table and turning, with the easy deference of a trusted staff officer, to ask the richest man present his opinion of the last government intrusion upon industry. He knew little of such matters, but he knew how to ask a good question.

It may have been precisely Father's trouble that he had too much imagination. It may have been why, in the short run as well as the long, his brothers did so much better. Bellevue Ave-

nue and Fifth must have been at times the least bit nervous at
what their images might be in Percy Prime's bright, blank, serenely gazing, sky-blue eyes. Society people, at least in that day,
like to glaze their materialism under the icing of religiosity
and the spun sugar of a late Victorian sentimentality. But Father refused to apologize for his own materialism; he reveled in
it, boldly baring the very facts the others sought to hide. He
conceded with a blatant cheerfulness the sisterhood of the Colonel's lady and Rosie O'Grady and deduced without a qualm that
only a bank account separated the New York top from the New
York bottom. What then, he would conclude, was more glorious, more worshipful than money? New York worshiped
money, to be sure, but not in public or on Sunday, and Father
caused uneasiness with his vigorous genuflections to the golden
calf.

Why then did this paragon of the age of elegance, who could
have dipped his beaker in those fulvescent waters on whose surface his words were always skipping, bear it instead to the stag-
nant shallow pools of old New York? My maternal grandfather,
Jonas Fearing, had been accounted a merchant of substance; he
had a Swiss chalet at Bailey's Beach and a chaste red brick town
house on Washington Square; he was a charter member of the
Century Association and a friend of William Cullen Bryant.
But what was all this in the dawn of Standard Oil? What was so
fascinating about my mother, of faded prettiness and gentle
ways, dowdy of dress, utterly unaware that it was not still a
world of Fearings, already thirty-six years old and distinguished
solely for having once won the ladies' archery contest at Mrs.
Julia Ward Howe's?

Perhaps it was her very unawareness of the times. Perhaps it
was Father's nostalgia, born of the bitterness that must have
lurked beneath his flamboyant philosophy, for that simpler society which Eunice Fearing represented to him, the New York of
quiet afternoon calls in brownstone streets, of a mild rubbing of

elbows with landscape painters and even Shakespearean actors, of long midday meals with Madeira to which the men came home, of insularity and integrity, of small minds and high principles. I have always treasured my Grandfather Fearing's scrapbooks and still spend an occasional evening, with a pleasure that Carmela can never fathom, turning the pages of old hotel menus and calling cards, of photographs of gabled houses and crowded porches, of huge engraved wedding announcements and diminutive *Times* obituaries. Mrs. Wharton knew what she was doing when she called this era the "age of innocence." It may have been its evocation that Father in a sentimental moment, surfeited with Mammon, considered his salvation. He should have reflected that sentiment is short and salvation long.

They were married, at any rate, Percy Prime and Eunice Fearing, the exquisite forty-year-old bachelor and the stately, demure virgin, and all Newport went to the wedding in the summer and gathered afterwards on the lawn around the chalet and drank the couple's health by a shimmering sea. It was a question of their starting at the top, for thereafter everything seemed to slide, inevitably if almost imperceptibly, down the long gentle velvet incline of a life in which there was never quite enough to do but just enough to keep one from doing more.

From my beginning, all Father's hopes centered in me. My sister Bertha, Mother herself, being women, could not help. He made it clear that everything he had was mine: all of his little money and his greater ambition and all of his peculiar brand of love—peculiar in that I shared it with no one else. He never hurried me, never pushed me, rarely complained that I made no higher grades or grander friends. I could take all the time in the world and have all the fun in the world, but when I was ready, he wanted to know. That was all.

And when I was ready, he set me up; he established me in the firm which thereafter bore my name. He bought my seat on the

Exchange and put up the capital. He did it by using all the money, in a single magnificent gesture, that he had *not* borrowed from his rich brothers in all the long hard years of his married life. Never once, even when mother was at her most ailing, did he take a single penny for her doctors or for her pleasures. On the contrary, he poured out sums that he could ill afford in presents for his wealthy sisters-in-law and nephews and nieces, on birthdays and on Christmases, and nearly bankrupted himself paying tips to their servants and buying outfits for their sporty weekends. It was bitter tea, keeping up with his rich relations, but he did it all with a view in mind of the day when he would be able to go to his brothers and say: "Never have I dunned you before. What will you do now for my only son?" And when that day came, the money was forthcoming as readily and as willingly as he had foreseen. My uncles were not imaginative, but even they could appreciate so perfect a father's love.

In all the wreckage of my career there remains one thing for which I continue to be grateful to the dark deities who presided over my collapse: that Father never lived to see it. He died, at ninety, in his room at the Glenville Club, which I always reserved for his spring visit, after attending a great dinner that I had given in honor of the visiting King of Siam. He had seen me reach a social altitude never attained by his brothers, and he expired with his own particular *Nunc Dimittis* on his lips. It is perhaps of some significance that the only person I never let down was the only person whose faith in me was complete.

4.

I WAS ALWAYS very proud of my office, which was unique for Wall Street. Prime King Dawson & King occupied the top floor

of No. 65, but the banal, if splendid, view of the harbor and the
Statue of Liberty I had abandoned to my partners and employees. For myself I had kept the noble chamber in the center of
the floor, forty feet by twenty, possessed of no window but entirely covered by a great skylight. On the walls, painted a glis-
tening white, I had hung my Grandfather Fearing's collection of
Hudson River canvases: "Source of the Amazon" by Church,
"Storm in the Catskills" by Cole, "Indian Bivouac" by Durand.
The effect of these, with their rolling mountains, broad prairies
and tumbling rivers, was to make one feel as if one were rushing
across the American continent in a low-flying, open plane.

The first of my callers, on that spring Monday morning of
1936, after the Sunday revelations at the Glenville Club, was my
junior partner, Bert King. He brought the sorry news of another terrible slide in Georgia Phosphates. His long handsome
face, still boyish at forty, had become pinched and dry with
eight years of anxiety.

"You make me wonder if the ancients didn't have a point," I
complained. "They used to put the bearers of evil tidings to
death. If I'd tossed you out the window years ago, do you think
my luck might have turned?"

"I'll save you the trouble, Guy. I'm ready to jump now."

I tried to picture how he would look if he knew what *I* knew.
Decidedly these younger men, depression weary, lacked the
bounce of my generation.

"Buck up," I told him. "It can only get worse."

My grandsons will learn from their elders and betters that
foolish investors always blame their failure on bad luck. But I
wonder if even the wisest watcher of the market could have foreseen the hurricane that wrecked my Caribbean resort island, the
patent suit that delayed the production of my Vita-Glass houses,
the title flaw that paralyzed my phosphate mines, the federal investigation that slandered my tranquilizer pills. If only one of
these projects had been realized in 1936, my troubles would

have been over. All were realized ultimately—that is the killing part. If I owned today the stock in those four companies that I owned twenty-three years ago, I would be richer than any partner in de Grasse.

When Bert left, my secretary rang to say that she had Jo Beal, treasurer of the Glenville Club, waiting on the line to talk. Jo was one of those serious-minded insurance executives in whom the need to please is at constant war with their natural sense of the bleakness of things.

"Sorry to bother you, Guy," he started straight off, "but Elkins said you wouldn't discuss the America City bonds with him at the club yesterday. I know he had no business bothering you on Sunday, but we are a bit pressed with the board meeting tomorrow. Do you think I could possibly make an appointment for the auditor to see those bonds this afternoon?"

"I won't be in this afternoon, Jo."

"Couldn't someone in your office take care of it?"

"Handling securities? Certainly not. I always like to take care of those things myself." My tone was mild, but my fingers were gingerly tapping my rapidly dampening brow. Was it possible that my margin of operation had dropped to a single day?

"What about this morning, then? Suppose I bring him over now?"

"I'm afraid I have appointments all morning."

"But, Guy, that makes it a bit tough on me, if you don't mind my saying so. I put it on the agenda of tomorrow's meeting that we would ratify this merger with Dellwood Beach. If it has to go over to the fall meeting, the whole deal may fall through."

"Well, I don't see how we can do it, Jo. What about next week? I'll be freer then. If Dellwood doesn't like it, to hell with Dellwood. We can find plenty of other beach clubs to merge with."

"Now, Guy, what kind of talk is that?" There was a sudden sharp whine in Beal's tone, and I sensed the immediate diminution of his old-time awe of me. How fast we fall when we fall! Like comets, as a thousand poets have said. "You're not going to make us lose Dellwood because you can't find two minutes for an auditor, are you? Besides, it's not Dellwood's auditor who's requesting the check. It's ours."

"I still don't see why next week isn't just as good. We could call a special meeting of the board if we have to."

"Look, Guy, those bonds are *there*, aren't they?"

I had to catch my breath at this. What could have happened to make Beal so bold? Were there other losses besides Georgia Phosphates of which I was ignorant? Had word got about that I had pledged the bonds? Or was there some bit of bad news in the air, perhaps unjustly attributed to me, of which no one would speak? That is the hell of the market: everything affects it, most of all untruths. "Of course, they're here. But they're down in the vault, and it's not convenient to dig them out. Not today, anyway."

"Well, I don't see it, I'm sorry. You won't let the auditor check them and . . ."

"I didn't say that, Jo."

"That's what it seems to boil down to. I'm going to report to the club board tomorrow that you've had those bonds for six months and can't find two minutes to exhibit them!"

"Very well, Jo," I said softly. "You do just that."

"I'm sorry, Guy."

"*I'm* sorry, Jo. That you should feel compelled to push me around this way. But I shan't put up with it. I have not organized and developed a great club to be treated in this fashion by one of its junior officers. We will *both* have our reports to make tomorrow. Good day, Jo."

As I sat, contemplating the telephone that I had replaced in its cradle, I considered what else I might have said or done. It was a bad hand to play, but it seemed to me that I had played it for all there was in it. What more could be expected of a man?

And now, for the first time, I faced with unblinking eyes the possibility that I could go to jail.

I am happy to record that my nerves steadied as my sense of the danger intensified. Leaving my office for a walk, I found that I could even take a curious interest in the totality of my disaster. With Georgia Phosphates down and only twenty-four hours before the Glenville board meeting, I was in a hopeless position to raise three hundred and fifty thousand dollars, unless I could get them from Rex Geer. It was out of the question now to go to Karl Vender. It was out of the question to go to anyone to whom I could not make a full confession. And how few would be those of my friends and acquaintances who would not be secretly delighted at the spectacle of my catastrophe! Oh, I did not kid myself. Nor did I blame them. Only in war, when disaster is the rule, do men lose their taste for it.

I walked west toward the big black Gothic spire of Trinity that loomed at the end of the narrow corridor of Wall Street like a giant phallus, fitting symbol of the ruthless world of male competition. It was much more to me the house of my family than the house of God, for my grandfather had been Rector there before he had been Bishop and my ancestor, Lewis Prime, was buried in its graveyard under a chaste black stone. As I passed beneath the portal of the twelve apostles I slackened my pace and squared my shoulders, trying to look as if my visit was a usual occurrence. It is always risky for a financial man to be seen entering a church on a weekday.

I sat as usual in a back pew near the marble bas-relief of my eagle-nosed grandfather. It had been the seat of my few market inspirations. I felt no impropriety in using a church for such purposes because Trinity seemed to me to stand for what the Primes stood for: the survival of a small, tough piece of Knickerbocker New York on an island overwhelmed with the old poor of the old world and the new rich of the new. Of course, Trinity was not itself very old, being the replacement of a twice-burned church and designed in the eighteen-forties by that same Up-john who had built my grandfather's Newport villa, but it was still older than anything else in the street, and richer, too, for it owned blocks of the very downtown land on which the new money was being made. Yes, it was a kind of Prime.

But Trinity and I were not in tune that morning. I felt that it might forgive me my crime but never the exposure. Old New York knew too much about the value of appearances. And would even my physical appearance pass? I remembered the image in the mirror over the Glenville bar: the ruddy face, the tweedy look, the vulgar health, the seeming loudness. What had any of that to do with the lean dark meanness of the early Primes? Had honesty fled with boniness, and virtue with the stiff collar? Would not my own father have distrusted a broker who went to work in a colored shirt? Was it any real argument that fashions changed?

There remained the Almighty. His only begotten Son in the altar window, flanked by the four evangelists, was richly caparisoned in sapphire and scarlet. All the other windows in the austere church were as plain as Primes; only over the altar, only in the Redeemer was there color. Could that mean there was redemption for me? It is a curious fact that in all my visits to Trinity Church, only in this last one did I pause in all my giddy associations to consider my relations with God. It was no time to neglect potential allies.

In my childhood Mother had been the one who had cared about matters spiritual while Father had concerned himself exclusively with the here and now. As she had always ailed and as Father had enjoyed robust health, I had grown up to think of God as a rather heedless being who neglected his devotees. If only Mother had depended on *me,* I would mutter to myself as I watched her bowed in prayer, *I* would not let her down! But Mother seemed aloof to terrestrial help. Her eyes sought only eternity.

I have a photograph of us, taken when I was fifteen, which has always graced my bureau, even in jail, even in Panama. Mother is seated stiffly in a high-backed chair, her waved white hair and diamond choker recalling the style of photographs of royal persons, but her thin cheeks and rather haggard intensity bespeaking a world of worries. And I, round and uncoordinated, with blond straight hair parted in the middle, seem to have strength to spare, life to throw away, as I lean awkwardly over the chair, one arm about her seemingly quivering shoulders, as if by hugging her I could give her some needed transfusion of vital energy. Yet she, erect, uncompromising, willful in the agony of her love for me—agony because she knows that she will die and leave me and that big as I am, strong as I am, I cannot do without her—seems with desperate gaze fixed on the camera to deny my help, not only because she is doomed and beyond it, but because she knows that I will need every scrap of strength that I can offer her for myself.

Father never objected to Mother's religiosity until it threatened to affect his plans for me. Then he acted quickly and decisively.

One Christmas vacation, down from St. Andrew's, I got drunk at a debutante ball with two of my cousins. They were sober enough to see me home and up the three narrow flights of stairs in the family brownstone without awakening anybody, but they could not help what happened afterwards. I was sick to my stomach, abominably sick, and Mother, whose room was directly under mine, appeared in my doorway as white and terrible as an angel on Judgment Day.

"Go down on your knees!" she cried in a hoarse, unfamiliar tone. "Go down on your knees in your vomit and pray God to forgive you for this night's wickedness!"

And down I went on my knees, and she too, in my vomit, by the side of the bed, while she prayed aloud.

"Dear God, may this disgusting performance convince this sinning child of the error of his ways. Lead him from the gutters of Mammon to the clean avenues of Thy presence. Teach him

the dangers of the frivolous pursuits of society and make him see
the stinking cesspools that lurk below its lacey covering."

Yes, people in 1903 could still talk that way. But one person
who never had any use for it was Father, and by my third piece
of bad luck in one night, he too was aroused by the events on my
floor. When he appeared in the doorway, in his red and black
silk dressing gown, he might have been playing Mephistopheles
to Mother's Marguerite.

"For heaven's sake, Eunice, what are you doing out of bed at
this hour? Do you want to catch your death?"

She turned to him, still on her knees. "Can't you smell it?"

Father raised a handkerchief to his nostrils. "I can detect the
aftermath of an evening where boys seem to have been rather
too boyish. But surely you don't expect God to clean it up, do
you? That's a lot to expect, no matter how hard you both pray.
May I suggest that we move Guy to the guest room and close the
door here until our faithful Agatha can get to this mess in the
morning? Unless, of course, you want to rouse her now?"

"Percy, have you no concern for our boy's soul!"

"Really, my dear, at three in the morning? There's a time for
everything. Let us all get to bed."

Mother was on her feet now, almost distracted with her concern. "Percy, this may be our last chance to save him! Don't
you *see* what's happening?"

And then, suddenly, the operetta was over. Suddenly a very
different sort of drama began to unfold. For the first time in my
life I saw Father drop the air of faintly mocking gallantry with
which he habitually treated Mother.

"I'm afraid I *do* see, Eunice," he said in a chilly tone. "I'm
afraid I see that you're trying to turn the boy into a molly-
coddle. He's got to learn to live in this world before he learns to
live in the next. You, my dear, have always avoided that, but
you are not a man. It is my job to see that Guy understands the
things a gentleman must understand. Religion is only one of
these. Drinking is another."

"Percy!"

"I realize that shocks you, my dear, but you've brought it on yourself. You know that I brook no interference with my plans for Guy. Not even from you. I am quite determined that he, at least, shall enjoy the experience of living."

"You call what happened tonight *living?*"

Mother was leaning forward now, one hand over her mouth, as though she, too, were going to be sick, her other hand and arm jerking sharply up and down in a gesture that seemed desperately to protest any answer that he might make. My agony at hers tore at my stomach like a saw. She seemed to be having a kind of a seizure, but when I ran to her she thrust me roughly off.

"Father!" I shouted. "Don't you see you're killing her?"

Mother swayed to the doorway and down the stairs, clutching the banister as she went. I hurried after her, with little groans of commiseration, but she would not turn, and when she reached her door she shut me firmly out. I even heard the key turn in the lock. I think I would have pounded on it in hysteria all night had Father not followed me and turned me around to shake me by the shoulders.

"I'll tell you something important, my boy. Women are a good deal tougher than they look. Watch how mercilessly they treat each other. If I hadn't learned that, your mother would have long ago turned me into a lapdog."

The next day he was as charming and courteous to Mother as if nothing had happened, but there was no question in anyone's mind as to who had won the bout of the night before. Mother continued to fight for God in dozens of little ways, reminding me to go to church, putting a Bible on the table by my bed and warning me never to place another book on top of it, applying Scripture to all kinds of small humdrum problems, but she never again came to my room at night to urge me to pray for forgiveness. God, her God, had been put in His place.

What could a man do but stand on his own two mortal feet? What could a man not do but not drivel and fawn and weep? I rose now and left Trinity for what turned out to be the last time. Neither Christ nor His evangelists, nor Peter with his keys, nor the good bishop behind me with his fine aquiline nose, had any message that I could carry to my creditors.

Returning to my office I dialed Rex's number myself. The de Grasse operator told me that he was in a partners' meeting, but I insisted that she tell his secretary to get him out. When he finally came on the wire, he sounded very cross. "What is it, Guy? Can't it wait till tonight?"

I had quite forgotten that he and his son George were dining at Meadowview. It was to be a family party for a discussion of wedding plans with George and Evadne.

"I've got to have three hundred and fifty thousand dollars by tomorrow morning," I said flatly. "It's a matter of life and death."

"God, man, what's up?"

"I'd rather not tell you over the phone."

"Can you give me an idea?"

"Well . . ." It was before the days of universal wire tapping, and I knew that our old switchboard girl did not listen in. "I've got to get hold of the America City bonds in my security account at your shop."

"All of them? Why?"

I moistened my lips and then threw it at him. "Because it so happens that they're the property of the Glenville Club."

"You mean the Club *allowed* you to pledge them?"

"I mean no such thing. The Club doesn't know."

"Jesus, man!" Rex's tone was high and piercing, as it always became, soaring from its usual low gravity, in moments of crisis. It had an immediately calming effect on me.

"You see my problem."

"But, Guy, how *could* you?"

"What's the use of that, Rex? You're my last chance. It's you or ruin."

"I'll have to think about this. Good God, it's not easy, you know! I'll talk about it tonight."

"But, Rex, I have to have those bonds in the morning. *If* I'm to have them at all."

"You will. *If* you have them at all."

"I knew I could count on you, old man. Friendship is thicker than blood."

"I haven't promised anything."

"Of course not. You never do."

No sooner had I put down the receiver than I picked it up again to ask my secretary to call Jo Beal. She got him before I had even had time to gauge my reaction to Rex's reaction.

"Jo, I've been thinking about those bonds," I started off. "I guess it was silly of me to let you get my back up. After all, you were only doing your job. The board meeting tomorrow is at five, isn't it? Suppose you round up that auditor and bring him here at noon? I'm going to the vault at eleven, and I can pick up the bonds then."

Jo simply collapsed. It was surely the worst diplomacy in a man of his supposed business acumen to reveal so baldly what his suspicions had been. "Oh, Guy, that would be just swell! Of course, I'll bring him. But if it's really inconvenient for you, I'm sure we can arrange it for another time. Dellwood can wait. Hell, they're only too glad to merge with us, anyway."

"No, as you said, there's no point making an issue of something that's going to take fifteen minutes. Tomorrow at noon, then. And bring an armed guard so you can take the bonds back with you. I had thought they were as well off in the president's vault as in the treasurer's, but after all, I *am* a broker. Let's do everything according to Hoyle."

I hung up and stared at "Storm in the Catskills" and wondered sadly what was left of Guy Prime now that he, like his daughter, was to be delivered to the Geers.

5.

FATHER ALWAYS felt that my best friend, Rex Geer, and my wife, Angelica, were the two great mistakes of my life. Certainly, my relationship with each was entered into over his open protest. I think I can see now that they represented, not so much my conscious desire to defy him—for Father was rarely so arbitrary as to put himself in a position where defiance was a feasible act—as my desire to impress him. I wanted to show him that I could acquire something on my own, that I could pick out of the corners of a world into which his elegance did not shine some golden nuggets of whose very existence he was ignorant, yet whose value, thrust under his nose, he could hardly deny. Of course, I should have known that Father was a past master at denying values.

If Angelica's family were to stand for the corner, unvisited by my parents, of cultivated and cosmopolitan living, Rex's were to fill up the corner, unvisited at least by Father, of evangelical religion. The Reverend Jude Geer was a fine, big, spare, clean man of God, the Congregationalist minister of a small Vermont parish, and his wife, as large and spare as he, had borne him eight splendid children of whom my friend was the senior. In middle age Rex was to publish privately for his friends and relatives a memoir entitled "My Boyhood in a New England Rectory," which I privately subtitled "From Lux to Lucre." But in sober fact the Geers were almost too good to be true.

We did not become friends until junior year at Harvard. Our lives were too different. I existed luxuriously on the liberal allowance that Father, for all his scrapings, managed to put aside for me. I took courses in English and history of art and submitted gaudy poetry to the *Advocate;* I entertained liberally at restaurants and fancied myself a terrific dandy. But, for all my social efforts, I had few real friends. Oh, true, I had dozens and dozens of the friendliest acquaintances; I was probably welcome in more rooms than any other man in the class. Why not, with high spirits and a bubbling laugh that could pass for wit? Nor was I the Philistine that many people later supposed; I could quote copiously from Matthew Arnold, Ernest Dowson and Oscar Wilde, and I considered "The City of Dreadful Night" the most powerful and terrifying poem ever written. I could talk until dawn about life and sex and go freshly to class without having slept an hour. I knew all my professors and called at their houses. Was I simply too bright-eyed, too anxious to please, too much the young aristocrat, the Pendennis, the Clive Newcome, to be quite believable?

Today I would have been considered ripe for a serious love affair, but in 1906 this was not so usual a solution. I had held hands and necked with the less discreet debutantes of the period and had imagined myself the summer before (to Father's disgust) passionately in love with one of my poor Fearing cousins, and I had passed, with bursting pride, the customary tests of manhood in Boston cat houses. But to fill the great gap in my young and surging heart I needed a friend, a particular friend, a Pythias, a Jonathan, who would direct me as well as understand me, who would help me prove to myself that I was a man as well as a Prime. And just such a friend did I think I had found in Rex Geer.

This is not all hindsight. I knew what I needed at the time, young as I was, and when I saw Rex I seemed to recognize at once my solution. He was already one of the prominent men of '07: a powerful debater, a first-rate boxer, and, academically, first in the class. Only a reputation for extreme sobriety and toiling industry (he was, of course, a scholarship boy) dimmed his popularity. Rex, like his family, was, if anything, a bit too worthy.

Yet I liked his worthiness. I had plenty of qualms about my own frivolous existence—Mother's shafts had not all been thrown away. I was attracted to a man who was as ascetic as even her standards could require. And Rex was a fine fellow to look at, too. He was handsome, not with the bursting blondness of my brief moment in the sun, but with a taut, tight cleanness that has lasted through the years. His later became the face that magazines like *Fortune* always wanted to illustrate articles on Wall Street. It hardened; it was hardening even at college, but it was the rigidity of justness and clear thinking and exact application. Rex had short, stiff, wavy, inky hair that he never lost, and wide-apart, brooding, gray-green eyes that rarely committed themselves. His brow was high and fine, his nose Roman, his complexion pale and clear. When he became angry, his features settled slowly into a formidable, craggy expression. But in college his high cheekbones and pallor still gave him at moments an almost romantic air.

We had known each other from the beginning in that smaller Harvard, but Rex had little time for friendship and less for butterflies, in which category he had obviously placed me. I might never have bridged our gap had I not called in his room one night, on the excuse of borrowing a book, and found him in such a funk that he was willing to talk to anybody.

"I've got to chuck it, the whole thing, college and all. I've got to go home and get a job. My baby sister has developed a spot on her lung, and Dad's at his wit's ends. She may have to be sent out west . . ."

"But I thought you supported yourself," I interrupted.

"I do. But it's a question now of my having to help out."

"I never heard such a thing!" I exclaimed indignantly. "It's bad enough that you should have to pay for your own education, but must you support your parents, too? Haven't you got things just a bit topsy-turvy, my friend?"

"In *your* world I would have," he snapped back with a ferocity that made me jump. "It's dog-eat-dog on Fifth Avenue and Newport. But we poor don't know any better. We honor our fathers and our mothers!"

"I'm sorry," I said humbly. "Please tell me about it."

Which he finally did. A Boston millionaire named Bennett had offered an annual prize of a thousand dollars (in those days a considerable sum of money and to Rex a small fortune) to the Harvard undergraduate who should submit the best paper on economics. The judge was a professor of history, and the prizewinner was selected in March. Rex had submitted a paper on the Sherman Act, for which he had high hopes, but now he did not see how he could afford to wait. It was only January.

"But all the papers are in?" I asked.

"Oh, yes, they've been in a month."

"Then there's no reason Professor Henderson couldn't read them and let you know if you'd won?"

"What professor ever read a paper before he had to?"

"But he *might,* mightn't he, if someone asked him?"

"Dream on, my friend."

I sat with Rex another hour, but when I left, instead of going to my rooms, I went boldly to call at Professor Henderson's house. I found him working in his study on the papers for the competition. He was a small, silent, wizened old fellow, surrounded by a terrible mess of books and papers, and though we had never met, he listened to my introduction and my story without apparent surprise. When I had finished, he thought for a while.

"I daresay most of my colleagues would regard your request as outrageous, Mr. Prime. But it happens that I don't. I like friends who do things for each other. My trouble is simply this. I have already read Mr. Geer's paper and been impressed with it. If I read the others now, will not your sad tale have prejudiced me?"

"I shouldn't think you were so easily prejudiced, sir."

"Nor would I. But people talk. What assurance have I that this matter will be a secret between the three of us?"

"My word of honor, sir!"

And indeed Professor Henderson did not rely in vain upon it. Only as I write now has our secret been communicated, three decades after his demise.

The professor sent for me in two days and told me that Rex's paper was the winning one. My difficulty was in making Rex believe it. He thought at first that it was some hideous practical joke, and we came very near to having a fist fight. But when at last I took a Bible from his bookcase and solemnly swore on it, he was convinced. He threw his arms about me and let out a shout of joy. It was my first inkling of how much emotion this sober young man was capable of.

Celebration was my field, and I took him on the town, where I made another discovery. Rex was one of those men who find it impossible to stop doing anything they have started. If he was working or taking physical exercise, or arguing or playing cards or even drinking, his enormous energy and momentum would not allow of cessation. Rex was actually a man of great violence, if of great self-control. I remember him in the early hours of that next morning, as we finished off a fourth bottle of champagne, fixing me, still sober, with glittering eyes.

"Frankly, Guy, you amaze me. I thought I had you all figured out. The kind of plush New York snob who feels he has to booze his way through four years of Harvard and make an acceptable club before settling down in a brokerage house and waiting for his old man to kick the bucket. But, damn it all, you have a heart. As big as a mountain! Shall we have another bottle of champagne? Are you sure you can afford it? Are you rich? Oh, yes, you told me—the poor branch of a rich tree. Yet in *your* poverty you can buy champagne. Do you know this is the first time I've ever tasted it? But I won't boast about that. I mustn't be that kind of prig. Damn it all, Guy, shall we be friends?"

Basically, he needed a friend as much as I did. He had been too busy and too poor for college social life. From that evening on we saw each other daily. I induced him to relax, to go on hikes, to have a few drinks on Saturday night, even to go to an occasional party. He kept me from cutting classes and from going to New York on too many weekends. What it boiled down to was that he helped me to work and I him to play. There was always a grasshopper and cricket aspect to our relationship.

But I was a good deal more than a grasshopper. I planned for the future quite as intensely as he did, probably more so, for Rex was engrossed in the toil of his present. As spring approached, I opened a campaign to make him promise a summer visit to my family in Bar Harbor. He protested violently that he had neither the right clothes nor the right manners for such a swank resort, that he could not play the right sports or even dance, that my parents would be ashamed of him and, finally, that he could not afford the railway ticket. All was in vain; I tore down each excuse as he put it up. I had enough summer clothes for both of us; I exempted him from social life and promised that we would not play tennis or golf, but simply walk, swim and fish; Mother herself wrote to invite him; Father procured a railway pass. What could my poor friend do in the end but submit?

6.

MY WHOLE small Machiavellian scheme was simply to install Rex in the good graces of Mr. de Grasse. The great man had al-

ready offered me a job in his firm after graduation, and I intended that he should do the same for my friend. I knew my
own limitations and Rex's capabilities. I knew the fault of his
stubbornness and the virtue of my flexibility. I knew the advantages of my connections and the indispensability of his industry.
We were a team made in heaven. But I had sufficient acquaintance with my friend's demonic pride to know that matters would
have to be arranged so that Mr. de Grasse's offer, if it came,
should appear to have come spontaneously. It would not be easy.

Marcellus de Grasse, head of the banking partnership that
bore his name, had been my parents' summer landlord since I
could remember. He owned a pine-covered hill, overlooking
the village of Bar Harbor, with a magnificent view of the bay
islands and sea, on the crest of which perched his big, stone,
multi-porched, styleless mansion, "The Eyrie." There were three
much smaller shingle villas on the hillside abutting his mile-
long driveway, one of which he leased to my family. Father was
never one of his intimates, but as a contemporary of the large,
shy, giggling de Grasse daughters I was frequently invited to the
big house. In time, however, my invitations came from the
master himself. The boy and the tycoon had formed an odd
friendship.

He seemed on a first meeting almost effete. He was tall, thin
and very languid, with ivory skin and brown, wig-like hair; one
half expected him to raise snuff to his nostrils with a rustle of
lace cuffs. He professed to despise everything that had happened since 1850, and he found New York and even poor little
Bar Harbor hopelessly vulgarized by the stampede for wealth
that, to his eyes, had blotted the fair and promising copy book of
American history. Because his grandfather had owned a fleet of
clipper ships, he always tried to identify de Grasse Brothers with
the China trade and what he deemed the cleaner marine atmosphere of those earlier days. He had filled the little Doric temple
at the corner of Wall and Pearl Streets, which housed the family

bank, with prints of sailing vessels and the harpooning of whales, with paintings of Chinese ports and of Chinese merchants, with cases of rare porcelains and golden dragons. Not for him were the spittoon, the ticker-tape, the dreary photographs of bearded, dead partners.

Yet the little airs and mannerisms by which the world makes its judgments and which should mean so little to the seeker of truth, meant even less in his case than in others. The essence of Marcellus de Grasse was in the speculative quality of his intellect and in his own delight in its exercise. He hated reference books and compendia of statistics. When a question arose, he liked to sit back, clasping the arms of his chair with his long white fingers, and seek the answer by pure deduction.

When I first struck his attention as something more than a friend of his daughters, we were sitting in his study after a de Grasse family Sunday lunch at which he and I had been the only males. He happened to apologize for speaking sharply to the butler, who had brought the wrong brandy. I suppose he was embarrassed to have shown his irritability before a boy.

"One should never be impatient with servants," he told me when the man had gone. "They can't talk back. Besides, one doesn't pay them enough to abuse them. They're not like lawyers or doctors."

"But they have their commissions," I pointed out. Father had made me worldly wise in such matters.

"Commissions?"

"They get a percentage in the village on everything you buy."

"Dear me, is it as definite as that?"

"Oh, yes, sir. To be the de Grasse butler is a very great thing in Bar Harbor. Ida, our cook, told me he could retire after five years."

"And what would you do about it if you were de Grasse? Fire him?"

"Oh, no, sir. But I might make him divvy up!"

Mr. de Grasse was amused. "I see you should be the banker, young fellow. You make me feel very naïve."

"But it's not your fault, sir. Father says it's simple to steal a dollar from a man who is always thinking of millions."

"Does he so? And if I was always thinking of dollars, I suppose somebody might pinch a million."

"Yes, you have to be careful. Father says everyone thinks a man who was born rich must be a fool."

Mr. de Grasse's lips just parted in a thin smile. "I confess I have sometimes taken advantage of that very prejudice. On occasion it can be extremely valuable to be thought a fool."

It amused him to find out what Bar Harbor thought of him, and I was very candid. From that time on he would invite me up of a rainy afternoon to read in the big library where he did his work and where there was a bookcase of excellent boys' books that had belonged to his oldest son, who had died. Sometimes we would read silently to ourselves and sometimes talk. Mr. de Grasse was a novelist *manqué*. He could tell wonderful stories of his father and grandfather, of clipper ships and the Orient, of the West and wars with the Indians, of the building of railroads and the laying of cables. We were both romantics. And then, too, we were both nature lovers and kept bird lists and, despite his aversion to all forms of exercise, I once got him halfway down his own hill in quest of warblers.

As I grew older I began to anticipate the inevitable time when Mr. de Grasse would become bored with me. I had a sure instinct in such matters, and I knew that my youthful liveliness would not always make up to him for my lack of a genuinely philosophical mind. I kept him as much as possible on the particular and away from the general. In history I liked to talk about the kings, in religion, the martyrs and in economics, the great robber barons whom Mr. de Grasse had known. Not for me was the colosseum of general ideas. When I complained to him that I had been born too late in American history for true adventure, he chilled me a bit with the sarcasm of his sympathy.

"Yes, I can see, Guy, that you should feel that. The slaves have all been freed, and the West has been won. The railroads are built and every beggar has his flush toilet. But I think you may find, if you come to work for me, that there's still some adventure left. You were born to the great age of the dollar, of the speculator, of high finance! It should take us a century to plunder our new land, and don't worry, the banker will be in the vanguard. Ah, yes, you look askance at my levity. That's right: young men should be serious. And it's a very serious thing that no matter what virgin forest any pest of a speculator may wish to cut down or what stinking mill he may wish to put up on its site, he will always find a banker to give him his money!"

"But not you, sir!"

"No, Guy, not me." He shook his head almost wearily. "But I am a privileged person. At de Grasse we are small enough and old enough to do our own picking and choosing. It is not really a moral choice. It's more that life's too bloody short not to do the worthwhile thing. That's a rich man's luxury."

How he inspired me! The detached contemplation, the bemused induction, the ultimate decision taken in silence and calm; that was how I pictured him at work. A great, grave doctor by the bedside of our economy, finger on pulse, meditating a transfusion. Was it wrong of me to have plotted to share that with Rex? I never fooled myself that I was Mr. de Grasse's intellectual equal, but I was convinced that Rex was. It seemed logical to suppose that if I brought him into my relationship with the older man, he might fill in its empty corners, and indeed for a time it worked out just this way. The start, however, was inauspicious.

We were asked to lunch at the big house on the first Sunday after Rex's arrival. I persuaded my friend that this was not really "social life," so he reluctantly went. Our host, unfortunately, was in one of his sullen, silent moods, and Rex plunged into a similar one in the unfamiliar atmosphere of the dining room with its yellow and brown clothed walls, its dark angry lithographs of bears and lions in their native habitats (Mr. de Grasse did not waste his taste on country abodes) and its bay window through which shimmered the glory of Frenchman's Bay, but unreally, like the view from a prison castle in a child's picture book. Mrs. de Grasse, Boston bred, whose father had built "The Eyrie," presided benignly but uncommunicatively over our sparsely enjoyed meal, and the three girls, still shy but now grown sentimental, like so many of the daughters of intellectual men, giggled at private jokes among themselves. In desperation, I brought up a topic that Rex had forbidden me.

"It might interest you to know, Mr. de Grasse, that my friend here is the winner of the Bennett award."

"Oh, for pity's sake, Guy!" Rex hissed.

"And what, pray tell, is the Bennett award?"

"It is a prize for the best Harvard economic paper of the year," I persisted. "Rex wrote his on the Sherman Act. You know, the law that's putting the fear of God into all those highhanded tycoons you complain about?"

"I know the Act," Mr. de Grasse said drily, "and I admit the complaints. But I wonder if the cure isn't worse than the disease. It may be one thing to suffer the slings and arrows of outrageous magnates, but it's quite another to live in a police state where no man is allowed to distinguish himself from the mob." He turned one eye now on Rex. "I suppose, Mr. Geer, as a young intellectual, and no doubt as a radical, you approve of this legislation?"

"I think the weak should have some protection from the strong, sir. If that makes me a radical, I suppose I must be a radical."

"And the constitution, what of that?" Mr. de Grasse had flared a bit at Rex's tone. "Or do you subscribe to Wendell

Holmes' theory that it is a mere barometer of public opinion, to be interpreted according to the whim of the prevailing majority?"

"I don't understand that to be Justice Holmes' theory, sir, but then I don't claim to be an expert on constitutional law. Still, I can't see why it should be wrong to save little businesses from being eaten up by big ones. Unless the founding fathers meant to codify the law of the jungle."

"You don't think a man should look out for himself? You think he should run to the government every time he takes a licking?"

"Do you know what you put me in mind of, Mr. de Grasse?" Rex had by now lost what little awe and reticence he may have had. "An expert swordsman in an age of musketeers. You know there are bullies about, but so long as you can defend yourself, you don't worry about those who can't. And you oppose any ban on dueling on the ground that it will turn men into fops."

"One can make a very good case for dueling . . ." I was beginning, but nobody listened to me. Mr. de Grasse and Rex were too thoroughly engrossed in their own fight.

"You would run society, Mr. Geer, for the benefit of its weakest members?"

"For them, sir, as well as the strong."

This was Rex Geer speaking! Rex, who in another quarter century would be one of the principal critics of the New Deal, one of the last champions of *laisser faire!* But we should not be surprised. Such transitions are common enough. The twentieth century has moved much faster than its citizens.

"That attitude spells to me the end of everything exciting and colorful in the world," Mr. de Grasse now protested. "I don't say that I want a world populated only by Borgias and Medicis, but if you legislate them out of existence, don't you lose your Da Vincis and your Michelangelos too? There must have been some connection between the two."

"If there was, we've lost it today. I doubt if Saint-Gaudens makes up for Jay Gould." Here Rex actually slapped his hand on the table as he moved into the offensive. "But the real point against the Borgias, Mr. de Grasse, is not so much that they rob us as that they corrupt us. You think, sir, that you can conduct a gentleman's banking business in a world of swindlers. But you can't. In a market place the lowest permitted standard is bound to become the prevailing one."

Mr. de Grasse at this turned away from Rex altogether. "Of course, if you're going to call a man a swindler in his own house," he muttered, and then he said no more.

This was very bad, and for the balance of the wretched meal I made nervous conversation about the new pool at the swimming club with Mrs. de Grasse.

Rex apologized to me in sulky fashion on the way home, but I told him, a bit shortly, to forget it. That afternoon I took my copy of his award paper up to the big house and left it with a note for Mr. de Grasse saying: "It may be better to read Rex than to hear him."

In the morning I went up again and found the old boy in his study, actually reading the paper. I say "old," for so he always seemed to me, though I doubt if he was more than fifty-five at the time.

"I heard a great horned owl at two this morning," I told him. "I have an idea he sleeps in the big elm by the old stable. Would you care to walk down and see?"

"What about your friend? Won't he come?"

"He thinks he's not exactly *persona grata*."

"Is he such a sensitive plant?"

"Not in the least. He simply doesn't like to push in where he's not wanted."

Mr. de Grasse sighed. "Doesn't he know anything about the petulance of the elderly? Tell him to make allowances. And give him this." He opened the superb leather-bound

copy of Herbert Spencer's *Social Statics* that was always on his desk and wrote on the fly-leaf: "From d'Artagnan to Richelieu: 'Almost thou persuadest me to give up dueling.'"
"There. Bring him up for lunch. If he'll come. I don't feel up to the great horned owl today."

From then on, for the rest of Rex's visit, everything went beautifully between him and Mr. de Grasse. Inevitably, I felt excluded from their technical discussions of economic matters, but I consoled myself by remembering that they owed their friendship to my machinations. My satisfaction was complete when, after Rex's return to Vermont, on a Sunday night after supper in the big house, Mr. de Grasse asked me:

"Do you think your friend would be interested in coming to work at de Grasse?"

"Why don't you write him and ask?"

"Because he's so prickly. But I'll certainly try."

My scheme, however, was still not implemented. Back at Harvard I found that Rex had received Mr. de Grasse's offer but had not yet accepted it. He was suspicious.

"I can't owe *everything* to you, Guy. You get me a prize that keeps me in college . . ."

"I had nothing to do with that."

"Well, anyway, that's the way it's beginning to seem to me. You give me a summer vacation, you launch me in a swank resort, and now you get me a job. You'll probably fix me up with an apartment in New York and a rich wife!"

"But don't you see what you do for *me?*" I retorted with mock gravity. "I was a libertine, and you've made me serious. I was a prodigal, and you've made me respectable."

"You don't even know me," Rex continued gloomily. "You've never met my family. You probably can't imagine how different they are."

"Why don't you invite me to your home?"

"Would you come?"

"Ask me!"

And so it was arranged that we should go to Vermont on the
first weekend when Rex thought he could properly cut his
Saturday classes, which was not until November. In East Putnam I shared his bedroom on the third floor of the old Gothic
rectory that was attached to the church, and, for the first and
last time, I met his parents. It was not, in later years, that
Rex was ashamed of them. On the contrary, he was tremen-
dously devoted and tender. But they were simple folk, very
pure and very silent, and he saw nothing to be gained by dis-
turbing them with the company of more sophisticated souls.
He did not hide them; he protected them.

Jude Geer was afraid that his son would be corrupted by
New York sharks; his wife, that he would be corrupted by
New York women. I thought they were both very dear and
very naïve; later, I was to wonder if they were not rather
shrewd. The girl whom they favored, the girl "next door,"
Lucy Ames, as bright and pert and good as the heroine of a
Trollope novel, was obviously in love with Rex, and he,
equally obviously, was not in the least in love with her. The
three of them made rather pathetic efforts to win my favor, as
if I represented Rex's future and they only his past. They did
not understand that nobody represented Rex, I perhaps less
than any.

It was nice of them, however, not to identify me with the
evils and temptations that would await Rex in New York.
They seemed charmingly to take for granted that his best
friend must have all the virtues and not the vices of the dangerous new world that he hoped to conquer. Lucy discussed
with me whether or not Rex should go to law school before
becoming a banker, his mother asked me if he ate regular
meals at Cambridge, and the Reverend Geer, to whom I devoted my particular attention, ended by consulting me about
his next week's sermon. When Rex discovered me with his fa-

ther, in the latter's study, examining on a biblical map the route of Moses from Egypt to the promised land, he burst into a hoot of laughter.

"I think, Dad, we're giving the poor man quite a dose of East Putnam!" he exclaimed. "But he's passed every test with flying colors." As he led me forcibly away, he spoke in a tone that was almost gentle: "You win, Guy. You've seen me everywhere now: at school, in Bar Harbor, at home. You've seen me every place I've ever been! If you think de Grasse is the spot for me and that I'll fit in there, well then, let's try de Grasse. Who am I to slam the door in opportunity's face?"

7.

REX AND I took an apartment together when we came down from Harvard to work in de Grasse. My uncle Lewis Prime let us have the commodious third story of his carriage house just off Lexington Avenue in Sixtieth Street for a nominal rent, and I decorated it gaily, as I hoped, with *art nouveau* theatrical posters and odd bits of Tiffany glass. Father wanted me to live at home, and he looked askance at my continued friendship with Rex, whom he had found a surly, socially unprepossessing fellow in Bar Harbor, but he was much too wise openly to oppose the arrangement. He thought it entirely fitting when Rex informed him that he would always regard the apartment as mine and himself as merely the subtenant of a single bedroom. But I, of course, could have none of that. I would have shared anything with Rex, even my girls.

Most fathers of that day worried that their sons' friends would lure them to pleasures; mine was afraid that Rex might

entice me to overwork. Father seemed to see my poor subtenant as a clerkish Lorelei with an account book instead of a
golden comb, and, as an antidote to Rex's influence, he reminded me constantly of my duty to take up what he called
my "position" in New York society.

"Success, my boy, isn't only a matter of grinding away at
the office. That's all very well for a fellow like Rex Geer who
hasn't any other way up. You mustn't forget that we live in
an overpopulated, overeducated world where it's always possible to hire a hack to do the technical job. It's *getting* the
job that counts. And where do you get the big jobs? Where
the big people are, of course!"

I pointed out that Mr. de Grasse seemed to care very little
about the business that his clerks brought in and quite a lot
about how they did their work.

"I don't say you're not to do your work properly," Father
retorted testily. "Of course, you are. And de Grasse is an excellent place to be apprenticed. But I have greater plans for
you than to spend your life as junior partner to some de
Grasse heir or nephew, looking after old Marcellus' daughters' money!"

I knew what Father's "greater plans" for me were: he
wanted to set me up in a brokerage house to be called "Guy
Prime & Company." My next question was indiscreet enough
to bring on one of our rare quarrels.

"Will there be room for Rex in those greater plans?"

"My dear boy," Father answered, with his most provoking
condescension, "you will forgive me for saying that you seem
to be quite infatuated with that young man. If I am to set you
up on Wall Street, it will be with men of your own class. I
haven't worked all my life for the future of Reginald Geer."

"Worked!" I could not help exclaiming. "Excuse me, sir,
but when did you work?"

Father's face turned a faint pink, a most unusual phenomenon with him, and those long agile fingers twined and re-twined themselves around the silver handle of his walking stick. "Never mind how I've worked," he reproved me sharply. "One day you'll find out and beg my pardon for your impertinence. One day you'll learn which is your truer friend: your father or that young man."

"Do you imply that he's using me?"

"Certainly, he's using you, and I don't blame him in the least. These things aren't done in cold blood, mind you. The circumstances create them. You will understand that when you've watched the human ant heap as long as I have. Young Geer is by nature a self-aggrandizing animal. He moves up-wards wherever you put him. Of course, he'll crawl over you, if you let him. He can't help himself. He wants the moon. He wants to be first in de Grasse, first in Wall Street, first in society."

"Rex cares nothing for society!" I cried indignantly.

"Rex cares for anything he hasn't got," Father said emphat-ically. "You think, because he doesn't enjoy things, that he doesn't want them. You're dead wrong. He may want them just because someone else has them, but he still wants them."

None of Father's suspicions, however, could cloud my relationship with Rex. In that first year of our apprentice-ship our friendship was at its apex. He came with me to my family's for Sunday lunch and was asked to my uncles' on holi-days and special occasions, as if he had been a Prime. Some-times I took him to parties, but more often he preferred to stay home and work and hear about them later from me, sit-ting up over a cigar and a glass of brandy. Our only disagree-ments were over my failure to work as hard as he. One night, after a particularly grand dinner at Uncle Lewis', I must have described the guests with some of Father's fulsomeness, for I provoked him into retorting:

"Those men didn't get where they are by going out to din-ner parties when *they* were young."

"Didn't they? Where would Chauncey DePew have been without the Vanderbilts? Where would the Pratts and Paynes have been without Mr. Rockefeller?"

"You think too much of money-making, Guy."

"But we're in the money-making game! You may not judge a doctor or even a lawyer by his income, but how can you rate a money-maker except by the size of his pile?"

"Banking isn't just money-making. Banking is starting new businesses and saving old ones. Banking is helping the right man over a bad time. Banking is keeping the heart of the economy pumping. If you don't feel that way about it, you ought to quit and become a stockbroker."

"You and Father!"

But I had no idea of becoming a stockbroker, and seeing that I had really irked him, I held my peace. I was determined to make good at de Grasse, and Rex, in his own way, was trying to help. He was constantly checking on my work, reading over my market reports, suggesting areas of additional research, filling up our brief lunch periods with talk of stocks and bonds. His attitude was rather irritatingly tutorial, but I knew that it did me no harm.

What *did* do harm was the contrast that he unconsciously obtruded between himself and me, not so much to other eyes as to my own. There was something about Rex that made all non-Rex activities seem foolish. And so I was constantly pretending to be something I wasn't, nodding my head and clearing my throat and starting sentences, statistic-laden, that I could never seem to finish. I read much of what Rex read, but I could never retain it as he so uncannily did. His mind was a whole glittering philosophy of finance, and every customer of de Grasse, like one of Browning's broken arcs in the poem he loved to quote, seemed part of a perfect round above. It was only away from Rex that I could abuse him as an astigmatic who saw order in the jungle and Christian discipline in the wolf pack. In his presence, his relentless logic and inexhaustible figures reduced me to sullen acquiescence.

I see now that he should have had more sympathy for the role played in Wall Street by men like myself. I was a salesman and he was a moneylender: that was the basic difference. What he should have encouraged me to do was to develop myself into a salesman of de Grasse. My view of Wall Street may have been naïve compared to his—I admit that I took a childish pleasure in the crisp heavy paper on which securities were engraved and in the promises of fairy tale wealth that they seemed to contain—but a naïve view can still be a contagious one. Reading and study, at least of business facts, were not my *forte*. My mind simply turned off after too many pages, and I would be torn between angry resentment and drowsiness. When I came home I was glad to go out again to dinner, any dinner, to sit next to a pretty woman and drink a good deal of champagne and talk gaily. Was that not youth? What else was youth for?

Our best times together were on weekends. Rex loved of a Sunday to take a train down to the South Shore of Long Island and hike through the marshes and along the beaches of Cedarhurst and Lawrence. On these occasions he would throw off the monastic earnestness of his banking hours and behave with a gay and infectious enthusiasm. He would even sing, loudly and off tune. Like many men of large intellect and moral seriousness, he could be very boyish when he relaxed. One had to have seen him in such moods to understand the attraction that he was capable of exercising.

All of this brief gaiety, however, blew away with his first love affair. Of what use is the wisdom of the ages? Young men will still go to war and still fall in love with the wrong women. They will believe, till doomsday, that dolls like Alix Prime will catch fire from their fire and learn love from their ardor. It is really hardly fair to the dolls, who are not to be blamed for their doll-like natures. Rex, like many impov-

erished, ambitious young men of his day, had kept sex too
long at bay. To cause an explosion within him, Alix did not
have to be either beautiful or charming. She had only to be
female.

She was an heiress, the daughter of Uncle Chauncey, the
stiffest of my uncles and the one who had made the greatest
match. She was pale, blonde and well shaped, with a high
chirping voice that expressed enthusiasm for all the things
over which a debutante was supposed to wax enthusiastic.
You couldn't fault her; she liked the best books and the best
plays and the best scenic views and the best people. It might
have been forgivable, even in a first cousin, had she only been
dumb. But Alix wasn't dumb. None of the Primes were dumb.

I knew, of course, that she and Rex had met. He had been
with me to Aunt Amy's and Uncle Chauncey's on two or three
occasions. What I did not know was that he had gone back
alone. One Sunday afternoon, in early spring, as he and I
were exploring a marsh near the sea in Lawrence, our conversation fell, accidentally as I then thought, on my cousin. I described her casually as a stuck-up mannequin. Before I knew
it, he had jumped on my back and thrown me to the ground.
I wrestled desperately for some minutes before he was on top
of me, his knees pressing my shoulders down. Of course, he
had surprise on his side. I could not at first believe he was in
earnest.

"Take it back," he demanded hoarsely.

"Oh, Rex, for Pete's sake!"

"Take it back or I'll stuff your mouth with mud."

"All right, all right, she's anything you want, an angel, a
goddess, what the hell!"

I got up sullenly while he excoriated me. "The trouble with
you, Guy, is that you're a cynic. You can't see that girl's a million miles above the usual debutante type. Oh, she lives in
your silly social world, yes. Where else can the poor creature

live? She has to do what her parents say. But that doesn't
mean she wasn't born for better things."

"Like Rex Geer," I suggested sulkily, brushing off my
pants.

"Don't even think it!" he exclaimed wrathfully. "How
would I dare aspire to the likes of her?"

"That's right, she's a Prime, isn't she?" I retorted. "Forget
her, peasant."

Well, obviously he wasn't going to do that, and how could
he court Alix without my help? We were in 1908, and Uncle
Chauncey was not about to hand over his finest flower to
adorn the buttonhole of the son of a penniless rural parson.
In a few more minutes he had to beg my pardon, and when I
grudgingly accorded it, he threw an arm over my shoulder and
gave me a squeeze and then hurried off to lose his embarrassment in a rapid walk. We did not speak again until the station, and then, as we sat waiting for our train, he asked me a
dozen questions about Alix. In the crowd of hot excursionists
returning to the city, amid soft drinks and crumpled newspapers and howling babies, we talked of Alix at dancing class,
Alix at Miss Chapin's, Alix reciting "Evelyn Hope" at Aunt
Amy's Christmas party, Alix in pink and white sitting with her
mother for a portrait by Porter. I did not tell him of the
time Alix did wee-wee on the rug and let me be punished for
it, or of how we used to make fun of her for her crushes on
older girls, or of her temper tantrums or of how Aunt Amy was
supposed to have wept before Miss Chapin to keep her from
being suspended for cheating. No doubt Alix no longer remembered these things herself. When the violence of the
teens congeals into the kind of sandy surface that she presented to the world, it is possible that the memory itself may
be affected.

What I found difficult to make out from Rex's version of his
romance was to what extent his emotion was reciprocated. I

suspected that Alix was probably both flattered and surprised by the passion that she had aroused, but that she did not know what to do with it. What does one do, after all, with a real stove in furnishing a doll's kitchen? Yet I was sure of one thing. I was sure she was Prime enough to appreciate that it had some value.

"You'd better let me work on it," I told him later that night. "We'll see what ideas I come up with. After all, it's more my field than yours."

The following Wednesday was Aunt Amy's "at home," and I left the office early to call at the great red and white brick Louis XIII *hôtel* that Uncle Chauncey had reared with her money on upper Fifth Avenue. Aunt Amy was the biggest, simplest, nicest, plainest old shoe in New York society. She looked like a cook dressed up as a duchess; she had pink hair and a round brown face that was inclined to be sad when it was not very merry, and she kissed half the people who came into the room. Unfortunately, she was also a secret drinker and had little of the will power that one usually associated with hostesses of her type. My uncle, small and dour and generally absent from her receptions, controlled her absolutely.

"Guy, honey," she exclaimed when she saw me, "you're cute to come! Tell me about that handsome roommate of yours. He's become quite a caller here. How do you make him talk? I declare I can't get two words out of him."

"Rex is not a ladies' man. I suppose he chats with Uncle Chauncey?"

"With Chauncey? I don't think Chauncey's even met him."

This was good. Certainly, the less Rex saw of Uncle Chauncey, the better. "Maybe you scare him, Aunt Amy."

"Me? As if I could scare a fly!"

"Perhaps it's your pearls, then. They are ominously large."

I found Alix in the library and took her to a window embrasure. As the oldest of my generation I was rather a hero with my female cousins. I used to quiz them and advise them on all their little love affairs.

"You've been holding out on me," I said severely. "Did you think I wouldn't find out?"

Alix cast down her eyes with a demureness that I was supposed to be stupid enough to take seriously. "I can't imagine to what you are referring."

"You can't imagine that, sharing an apartment with my best friend, I might have a suspicion when he's smitten?"

Alix's oval, pale face became almost stern. What did he *see* in her? She twitched her shoulders, and her satin crackled. More than ever she was like a doll in an expensive dress. "I fear that Rex has been indiscreet."

"If you call infatuation indiscretion. The poor fellow's in such a bad way that he almost beat the life out of me for abusing you."

"I wish he had!" she cried indignantly. "How were you abusing me?"

"I was only telling him that old story about your trouble with the boy who took away the wet bathing suits at Bailey's Beach."

"Guy Prime, you made that up!"

"And then about the footman with the big calves whom Uncle Chauncey had to get rid of."

"Really, you're too disgusting to be borne. I'm glad Rex beat you up."

"Look at the glint in those eyes! What a pity poor Rex didn't pick a simple girl from his own home town. But seeing he's stuck on a 'sassiety' type, I suppose I must plead his cause."

"Some pleader," Alix retorted with a sniff. She was beginning to realize that she would not get anything out of me without betraying some interest, but she still tried. "Tell me about this unhappy swain," she continued airily. "One knows so little about him. His father, I gather, is a minister?"

"His putative father."

"His *what?*"

"It's all part of the mask. Rex is in reality the son of a very great man."

"He *is!*" Alix's eyes were now really popping.

"Yes, his real father is the Stuart pretender to the British crown. But don't tell anyone. His life wouldn't be worth a plugged nickel if fat old King Edward were to catch him."

Alix's little red puff of a mouth formed poutily into an oblong like her face. "Oh, Guy, you can never be serious."

"But I am serious. I was just trying to find out something, and I succeeded."

"What?"

"That the only thing you have against Rex is his humble birth. If he were an eligible millionaire, you'd fly into his arms soon enough."

"I'm not flying into anyone's arms, thank you very much," Alix responded tartly. When I had no comment to make on this, she continued with a shrug of impatience: "Well, of course, one cares who people are. I have Pa to face. You have your pa. Be fair, Guy."

"Oh, my pa." I dismissed him with my own shrug. "He married for love."

"You're perfectly odious today! I won't talk to you."

"Then I'll talk to *you*," I said, catching her by the arm. "Where do you think your branch of the family would be today if a young man called Thompson, born in much humbler circumstances than Rex, a tailor's son, had not robbed his way to the top of the textile industry?"

"How can you talk so vulgarly? Grandpa Thompson was a most distinguished man!"

"He was when he died." But people of recent fortune in that day lived so utterly in the present that the past did not exist for them, even as a thing to be ashamed of. "Tell me, Alix, do you ever stop to consider that when you marry, you'll be marrying a way of life as well as a man?"

"I hate to consider what sort of a way of life *your* wife will be marrying!"

"No, be serious, please. Who do you think had more fun: your grandparents in their clamber to the top of the pile, or your parents in their dull existence at the summit? Which would you want for a husband: a man who would take you with him to the places where the exciting things of our century are happening, or a pink-faced boob out of a Turkish bath at the Racquet Club?"

"A pink-faced boob out of a Turkish bath at the Racquet Club!" Here she stretched her arms mockingly towards me. "Marry me, Guy!"

It was this gesture that gave her away, that made me suspect that she might, after all, care a little bit for Rex. Love him? *Could* she? I was not sure. But I knew that this bolder humor, this stretching out of her arms, was not characteristic of the old Alix. Someone had given her a confidence that she had quite lacked before, and I began to wonder if Rex might not, after all, make something of her. It was not promising material, to be sure, but in the hands of a man who cared—well, who knew?

I examined Rex about it that night and elicited the fact that he and Alix had already met twice alone for walks in Central Park. This, in a girl so cautious and so protected, was evidence of a considerable involvement. Rex also admitted that he had proposed to her and that she had accepted his commitment without in the least committing herself. I could not help laughing.

"She's as sly as her father," I said. "I don't suppose you've spoken to him?"

"Spoken to him! He's hardly aware that I exist. How could I speak to him when I'm not in a position to support a wife? Not a wife like Alix, anyway."

"Oh, I suppose Alix has her own money."

"I wouldn't touch a penny of it!" Rex exclaimed excitedly. "All I want her to do is to wait until I've got on my feet. I'll get there. You'll see!"

"My dear fellow, I have no doubt I'll see it. My only question is how long Alix will be allowed to wait. Particularly if Uncle Chauncey finds some duke for her."

"Her mother's on my side."

"Aunt Amy's a cipher. As an ally, she's more of a liability than an asset. I'll have to sleep on this."

But instead of doing that, I lay awake much of the night. Why, really, should it not be a match? Alix was a goose, but so long as Rex did not mind, why should I? He had more than enough brains for two. And if I had had faith in the power of a poor Rex to move mountains, what ranges might not a rich one move?

Their only hope, I concluded, was in elopement. It would be pointless even to ask Uncle Chauncey. The American rich of his generation were too unsophisticated in their worldliness. A French or English father might have scented Rex's future; Uncle Chauncey would have seen no further than his present bank balance. But what would Uncle Chauncey be able to do with a *fait accompli?* The fortune, after all, was Aunt Amy's, and would go in time through trusts to her daughters.

Summer was upon us; my parents had already left for Bar Harbor. Aunt Amy was to pay them a visit early in July, taking her three daughters, while Uncle Chauncey was to go cruising with his bachelor brother-in-law, Commodore Thompson, on the latter's steam yacht, "The Wandering Albatross." In the morning I suggested to Rex that we take our vacations simultaneously and go to my family's in Bar Harbor during Aunt Amy's visit. The poor fellow was pathetically grateful. There was no talk now of any lacking of the right clothes or any deficiency in the social graces. Alix's prospective visit to Mt. Desert Island had endowed the despised summer colony with the aura of a shrine. Of course, I did not tell him my scheme. I hoped that events in Bar Harbor might take care of themselves.

8.

WE WERE tightly packed in the little shingle villa halfway up Mr. de Grasse's hill, but Aunt Amy's enthusiasm made it a cheery houseparty. It was touching to see how eagerly she shed the grandeur in which Uncle Chauncey kept her so sternly invested. She had her bed pulled out on the sleeping porch and put her younger daughters in her room; Alix shared a room with my sister Bertha; Rex doubled up with me. Father was perfectly content so long as none of our arrangements interfered with his own room and dressing room. The era of "children first" had not yet arrived.

The natural foursome, as I had planned it, was Rex and Alix, on one side, and my sister Bertha and myself on the other. Four young people for tennis, for walks, for swimming parties, what could have been more natural or more innocuous? It was no fun for me, for Bertha, at a stout, solid nineteen, had still much of the explosive self-pity that had marred her maturing years, and it was hard on my male vanity to be seen constantly in the company of such a wallflower, but I was resolved that for two weeks at least I could bear it.

Yet it was Bertha who upset my plans. She proved not to be content to linger behind with me on a tour of Jordan's Pond while Alix and Rex sauntered ahead. She was as bored with my company as I with hers and had none of my motives for concealing it. On the contrary, she had developed a violent crush on Rex and was always trying to edge her way between him and Alix. And to make matters worse, whether it was from maidenly timidity, lack of imagination or simply innate good manners, Alix appeared to tolerate her intrusions.

Alix was indeed an enigma. She accepted our house and household, not with the disarming enthusiasm of her mother, but more daintily, as if she were being very gracious on some annual organization outing, some special anniversary picnic, where the servants, once a year, sat down with the princess. I wondered if she did not enjoy her visit to the Percy Primes in some of the same way that she seemed to enjoy her flirtation with Rex, as things that were pleasant, titillating, perhaps even exciting, but not, in the last analysis, quite real, things that belonged to summer and to a sea resort and to brightly colored umbrellas on a beach, things that one had, by implication, to put away in the crisp days of early autumn when one took up city things, social things, *real* things. Where did reality go in summer? Ah, that was just it, reality was off cruising up the Maine coast aboard "The Wandering Albatross." Rex would not have had even the little that he did have if Uncle Chauncey had been there.

He did not think, certainly, that he was getting much, and he became progressively gloomier as the visit wore on.

"I sometimes think Alix cares more for her clothes than she does for me," he grumbled one night after we had gone to bed. "Do you realize we've been here nine days, and she hasn't worn the same dress twice?"

"You must really be in love," I muttered. "I never knew you to notice a dress before."

"Is it possible, do you think," he persisted, "to break through the barrier girls like her put up? It's like a wall of pink and yellow ice cream, with spun sugar for barbed wire, on top. But don't let that fool you! It's as impenetrable as steel."

"Love seems to have given the banker's language a colorful turn."

"But you know what I mean, Guy," the anxious voice came to

me through the darkness. "After all, you're a Prime. You know the society attitude that identifies the unfamiliar with the comic. All I have to do to make Alix smile is to mention East Putnam or the public school that I went to there or the fact that my father's a Congregationalist minister. She doesn't mean in the least to be unkind. But middle-class things are supposed to be funny, like hay fever or hives."

"And lower-class things?"

"Oh, they're different. They're sad—when they're not dangerous. We shake our heads over the poor." He snorted in derision. "Of course, it's simply childishness at bottom. I remember the first time I discovered that every boy's father wasn't a minister. It struck me as very funny. But I've grown up since. Alix still feels that to mention any denomination but Episcopalianism is to say something, well if not exactly crude, certainly embarrassing."

"Ah, my poor fellow, I can see you've learned the ways of society! And to think what a simple unspoiled creature you were a year ago! Maybe you should give her up."

"Give her up? How can I give her up? Or give up the part of me that's bound to her? He sprang out of bed and paced angrily about the room. "It's easy enough for you to say that. You're not in love with Alix, and, besides, it's incredible to you that I should be. Oh yes, I know how that is. I never really believe in my sisters' beaux. And then you don't appreciate Alix. You don't recognize her enormous potentialities . . ."

"But, Rex, you know I've changed my mind about all that!"

"You say you have, perhaps you think you have, but have you really? I'll never forget what you said about her before you knew how I felt!"

The unfairness of this got me, too, out of bed. "You might at least have the decency to admit that I've been on your side in this thing!" I exclaimed angrily. "I've come up here on my vacation when I could have gone salmon fishing. I've spent all my days in the company of my dear sister which could hardly be deemed anything but a sacrifice. I've left you and Alix together; I've kept my father's attention distracted; I've played court jester to the whole damn family houseparty. And all for what? To be told that I lack sympathy. All right, Romeo, from now on you can paddle your own canoe! I'm going back to New York."

In a moment he had bounded to my side and gripped both my shoulders. "Please, Guy, forgive me. Make allowances for my insanity. You've been a brick. I know it's not your fault that the more you do, the worse things get. It's mine! No, honest to God, I'm not being sarcastic, I mean that!"

I stared into the darkness, but could make out no expression in the thicker gloom that was Rex's head. Then I decided that I wanted no further speculations that night. I was tired, upset, perhaps a tiny bit scared. "Go to bed," I said gruffly. "Maybe things will be better tomorrow."

"They could hardly be worse," was his only rejoinder.

I reviewed my conduct painstakingly as I lay in bed. Had I in any way, consciously or unconsciously, betrayed Rex's cause? I had certainly changed my habitual demeanor to Alix. Instead of treating her with the semi-contemptuous familiarity of an older male cousin, rubbing the nose of her pride in the dirt of my insinuations, mocking her, exposing her foibles, I had behaved to her with the seriousness due to my best friend's Egeria. I had asked her advice about my parents, my money troubles, my career, even my girls. Alix's advice on all these matters was, needless to say, quite worthless, and like most worthless things it had come in abundance. She had obviously been flattered to be asked. Had I in any way distracted her attention from Rex?

I was determined to find out the answer, and the very next morning, before breakfast, while Rex was off on a solitary early walk, I asked Alix to come out and talk with me on the veranda. It was one of those rare brilliant Maine July days, and Alix, in blue, looked for the first time almost like a woman.

"I want to tell you something. If you're playing with Rex, I don't know how much more he can take."

"Playing with him!" A faint pink of indignation appeared even under Alix's high pallor. "If a game is being played up here, why am *I* the person accused of playing it?"

"I suggest that you have given my poor friend, who's head over heels in love with you, reason to believe that you reciprocate his feeling. If you don't, you are most certainly playing with him."

"*I*'ve given him reason! I like *that,* Guy Prime. Who brought him up here? Who's always leaving us alone together?"

"But you were seeing him alone in New York, Alix!"

"Why should I not see him alone in New York? What business is it of yours whom I see or don't see in New York?"

I was certainly taken aback by this. "But if you were glad to see him in New York, why shouldn't you be glad to see him in Maine?"

"That's my affair! The point is, you have no business making plans for me. *Or* for Rex!"

This was very spirited for Alix, and I looked with sudden mistrust into those popping blue eyes. "You mean you have no idea of marrying him? That you never had?"

"I mean that I have no intention of telling you my marital plans!" she cried with a petulant little stamp of her foot. "When I have any, I shall tell them to my father. Can you give me any better advice, dear cousin?"

"Yes," I retorted, surly now. "I suggest that we go and have breakfast."

As I started away, I heard my name called in a sharp, tense voice, and I turned back in surprise, to find her apparently overcome with embarrassment.

"Yes, Alix?"

"Stop playing John Alden!"

Saying which she giggled, shrilly and foolishly, and hurried past me into the dining room, where Father was already seated.

Holy stars! What could she have meant but that I should plead for myself? I will never know, for I never asked her. All my wits had to be summoned for the emergency of soldering up this rapidly deteriorating situation. My grandsons may be surprised that it never occurred to me to be flattered by the possibility of such a passion in my heiress cousin. Yet it never did, not for an instant. I was too absorbed in helping poor Rex, and, besides, the idea of love between Alix and myself seemed incestuous. We had been raised together, more like siblings than cousins. Furthermore, Alix had no attractions for me, even objectively viewed. I was still a romantic, for all my gift of common sense, and I had the greatest dreams of what my wife should be: beautiful, brilliant, sultry, voluptuous. When I was looking for Cleopatra, could I stoop to the consanguineous fondlings of Victorian fiction?

But Rex, alas, poor Rex! How was I to detach him from his beloved without destroying our friendship? It was lucky for me, and I hope for him, that the same hour which brought the realization of my problem brought also its solution. Father, who had been silent and pensive all during breakfast, asked me now to go with him to his study.

"Close the door, Guy. I have something disagreeable to discuss with you. It concerns your friend Geer. Has anything been going on between him and Alix?"

"Going on, sir?"

"Well, I've noticed, of course, the usual dalliance that one expects of young persons on a houseparty. But this morning, as I was coming downstairs, I saw them below me in the hallway. She jumped away from him suddenly, as if they had been kissing or as if he had been trying to kiss her. I couldn't be sure which."

"Is that so terribly shocking?"

"It depends on the circumstances. When the young man is

Mr. Nobody and the girl is not only my niece but a considerable heiress, I think it is. At least when it happens under my roof."

"You think, then, that Rex has no right to look at her?"

"To look at her? You talk like a green kid. To look at her money, you mean."

"You're insulting him!"

Father slapped the surface of his desk hard. "You will mind your tone with me, sir!"

"I'm sorry, sir."

"Take care that you are and listen to me. I want you to weigh what I have to say and . . ."

"But, Father . . ."

"Shut your mouth, sir! When I tell you to listen, listen. Your friend Geer has taken advantage of your affections and your confidence to obtain a place in society of which he could not otherwise have dreamed. For that, as I have told you before, I do not blame him. But the trouble with Mr. Reginald Geer is that he is greedy. It's not enough that through your family he has had the entrée into some of our best houses and a splendid opening in a great banking firm. Oh, no. He must fly higher still. He must have a fortune to boot!"

Father paused here to observe the effect of his oratory. When I thought he was prepared to receive a comment, I suggested as mildly as I could that Uncle Chauncey had found his own fortune at the altar. He brushed this aside.

"The cases are not at all comparable. Your Uncle Chauncey offered your aunt a position in society which would never have been hers without him. Geer offers Alix nothing."

"Except a brilliant future."

"A brilliant future that he will buy with her money. I must say, Guy, your naïveté astounds me. Can you honestly stand there and tell me that a man with the accomplishments you claim for your friend would have fallen in love with a goose like Alix if she'd had no money?"

I confess I was silent for a moment.

"You see then!" Father exclaimed triumphantly.

"No, sir, I don't," I protested. "I know it must seem odd to you, but Rex isn't used to girls. He's led too restricted a life. That's why Alix could suddenly strike him as a goddess."

"What do you know about his private life? Men don't always tell each other about such things. But that is beside the point. Am I to take it from you that a proposal has actually been made?"

"Why don't you ask Aunt Amy?"

"Because you and I know all about Aunt Amy. And because I'm asking you."

I hesitated again, realizing at last that so simple a way out of my troubles might never again present itself. "Very well, then, a proposal has been made."

"Good God! And accepted?"

"I believe not yet. But Rex has reason to hope that it may be."

"We'll see about that. 'The Wandering Albatross' is in Dark Harbor today. If I telegraph now, your uncle can be in Mt. Desert tomorrow. How can I face him? But that must be. In the meantime you will give me your word of honor not to mention this to Geer. I want no attempted elopements from my house tonight!"

"If you will forgive me, sir, I think the duty of friendship obliges me to say something to Rex."

Father rose menacingly to his feet. "Do so, then, and tell him at the same time that he is to leave this house immediately. Tell him furthermore that I shall denounce him to Marcellus de Grasse for the unprincipled adventurer that I take him to be!"

What could I do but hold my tongue and pass a wretched day and a more wretched night? Early the next morning Commodore Thompson's great white steam yacht slipped into Bar Harbor, as ominously beautiful as an imperial cruiser in a half-savage Pacific port. As Rex and I watched her from our balcony we both knew, without exchanging a word, that it was the end of romance.

Uncle Chauncey was too magnificent to set foot ashore. He simply sent for Alix, with her bags and baggage, and she went. Oh, yes, she went. She went without a word to Rex or to her mother or even to me. She went, perhaps in tears, but she went. As I have said, she was a Prime, and the Primes, however individualistic at heart, recognized authority. They could and would on occasion fight, but they always knew when the game was up. Rex could not believe it. When, later that morning, a sailor from "The Wandering Albatross" delivered to him a little pink scented note of adieu, I thought he would go mad.

"I'm going after her if I have to swim!"

"There's no use, Rex, they won't allow you on board. I know my uncle."

"Do you? I suppose you do. You're all together, aren't you? Against me and against that poor girl. Did *you* send for him?"

"Rex! May God forgive you!"

He shook his head fiercely, his attitude more one of desperation than remorse. "I wouldn't trust my own mother today."

He hired a rowboat in the village and went out to the yacht where, as I had predicted, he was not received on board. Then, until "The Wandering Albatross" got under way, he rowed desperately around and around her, shouting appeals to Alix and imprecations against her father. It was a shocking scene and caused a terrible scandal in the summer community. Needless to say, my father never forgave it. The big white boat sailed off, and my poor friend was told at once to pack his bags.

Rex went back to New York and to a rented room. He refused to occupy, for even one night, his old quarters on Prime territory. Later, however, he unburdened his heart to me in a touching and apologetic letter. I have always kept it, for never again did Rex express himself (at least to me) with so little rein.

.

He told me that it was all over with Alix, that he would never try to see her again. He said that he would always love her and that she would be the inspiration of his life, but that it had been perfectly plain to him, seeing the calm fashion in which she had obeyed her father, that he could have meant very little to her. He said that it behooved him now to be a man and learn to live without her. He quoted from Browning's "The Last Ride Together." That was the way we were in those days. But it did not mean that he did not suffer.

When we met again in de Grasse, Rex was a different man, or perhaps it would be more accurate to say that he had simply reverted to the Rex of our pre-friendship days. He was very grim and serious again and thought of nothing but his work and his future. He was perfectly cordial to me, and no reference was ever made by either of us to the terrible accusation that he had thrown at me in his despair, but I could not help feeling that somehow, as a male Prime, I was identified in his mind with the forces that had kidnapped his beloved. In time a kind of intimacy was restored, and I was always considered by the world to be Rex Geer's closest friend, but things were not as they had been. Rex never, for example, bothered to chide me any more for my frivolity. He did not consider himself my keeper, nor me his. My consolation was that the position that I had occupied in his life was never taken by another. I am sure that Rex came as close to friendship with me as he ever came. Oh, there was Lucy Ames, of course. Lucy came to New York and took a job and went after her childhood sweetheart and caught him soon enough, with no competition. But Lucy, after all, was a woman, not a friend.

The Christmas season of our second year at de Grasse brought an event that ended for a time my social distractions. Poor Mother succumbed at last to her multitudinous ailments, but it was a hideously prolonged departure. She had a series of heart attacks, each causing terrible pain and panic, and the religion which she had succored all her life for this emergency now deserted her. When I was with her, she whimpered constantly about hell fire. I am sure I suffered more at her dying than I ever will at my own. It was not simply the animal terror in her eyes or the incessant roll of her head on the pillow; it was not even her ghastly sense of waste behind and punishment ahead. It was the total loss of communication between us. Not once in all that time did she ask me about my friends or my girls or my plans in the great world where she was leaving me. Mother's death may have made a man of me, but what sort of a man?

Rex was very properly sympathetic and called at the house many times. It so happened that he was with me when Mother actually died. I had been sent out of her room while the doctor was giving her an injection of morphine, and I found him downstairs in the library. In a sudden burst of my old feeling I made a suggestion that surprised myself.

"When it's all over, old man, what do you say we go around the world together?"

"What on earth do you mean, Guy?"

"Just what I say. Chuck de Grasse. Take a leave of absence. I can swing the whole thing with my share of poor Mother's little trust. We'll go to India. Siam. Tahiti. Think of it, Rex!"

"And Mr. de Grasse?"

"Oh, I'll fix it with him! He's always talking about enlarging one's vision. It may be your last chance to see the world, you know. Success can be very confining."

"That's it."

"What's it?"

"Yesterday, he took me out of Credit. I'm to skip Mortgages and be his personal assistant."

I stepped back. "Which means, of course, that you'll be a partner."

"In time, one hopes."

"Oh, in time, surely."

I saw Father's face in the doorway, nodding to me, and I dashed past him upstairs. Even in the moment that I knew was my dear mother's last, I had room in my mind for Rex's news. It seemed to me now that I had only his past and he my future.

9.

WHAT AN EVENING we had at Meadowview, to return to 1936 and the day when I broke the news of my misappropriations to Rex! My reader may remember that he was to answer my plea for a loan that night after a family dinner. The suspense was so great that I tried to minimize the pain by stepping outside myself and viewing what was going on as if it were a play. Lucy Geer, as usual, was too ill to come, and Rex arrived just before we went into the dining room. He was more taciturn and craggy than ever, and when, handing him a drink, I asked him if he had come to a decision, he simply brushed me off with a grunt.

"I'll talk to you later," he muttered.

It was hardly a gay party. Angelica, *distraite* as usual, listened vaguely to our son Percy's chatter. Our daughter Evadne and George Geer, the lovebirds, looked at each other. Rex said nothing. Stride, the old butler, who acted on the twitch of my eyelid, filled and refilled my glass with champagne. It was very hot, and through the wide-open French windows came, every few minutes, the roar of one of Angelica's black angus bulls which grazed in the pasture abutting the front lawn.

I understand that Meadowview has been condemned and a turnpike put through it, so I will say here, for the benefit of such of my grandsons who may not remember it, that it was indeed a dream place and all Angelica's dream. Left to myself, I would probably, like my uncles, have put up a French chateau or an Italian palazzo. But Angelica had built a poem, a long, rambling, two-storied, amber-brick manor house that was at its most beautiful as then, in an early spring dusk, with candelabra flickering in the high-ceilinged dining room and the scent of roses and geraniums in the air.

I lifted my glass to Evadne. "Every sip tonight is a toast for you and George, sweetheart."

"Then our health should be horselike," she responded calmly, her large gray eyes taking in my again empty glass.

"Have you fixed a wedding day?"

She glanced at George. "We thought November."

"But that's six months off!"

I always found Evadne very beautiful, though she was generally considered merely pretty. She had the pale oval face and rich blond hair of so many of the Prime women. At this time she looked somewhat as my cousin Alix had looked at her age, except that Evadne had more character. Her silences were the silences of a contented rather than a nervous woman. She had always been a perfect daughter: affectionate, neat, industrious, good tempered. She had extraordinary equanimity, almost at times placidity. But I suspected that she was more deeply in love with George than she cared to show, and her reserve irritated me. I quite concede that demonstrative affection would have irritated me just as much. I was as inconsistent as any fond father. Evadne was a one-man dog, but I suspected that she could change her attachment, like a poodle, from one owner to another. She was all George's now, and it bothered me that she was cool enough to pretend to the contrary.

"If George finds somebody else in that long cold wait," I pointed out, "you'll have only yourself to thank."

"I'll have myself to thank for finding out he's not the man for me. Before it's too late."

"That sounds so calculating."

Evadne gave a faint shrug. "I've noticed something about parents, Pa. They're always complaining that children have no common sense, but they hate it when we do."

"May I say that you seem particularly Prime today, my dear?"

"Where did I get it from, old sweet?"

"Don't worry about me, Mr. Prime," George put in. "I could wait seven years for my Rachel."

"But who would be Leah in the meantime?" Angelica demanded suddenly from her end of the table, and there was perfunctory laughter. It was the only laughter that I can recall that night.

Angelica was wearing the loose-flowing black velvet robe that she kept for family evenings. Except for nights when we went out together, which were rare now, she hardly needed other clothes, for she was in riding habit all day. Her brown, wrinkled skin and crinkly, glinting smile, her thin braceleted arms, her rough voice and raucous laugh, all cried her independence from the world—and from me. Fox hunting was her only passion now, and she was known in Nassau County for her daring jumps and persistence to the kill. So also, and less fortunately, was she known for her extravagance, of purse and of tongue, for her barbed wit, for her ability to drink like a man, for her fondness for younger company, particularly male. Yet Angelica's flirtations had only once been more than that. There was a curious discipline to her riot, a heritage of the Hydes.

She brought up a topic now, in all innocence, that had a grisly relevance to my situation: the failure and suicide of Count Landi. He had been one of those weird international manipulators, by birth an Armenian, by nationality a Panamanian, with a Vatican title, a French wife and a universal fortune. The papers had been filled that morning with revelations of his hoaxes: the nonexistent warehouses, the forged letters from crowned heads, the concealed youth of poverty and crime.

"I'm sure, if his wife suspected anything, she didn't give a hoot," Angelica was saying. "Women love men of mystery. Of course, it never lasts. One of the fascinations is precisely that it doesn't. Only dull things last. And dull men."

"Like stockbrokers?" I suggested with a smile, looking at Rex, who stared down into his plate.

"I don't see anything particularly fascinating about Landi, Mummie," Evadne protested. "His whole life was a cheap trick."

"Yes, but a trick that worked! For a while, anyway. Ordinary millionaires try to delude themselves into thinking they're happy with different kinds of private transport: planes or cars or yachts—vulgar things to carry them from distraction to distraction. Landi knew that the only point of money was to create a child's dream of fairy palaces with golden bathtubs full of asses' milk. He made the dream real—for a minute."

"Hasn't Meadowview been your dream, my dear?" I asked.

"Me? Dream? Why, Guy, I haven't even been to sleep!"

"You should have told me you wanted a pirate. I might have complied."

"What would your Sunday foursome at Glenville have said?" Angelica retorted.

I shrugged and sipped more champagne. I was beginning to enjoy the conversation. My sense of Rex's outrage, conveyed by his stubbornly lowered head and immovable shoulders, made up a little for my sense of moral inferiority. "What do *you* think, Percy?" I asked my son. "Does Count Landi appeal to the romantic in you? Or hasn't that side survived the impact of your too rarely visited law school?"

Percy looked up in indignation. "I'm hardly a romantic, Pa. If you'd ever bother to look at me, you'd see I am the coolest of realists. But families, naturally, are myopic."

"They are, my boy. They are just that."

Poor Percy had none of the Hyde charm. He had the looks of the Hyde men: the short, stiff, curly black hair, the pale long face, the thin cheeks that somehow never seemed to be properly

shaven, the large, aquiline, porous nose. But he moved awkwardly, and his tone was shrill. He was intelligent, even sensitive, but he was not brilliant. He had the knobbly personality
that is accepted in geniuses, but only in geniuses. At school and
college he had gone in for every activity: sports, dramatics, glee
club, journal, debate, but he had been remarkable more for the
energy that he had scattered than for the quality of accomplishment. He had talked at different times of becoming a composer,
a poet, an actor. But here Angelica had stepped in. The Hydes
liked charades, not theatre; they could write jingles, not odes.
When it came to a question of the artist's life there was not
much to choose between them and the Primes, except that my
family was franker. Angelica would never admit to what depths
of subtle persuasion she had descended to bring about Percy's
enrollment in Columbia Law.

Percy now treated us to his opinion of Landi.

"Gall on that scale is to me the highest kind of courage. I
would call his the perfect life. To be dealt a hand without a
single honor card, and to play it for a grand slam, knowing all
the time that it can never be made, that the most one can hope,
even by magic, is to take twelve tricks and lose the last! And
then when it happens, when one sees the ace of trumps finally
played, to retire without a word or a sigh, without even a joke,
to one's magnificent Renaissance library and there, after a sip of
Napoleon brandy and a nod to one's peerless Masaccio triptych,
to take out the jeweled revolver that one has bought years before
for just this purpose and put its single gold bullet in one's fertile
brain. How fine!"

"What about his wife, his children?" I inquired.

"Oh, *family*, Pa! What has such a man to do with family?"

Even at this Rex wouldn't look at me! I turned to his son
George, my about-to-be son-in-law. "What about you, my boy?
Does the Count excite your imagination?"

"Not in the least, sir." George Geer's soft brown eyes hardened like his father's. "Dress him up as you will, the man is a criminal, purely destructive, purely wasteful. And with all due respect to Mrs. Prime, I doubt if she'd have found him so romantic. I think it's sufficiently notorious that criminals make disappointing lovers."

"Ah, George," Angelica reproached him, "after a lifetime in the bogs of respectability and disillusionment, are you going to deprive me of my last hope?"

"Poor Mummie," Evadne murmured. "She has always wanted to be abducted by a knight in armor. And you tell her the *Decameron* was written by Sinclair Lewis!"

In many families of one boy and one girl, each child turns to the parent of the opposite sex. But if Percy followed the rule, Evadne did not. It was always singular that she loved me and Angelica equally.

"What about you, Vad?" I asked. "Would you have a spot in your heart for an old swindler?"

"Oh, I agree with George," she said flatly. "I see no romance in thieves. Even ones with jeweled revolvers. They strike me as merely stagey. But if you'll forgive me, Pa, I'm bored with Landi. I had thought we were going to have a whole evening of wedding plans after dinner, and now George tells me you and Mr. Geer will be tied up. What can you two possibly have to discuss that's so much more important than our wedding?"

"Money, my dear," I said grimly. "Without which there would be very few wedding plans for anyone to discuss."

It seemed to me, in the silence that followed, that the unfortunate Count Landi had created an unexpected unity in my little family, as if Angelica and I and Percy were all suddenly concerned in pulling a quilt of fancy colors over the dirty, unmade bed of our ordinary lives. We might have been almost united for the moment, our hands, so to speak, touching, our backs turned to anything as foolish as poor old reality. Only Evadne looked to George, who seemed, in turn, to be looking to his fa-

ther, raising his head at last like an angry Wotan and preparing
to hurl his spear.

After dinner Rex went directly to my study while I, per-
versely, lingered over a brandy in the dining room with Percy.
Not until I had quite finished did I rise from the table and
amble down the long library corridor to hear my fate. The little
study at the end of it was the only part of Meadowview that was
entirely mine. There I was allowed to keep my framed letters of
American presidents, my collection of bronze bears and bulls
(stock market symbols), my leather-bound sets of Victorian
novelists and the John Alexander portrait of my father (which
Angelica detested), a study of Edwardian elegance, with a cane
resting against his crossed knees.

Rex's back was to me; he was staring into the empty grate.
He did not turn until he heard the door close, and then I saw
that his small, green-gray eyes were as hard as emeralds. "I'll
never understand you, Guy. How could you sit there and talk so
glibly about Landi? How *could* you?"

"What does it matter? The question is: do I go under or do I
not? Of course, anything you advance me will not be lost. All I
need is time."

"But don't you know what all this means?"

"Who better?"

"Don't you realize you're asking me to compound a crime?
To be an accessory after the fact?"

I shrugged. "I suppose technically that's so. But you know
how often it's done."

"Technically! Don't you understand, Guy, that you've done
something that is *morally* as well as technically wrong?"

"Oh, Rex, what a time to preach!"

"I've got to know the answer to that."

"Well, of course, I know it was morally wrong. I'm not an
idiot."

"Has it happened before?"

I began to be irritated. "Maybe once or twice. Never on this scale."

"Once or twice! My God, man, what assurance do I have that it won't happen again?"

"Look here, Rex. If it were just myself involved, I wouldn't have even asked you. I'm thinking of Evadne and George."

"So am I thinking of Evadne and George! And of Angelica, too."

"Oh, yes, no doubt you're thinking of Angelica, too," I said with a sneer.

Rex ignored the sneer. "Have you told Angelica?"

"Certainly not. Why should I?"

"Then I suggest you call her in and tell her now. First, I should inform you that I *am* prepared to cover the amount of the bonds. I might even go further and help you settle your other debts. But only on the express condition that your firm be liquidated and that you give me your word that you will stay out of the market in the future."

I stared in astonishment at that square white face and those unblinking eyes. "Liquidate Prime King! Why, in the name of all that's holy?"

"It is the only way I can protect the public from a repetition of this kind of thing. If I am to stand between you and justice, I must certainly see that you get out of business and stay out. And I shall require Angelica as a witness to our compact and a guarantor that it be performed!"

My anger, which had been growing since the morning before when I had sent the glass hurtling into my staring image in the mirror over the Glenville Club bar, now tore its way out of my chest with a violence that left me trembling from head to toe.

"Has it occurred to *you*, Rex Geer, that it may be morally wrong to get so much pleasure out of humiliating an unfortunate friend? Was it not enough for you to have had an affair with my wife without dragging her in now to see me spiritually cuckolded?"

Rex seemed to congeal as I expanded; he turned back to the empty grate. "You know that I will never discuss that with you. If you want the money, those are my terms. They are not negotiable. Will you get Angelica or shall I go home?"

Looking at that stiff back, I felt the anger slowly subside. Had that affair not been over three years? What was the point *now* of scenes and protests? Rex had me in his hands.

"I'll get her," I said sullenly. "You can tell her the whole story."

Angelica and Rex were alone in the study for only twenty minutes before she called me. I was astonished to find her actually smiling, while Rex, standing with his back to the grate, looked hurt and embarrassed.

"But it's just like Count Landi!" she exclaimed. "Were you laughing up your sleeve at us all during dinner?"

I think for just that moment I loved Angelica as I had loved her when we had first been engaged. I went over to clasp her hand in mine, and then I turned triumphantly to our visitor. "You must forgive her, Rex. Women have no morals in business matters."

Had I gone then and there to the penitentiary, it would have been without bitterness in my heart. But life is not that way. Just give the gods time. They know what to do with it.

"Angelica's taking it magnificently," Rex said pompously.

"Oh, but, Rex, don't think I don't realize what *you're* doing for us!" Angelica now went over to him and turned to face me, one arm tucked under his. "It goes without saying, doesn't it, Guy, that we'll do everything he asks? From now on, we're at his orders. What do we need this big barn of a house for? Let's put it on the market and start living within our means. It should be quite a novelty!"

Now, this, considering what Meadowview meant to her, was very handsome of Angelica. She had style, great style. But what did I care for her style if the gesture was made for Rex?

"I wouldn't do anything too quickly," Rex said judiciously.

"While Guy is winding things up, it will be better not to alarm people. Tell them he's tired and needs a change. As to Meadowview, we'll wait and see. I hate to think of your not living here. Maybe you can sell some of the land and rent the stables. We'll think of something. Perhaps Guy could take a job as manager of the Glenville Club. Nobody else could handle it as well."

"I leave myself in your capable hands, Rex," I said in frigid anger, turning to the door.

"Where are you going?"

"I'm going for a walk, thank you very much. I'm going to clear my head. May I come to your office in the morning tomorrow for the bonds?"

"You may."

"Then I'll go now."

Angelica hurried over to me, as if I were a child behaving badly before company. "Guy, aren't you *grateful* to Rex?"

"Perhaps I should be," I said grimly, looking from one to the other. "Without him I should look forward to years in a striped suit. But human beings, my dear Angelica, are so constituted that they adjust themselves very readily to the most unlikely rescues and sink their teeth remorselessly into helping hands. You, of course, think nothing of my giving up a lifetime's work. To you it's just one of those silly things men do downtown, and, granted, I've made a mess of it. But botchers still have their pride. Guy Prime was somebody yesterday. Today he is Rex Geer's creature. It takes a minute to swallow that. Don't worry, I shall swallow it. But will you both be good enough to give me that minute?"

Rex at least understood. "Go ahead on your walk, Guy," he muttered and turned away. Angelica, like a woman, was inexorable. "But, Guy, don't you see it's all going to be all *right?*"

I slammed the door and strode across the hall to get out to the lawn. At a safe distance, in the dark, I turned and looked back at the long, lighted house. With all the mighty events of those two days and with all of the past that their events had churned up in my brain, what burned into it as the hottest needle of humiliation was Rex's suggestion that I should take a salaried job at my club. That I would never forgive. I cannot forgive it yet.

This may surprise my grandsons. They may take it as an example of lightness of character. Perhaps that is a difference between 1936 and 1960. Or perhaps it is merely a difference between me and saner men. But in any case it was of the essence of *me*, or of what I had tried to make of my own and my father's ambition, that I was at least a gentleman and not a servant. And Rex knew that. Or was it precisely the essence of Rex, and of his own blind egotism, that he did not?

Father had gone to his grave convinced that Rex and Angelica had taken advantage of me: that one had used me as a ladder to fame and fortune, and the other as a lifeboat from a mother's domination. On that feverish night, as I took off to roam the darkened fields of Meadowview, I went so far as to wonder if Rex and Angelica were not bound in some kind of unholy conspiracy to fetter me and reduce me to helplessness.

For had they not always despised me? Did I not make Rex's success cheap in his own eyes by representing too vividly the very world he had spent a lifetime trying to conquer? One toiled and toiled in order to be what? Guy Prime! Exactly, Guy Prime, the symbol of well-born affluence, of the grandeur of old New York! And did I not, by being as much of a gentleman as Angelica professed to be a lady, make mock of her airs and traditions? Even of her sacred family?

They could not take it. They could not take my honesty, as the generation before them could not stomach my father's. My grandsons may be embarrassed to read the story of my courtship of Angelica—sex, curiously enough, is not expected in progenitors—but I beg them to remember that they were raised in hypocrisy and that a little truth may do them little harm. They are probably immune to it, anyway.

10.

In 1910 I resigned from de Grasse Brothers. Armed with my small inheritance from mother, abandoning New York to my successful competitor, Rex Geer, and sighing with what I hoped was a sigh of relief at being free of a bank that was evidently going to be all his, I went off to see the world. The world turned out to be London and Paris. I went to a great many parties, hunted a great many foxes, had two flattering affairs with celebrated beauties and met all the people in politics, arts and letters whom one is apt to encounter in a fashionable memoir of the Edwardian period. In those days celebrities traveled in packs. I went to crushes at Lady St. Helier's and to small picked dinners at Lady Ottoline Morrell's; I visited the studios of Boldini and Helleu, and attended lectures by Bergson and receptions in the old faubourg that I was later to recognize in reading Proust. But as I never had another exit in mind when I rang each bell, it is hardly surprising that, like Omar Khayyam, I always came out by that same door wherein I went.

I was too robust, too young, too healthy, too handsome, if I may say so again, to be taken quite seriously. I particularly wanted to cultivate artists, but I found that young writers and painters, who were glad enough to play with me and drink with me and even, in the female cases, to make love with me, refused, except jokingly, to talk shop with me. When I at last realized how much outside the pool of European life I still was, after more than a year of diving in, clambering out and diving in again, I resolved unhappily to take myself home to the consoling arms of my always admiring father, and I would have done so had it not been for a lunch party that I attended, a week before my scheduled sailing, at the Paul Bourgets'.

Father had supplied Bourget with much of the material for his Newport chapter in *Outre Mer,* and the great novelist had been very gracious to me during my Paris sojourn. I think he may have been contemplating a story with an American setting, for on several occasions, in his perfect, ceremonious English, he questioned me closely about the frequency of adultery in the New York fashionable world. What I contributed, however, to his knowledge of my country, was nothing to what he contributed to mine. For I met a new America that day at lunch when I found myself seated next to Mrs. Lewis Irving Hyde.

"Going home?" she exclaimed, when I had told her my plans. I found out later that people always told their plans to Mrs. Hyde. There was something about her straightforward yet not inquisitive air that made one come to the point. "But my dear young man, you've only done the commonplace things. My daughter and I are going to Senlis tomorrow with Henry Baylies. I think you had better come along!"

"What is Senlis?"

"Well, there you are, you see. It's simply one of the finest small cathedrals in northern France."

I looked into those large dark snapping eyes that matched so perfectly with the raven hair and wondered if the latter was "touched up." Mrs. Hyde had already told me that she had known my mother as a girl and must, therefore, have been well past fifty. I had never known a woman of that age to be so forthright and knowledgeable. She was dressed in a dark suit with a black velvet hat that had a vaguely equestrian air. She was what was beginning to be known as the "well-tailored woman."

"You make me feel that my year abroad has been quite thrown away."

"Not at all. There are certain things that have to be got out of one's system. I think it's very sensible to begin with the sights that all Americans see. It's a kind of oat-sowing. After that you make the *real* start."

"But who will help me? Who will be my guide?"

"In the novels that kind of task is usually reserved for a sympathetic older woman."

"Would *you?* Oh, please!"

If anything could have surprised Mrs. Hyde, this might have. As it was, she burst into high, frank laughter. "Oh, I didn't mean that much older."

"You don't seem old to me."

This may seem crude, but I had noticed a little pink mother-of-pearl heart pinned to her coat, as incongruous as a daisy in a stern college quadrangle. Might not this tall splendid large-nosed woman want to be flattered?

"Would you be malleable?" she asked, looking at me more critically. "As I remember the Primes from my young days, that was not their distinguishing characteristic."

"But I don't want to be just a Prime!" I exclaimed in sudden heat. "I don't want to be just an American. I want to know things. I want to know the things *you* know. Please, Mrs. Hyde, won't you help me?"

"What a curious young man you are. Well, I won't undertake your education, but I'll take you to Senlis. That much I can do."

Even today I rarely think of Angelica for long without thinking of her mother. Mrs. Hyde dominated her offspring, not in the modern method of possessiveness (indeed, she was an indifferent parent by today's standards) but by the simple method of outwitting them. She was the most "superior" woman I have ever known. She had the feelings of superiority of the wellborn for the parvenu, of the erudite for the unlettered, of the devout Catholic for the agnostic Protestant, of the expatriate for the stay-at-home, even of the equestrian for the man on foot. She had an insatiable, ravenous appetite for the first rate; she wanted to explore the twelfth century with Henry Adams and the twentieth with Theodore Roosevelt. Small wonder that Lewis Hyde, an affable, red-faced clubman, adored of his own sex and a crony of T.R.'s, preferred, when not on minor diplomatic posts to which he was appointed by the latter, to remain in Tuxedo Park for golf and drinking and let his wife run about Europe on her heterogeneous quests.

I went with her and Angelica the next day to Senlis. Mr. Baylies, a rich old bachelor scholar, very kind and fussy and knowledgeable, whom Mrs. Hyde obviously had at her beck and call, acted as our guide. I had the good instinct to be silent, and it seemed to me, listening to him and Mrs. Hyde discuss arches and apses, that I was indeed only beginning my real European experience. Never had I heard from people whom, as Father would have put it, "one knew," such expertise so easily and so humorously bandied back and forth. I had always assumed that the only purpose of such talk was to "show off," but Mrs. Hyde, easily striding about the cathedral and talking in her normal tone even at the altar, was obviously indifferent to impressing me. And then there was Angelica. Angelica also was something I had not encountered before.

She never once spoke to her mother and hardly once to me. Even to Mr. Baylies, who, as I later learned, chartered yachts on which to take Mrs. Hyde and her family cruising, she was only grudgingly attentive. She seemed entirely concerned with herself and her mannerisms; she kept pushing back her long dark hair from her brow and running her finger tips along the wall and over the surfaces of whatever objects she happened to pass. Her deportment was in marked, probably intentional contrast to her mother's large, disciplined movements, but she had charm, the charm of a pre-Raphaelite *gamine*. If she spoiled some of her effect by a petulant restlessness, she made it up in the exquisiteness of her physical details: in her finely carved, upturned nose, in her aristocratic high cheek bones, in her large brown brooding eyes. She bore no resemblance to her mother, but neither, as I later found out, did her brothers. The distant clubman of Tuxedo Park must have had strong genes.

It was obvious, as we strolled about, that I was to walk with Angelica while her mother paired off with Mr. Baylies. It was equally obvious that this was her mother's plan, not Angelica's, for the latter made no effort to be even tolerably pleasant. Indeed, the mere fact that I was her mother's discovery seemed to brand me as a simpleton, if not an actual fraud. If I admired an artifact she would stare at it silently, as if she would never have otherwise observed it, and then murmur affectedly: "Yes, it's delicious, isn't it? Absolutely too yummy!"

"You sound as if you were in a pastry shop," I remonstrated the fifth time that she did this.

She turned to me wide-eyed. "But isn't that exactly how one is meant to sound?"

"See here, Miss Hyde, why do you take me for such a nincompoop?"

"But I don't, I assure you. I take you for an eager, up-and-coming American youth."

"Which to you is the height of inanity."

"Which to me, Mr. Prime, is the height of nothingness," she retorted in a sharper tone. "Don't worry. Europe isn't going to do you a bit of harm. We guarantee to send you back the same as when you came."

"We? Do you speak for Europe, Miss Hyde?"

"If I do, it's because I've earned the right. By having been made to swim all my life in seas of deliciousness. Oh, don't misunderstand me," she added with a surprising rush of anger in her tone. "I'm not being snooty. I'm simply sick to death of Americans who wander about in Europe ohing and ahing. I'm a jaded Daisy Miller if you like. A Daisy Miller who's stayed over here too long and lost her color. For that's what happens to us, you know. We don't die of fevers, as poor old doddering Mr. James thinks. We simply fade."

"Your mother hasn't."

"No, but then Mother's not quite human." Angelica, like all the Hydes, as I was soon to learn, could be quite independent out of her mother's earshot. "She actually *eats* culture."

It suddenly provoked me that this girl, who had thrust upon her all the things in Europe that I had come to seek, should be so churlish about them.

"I know your type," I said scornfully. "You're the kind of daughter who likes to slam Mamma without letting go of the apron strings. You can be as snotty as you like, but will you budge an inch without her?"

Angelica's surprise at this was not feigned. "Budge where?"

"Will you come out with me tonight and see Paris? Will you give up chapels and chaperones and have a look at life?"

"Men who suggest improprieties always call it living."

"Isn't it?"

"You're very pushing, Mr. Prime. I don't know what I've said to give you the idea I might be willing to run around Paris with you."

"Why everything!" I exclaimed. "You sneer at Europe and my presuming to want any part of it. You seem to regard it a kind of privately issued book that only you know. Well, I'll bet I could show you parts of Paris you haven't dreamed about, Angelica Hyde. Or only dreamed about. And it'll be a perfectly proper tour, too. You needn't worry. Only we won't take your mother."

"A pity," she murmured. "She'd love it so."

"I'm glad you'll concede her that much humanity. But tonight I'm just asking you."

She hesitated, and for a moment I thought she might actually be going to accept. Then she closed her lips suddenly in a tight little line and turned away to join Mrs. Hyde. "I'm sorry, Mr. Prime. I have letters that I simply must write tonight."

"Coward!"

She made no reply to this, but her silence conceded that the last word had been mine. From that moment there was no idea of my returning to New York. I had decided that I was going to see a great deal of Angelica Hyde.

The next day, I skulked about the Hydes' hotel until I saw Mrs. Hyde come out and walk to her victoria. Then I pretended to be passing by and raised my hat.

"Why, Mr. Prime," she said in her strong, pleasant tone, "what good fortune sends you just as I'm tempted to give up my shopping for a drive in the Bois? Get in. Now don't tell me you have business. No young man as well dressed as yourself could have business on a spring morning like this!"

We had not traveled as far as the Rond Point before I discovered that Angelica had revealed my proposition and that her mother had placed the worst construction on it. Yet she bore me no grudge. She was European enough to expect a young man to go as far as he could. Only the girl was blamed if he succeeded.

"I've been thinking about your mother," she now went on, a bit incongruously, to observe. "It brought back those dear dead days in Newport. I remember how well she did in the archery contests. We were all Dianas then. I was so sorry to hear she had died."

The tone was certainly matter-of-fact. Mrs. Hyde accepted many things, and death was one of them. Yet it was so long since I had been with anyone who had even perfunctorily mentioned Mother that to my mortification I found my eyes filled with tears.

"I'm sorry," I muttered. "I miss her so terribly."

"That's all right, dear boy. Those tears do you credit. I wonder how many of *my* brood would shed them a year after I've gone. Tell me now about yourself and what you're going to do with your life. Will you be like your uncles? I seem to recall that they went in rather heavily for the social game."

"They all married fortunes," I explained, glad of the chance to set the record straight. "I shall have to earn my own way. Father wants me to go into the stock market, and maybe I shall. But in the meantime I have this." I tried to take in Paris with a wave of my arm. "All this that you're going to show me."

" 'The time is short, the interim is mine,' " she quoted with an approving nod. "I like you, Guy Prime. Why don't you come cruising with us this summer? Darling Henry Baylies has chartered a boat to do the Greek islands, and I'm helping him make up the party. A handsome, unattached young man who wants to see beautiful things is always welcome. Come along!"

Obviously, I did not need to be asked twice. All that spring and summer I was part of Mrs. Hyde's travelling court. We cruised in the Mediterranean, but not until August, and in the intervening weeks I followed her about, staying in a hotel in Venice near the palazzo that was loaned to her and in another in Florence where she had rented a villa. In her immediate household were Angelica, two older sons who came and went, a dark old maiden sister of Mr. Hyde, an Italian courier and two Irish maids. Floating on the outskirts, besides myself and Mr. Baylies, were an old professor of Greek at Harvard and a beautiful dark Italian prince, with sleepy blue eyes, who bore the unlikely name of Giulio de Medici. But they had one thing in common. I had never before been with people who took such a serious interest in the art of living. I found it altogether exhilarating.

My father was less enthusiastic. He wrote me at length about Mrs. Hyde, saying that he could never trust a woman who felt she was too good for her native land and who sneered at her own antecedents. Mrs. Hyde, it seemed, did not scruple to speculate that her own ancient Knickerbocker family was of Jewish origin. Father had no patience with this kind of mockery. Also, he warned me, the Hydes had a lot less money than they seemed to have. "It's not that I want you to be a fortune hunter," he concluded, "but girls with extravagant tastes and small means make trying wives. Take it from one who learned the hard way."

I was not worried about Angelica's fortune; I could leave such considerations to her mother's obvious candidate, the needy Medici. I felt quite able now to earn all the fortune that Angelica would ever need; all I had to do was to earn Angelica. For that, in those first Italian weeks, had become my all-possessing ambition. I was giddy with the fantasy of taking her back to New York as a kind of captive bride, of returning to the golden capital of Philistia leading a beautiful hostage princess from the dark jungles of an old world culture. The New York that was beginning, now that I seemed indefinitely to have given up work, to regard me as another of its lotus eaters, would have to change its mind. Even Rex would have to change his.

Angelica had been very sullen when she found that I had attached myself to her mother's entourage, and for the first week in Venice she would not vouchsafe me a word. But under the double pressure of Mrs. Hyde's bland refusal to recognize her ill-temper and my own perpetual cheerfulness in the face of every snub, she began grudgingly to accept my presence and even to address an occasional sarcasm to me. I am sure that she had no intention of being coy, but her conduct was precisely the kind to inflame me. I had had enough easy conquests, and my romantic nature, Victorian in flavor, thirsted for an aloof heroine. By the time we embarked in Genoa on "The Loon" I was violently in love.

I do not wish to give the impression that my feeling for Angelica was entirely self-generated. She could be very charming when she wished. In the brief moments of that summer when she emerged from her moody preoccupation she gave us all a good time. She had a rough, rather rowdy laugh and an energy under her pallor that was exciting. Even that old eunuch Mr. Baylies was fond of her. Indeed, all of her mother's men friends were. She was markedly less popular with the ladies. Madame Bourget in Paris had told me frankly that she disliked her, and the Hyde aunt obviously disapproved. But what did I care for the warnings of older women? What did they really resent in Angelica but her sex appeal?

I could not make out her relationship with Giulio de Medici. He seemed content to be charming to everyone, in a lazy sort of way, without particularly distinguishing Angelica, and she treated him only a couple of degrees more warmly than she did me. Yet she was clearly concerned about him if anything was wrong. On our first two days under way he was violently seasick, and Angelica sent me half a dozen times to his stateroom to find out how he was.

"Is he really a prince?" I could not help asking her.

"Oh, yes. You can find him in Gotha, if you know how to look. It's not as simple as the Social Register."

"But surely there aren't any more Medici. I've read Colonel Young, and he says they're extinct."

Angelica smiled, but she did not immediately dismiss the subject as I had expected her to. "There's a younger branch. It even produced two rather obscure popes in the eighteenth century. Oh, you can be sure that anything Mother comes up with is pure as pure!"

"And I?"

She laughed her rasping laugh as she gazed over the dancing blue of the sea. "Oh, you're purest Yankee, of course. Purest New York. You might have stepped out of a novel by Harold Bell Wright. Just the way Giulio might have stepped out of *The Golden Bowl*. Do you remember Prince Amerigo's eyes, like palace windows thrown open to the golden air?"

"Or to a golden fortune," I suggested dryly.

"Yes, poor Giulio," she said with compassion, "he needs one, doesn't he? You must go sit with him. He's so wretched, and he doesn't like me to see him that way. It's his Italian pride."

"I'll sit with him all day if you'll do one thing for me."

"What's that, dear boy?" she demanded, in parody of her mother's tone.

"When we get to Naples let me take you out to lunch. Just the two of us. Just once."

"To lunch? What an innocent meal! How you've changed since Senlis. What could possibly happen at lunch? Very well. I hereby remise and release, or give, assign and transfer, as the lawyers say, to Guy Prime and the heirs of his body (is that right?) one lunch in Naples!"

Well, quite a lot did happen at that lunch, despite her sarcasm, for I proposed to her. I was certainly not accepted, but then neither was I insulted. It is a rare woman who resents a serious proposition of marriage from an eligible young man. Angelica was upset; indeed she was so nervous and agitated that she could not look me in the face. My finishing stroke was a masterpiece.

"I'm not going to talk about this any more now," I told her, "except to make one statement. You have insisted upon regarding me as a dilettante and an idler with no serious purpose in Europe or anywhere else. That may have once been true, but it's true no longer. I have a purpose in life now, and I'm deadly serious about it."

"But I wish you weren't!" she cried, looking up at me with tears in her eyes. "I never meant to do this to you!"

"But you have," I insisted, keeping my eyes fixed on hers, until she looked down again. "Will you concede that you have?"

I had to take her silence for consent, and we returned to the yacht. Angelica was too depressed to go to Pompeii. I had accomplished, however, all that I had looked for, and things thereafter were different between us. She no longer treated me as the village idiot, and it was tacitly agreed that I should thenceforth be a member of her little group on each expedition ashore. She sometimes even flirted with me, particularly if Giulio was present, which gave me my first hint that she might be trying to excite his interest. But that was perfectly all right. Competition had always aroused me to greater efforts. I would flirt back vigorously, even seizing her hand in front of Giulio, who did not seem in the least to mind, until she had firmly to pull it away. I did not delude myself that I was winning her, but I saw that I was tolerated. That was all that I needed for a start.

Everyone else accepted me now as Angelica's swain. Her brothers, Ted and Lionel, tall, bony, rangy dandies, with high shrill arrogant voices who condescended outrageously to all of us and still somehow managed to retain their Hyde charm, treated me with the friendly contempt that men mete out to those of their sex who have found favor with their sisters. And Giulio was positively outrageous in the pains that he took to show me that my path was clear.

I thought it was only fair to advise Mrs. Hyde of my intentions, which most probably ran counter to her own, but she refused to allow me. Sitting by her deck chair on a glorious blue and gold morning as we steamed towards Athens, the flow of my discourse was firmly arrested by the gentle placing of her large cold hand on mine.

"Do you know something, Guy, about our little cruise?" she asked. "The older people are much the happier. We are beyond the age of sentimental complications. It is popular to lament the passing of the 'heyday of the blood,' but how sad an occasion that is depends on what one has left. I find the quest of beautiful and ancient things in the company of those whose minds I respect and whose bodies I no longer desire a *summum bonum* that I could not have imagined in my younger years. You see, I am being very frank with you, dear boy. I spent my honeymoon on a yacht in this very Mediterranean, and I was deeply in love with my husband. Yet I find *this* the pleasanter excursion. I trust I do not embarrass you?"

"Not at all," I replied with a sigh. "There have been moments this summer when I would have gladly exchanged ages with you."

"Ah, but you must never think that way! That is not the way

to live at all. Life is like a good meal; each morsel has its particular savor and purpose. The sweet is just as vital as the soup.
You must concentrate on each minute of living."

"And then on eternity, I suppose. You Catholics have it both
here and there, don't you?"

"Do we strike you as Pollyanna? Don't worry. We have our
doubts. Oh, yes, hideous black ones. But I don't talk about
mine. I want to enjoy my life and enjoy this cruise. And I don't
think I'm going to enjoy them any more by hearing of romantic
complications."

So that was that, and she directed the conversation to the dis-
coveries at Tiryns and Mycenae that we would shortly be visiting. Wonderful woman! I knew even then, young as I was, that
hers must be the secret of living. How could I seize it? How
could I make it mine?

Angelica's mood seemed to darken as we approached the coast
of Greece, and when we docked at Athens she complained of a
fever and would not leave her cabin. She refused to have any
visitors, and I could only send her notes and flowers. She seemed
well enough, however, on the third day to join our caravan of
four motors to drive to Mycenae, and I was allowed to go in the
one that took her and Mrs. Hyde. All the way, over those long
fields, through purple hills and under a leaden sky, she brooded
behind her automobile veil. Mrs. Hyde and I talked of Agamemnon and his doomed family and discussed theories of the
fall of Troy.

It was not until the first morning of our stay in Mycenae,
when I followed Angelica alone to the Lion's Gate, that we had
any talk. She seemed pathetically white and sad in the white
dress that accentuated the darkness of her long hair.

"There's something I don't understand," I said. "Why, when
you make such a point of disobliging your mother in little
things, do you try so hard to oblige her in big ones?"

Angelica had been looking up at the great slabs of the gateway. She now turned and stared at me. *"Do* I? How?"

"By making up to Giulio."

"Ah, but how can I be sure she wants me to?" she asked with a shrug. "How can I be sure of doing something she *doesn't* want?" She waved a hand up at the gateway. "Electra had an easy time of it. She knew what would plague Clytemnestra. But modern mothers are foxy creatures. It's hard to know where to hit them."

Why was she so beautiful at that moment, in her white walking suit and black hair, a priestess of the House of Atreus? Did I think if I embraced her, I would be embracing poetry? All I know is that she seemed something that had to be caught and owned. Never have I felt desire as I felt it on that hot morning.

"You could marry me," I said boldly. "She wouldn't care for that."

Her brown eyes fixed me musingly. "And what, dear boy, in the name of Atreus, makes you think she wouldn't like *that?*"

"I'm a poor Prime, and she knows it."

"Indeed, if she doesn't, she'd be a half-wit, for you've told her often enough. I never knew such pride in poverty! But you underestimate Mother fearfully if you think she has such vulgar goals. To get rid of Angelica all she needs is a presentable young man who'll 'get on.' You'll 'get on,' dear heart. It's written all over you."

She must have read in my sudden anger the intent to grasp her shoulders, for she stepped quickly back. "What's wrong with 'getting on'?" she cried. "I thought it was a compliment."

"What is Giulio here for?"

"Oh, he's for Mummie. He's part of her collection. She has a whole gallery of European types. But there's no marrying him to Electra. He needs a bigger *dot.*"

"How much bigger?"

"Oh, oodles of times bigger. I don't really, properly speaking, have one at all. There are so many of us, and Mummie and Pa spend so much. It's all rather *Cherry Orchard*. You call yourself a poor Prime. Well, I'm a poor Hyde." She suddenly laughed again her low, rough laugh. "It's like a sentimental parlor comedy. And I who always yearned to play in Aeschylus!"

I seized her hand. "It can still be serious. I'm serious, Angelica. Marry me, and you'll see!"

She gazed into my eyes, half wonderingly. "Ah, my dear, you don't deserve that. No, not even an honest Yankee boy deserves that. But don't ask me too many times. You might tempt me."

"Tempt you! What the hell do you think I'm trying to do?"

"Listen to me, Guy." It was she now who raised her hands to my shoulders and gave me a quick shake. Her voice was low and biting. "I'm in a dangerous mood. I had a bit of a thing about Giulio, yes, but that's all over now. I hate him, and I hate my mother, and I hate Europe. I hate culture and beautiful little out-of-the-way places. I hate the whole fakery of it, sincere or insincere. I want to get out. I'd settle any day for a house in the suburbs and a husband who reads the *Wall Street Journal*. And I find you attractive, *physically* attractive. There! You're warned. You see what a modest creature I am. Leave me. Go!"

"I want to stay, Angelica."

"Don't be a fool. I'd make you a dreadful wife!"

"I'll be the judge of that."

"Go away, I tell you!"

I seized her in my arms and kissed her hard on the lips, but she fought desperately and broke away from me and ran all the way back to the car. This time, however, she did not tell her mother; in fact, she changed motors and went back to Athens with old Mr. Baylies. Giulio was in the same car, but I no longer minded about him. So long as she was afraid of me, I was all right.

Our cruise now moved into its final phase. We sailed for Corinth and Corfu and then steamed up the Adriatic Coast towards Venice, where we were to disembark. I knew that whatever was to happen between me and Angelica would have to happen before that time, and it did, on a cool, calm night as we were passing Ragusa.

I was ready for bed and standing by my porthole watching the dusky outline of the mountainous coast when my door opened and as suddenly closed again, and I turned to find Angelica, shivering in a white nightgown, her eyes burning, looking, with her long hair and clasped hands, for all the world like a Lucia or Ophelia about to play a mad scene. Without even speaking, I put my arms about her, if only to keep her warm.

"Angelica, dearest, what's happened?"

She burst into tears, and I led her to the single chair of the cabin, and sat on the deck beside it, holding her hands. "I've been playing with you," she sobbed. "I've been an absolute bitch during the whole cruise. I'm not going to marry you, Guy, but I'm going to make up for my bitchiness. It's the least I can do. I'm going to give myself to you. Here I am. Take me!"

"My poor girl. Be quiet."

I kept hold of her hands and leaned my head against her trembling knees as I thought. Men can think at such moments. Oh, yes, they can. I could see with perfect clarity the role of the young man as the romantic code of the day, or perhaps the yesterday, would have conceived it. I would have drawn Angelica to her feet, led her to the door, implanted a chaste kiss on her brow and told her: "No, my dearest, if you will not be mine, freely, of your own will and forever, let us part. I cannot take advantage of a mood that, however generous, is misguided."

And she would have gone weeping to her cabin and told me in a week's time that she would be my wife.

But would she?

I knew rather more about women than most of my contemporaries of my own milieu. It was my specialty. I sensed that Angelica, however passionate, was still a virgin, and I was quite sure that she had no conception of what might happen to her if a man made competent love to her. She had come to me out of desire, but she had still enough of the prudery of her generation to wish to mask it to herself as the discharge of a moral debt. She expected to lie inert on the altar of Venus, a passive penitent, a prim Iphigenia. She never imagined that she would participate lustily in her own sacrifice.

But that's what happened. When Angelica left my cabin in the early morning she was a confused but different woman. She was in a daze all the next day, and the following night, moored off Venice, we made love again. Before the break-up of our little cruising party a week later I was able to take her, secretly panic-stricken that she might be pregnant, to Mrs. Hyde and tell her that we were engaged.

Mrs. Hyde took it all just as easily as Angelica had originally predicted.

"I couldn't be more pleased. In my day it was always said that the Primes made good husbands. I had kind of an eye on Chauncey Prime myself once. We'll cable your father, Angelica, and what would you say to a Paris wedding? Or do you prefer Tuxedo Park?"

Angelica and I both preferred Paris, and it was decided that we would have a small wedding there in six weeks' time. The interim was not easy for either of us. Our physical bond proved strong enough to get us through it, but there were terrible gaps that had not been bridged. Angelica may have sneered at her mother and brothers, but it was a defensive kind of sneering, for basically she dreaded their scorn. She was always nervous when I was talking to Ted and Lionel, and I was hardly flattered to deduce that she was constantly apprehensive I would make a fool of myself. The Hydes were "special" people, and Angelica was sure that her brothers inwardly felt that she had let them down by engaging herself to a man who was determined to be a stockbroker. For that was what I had told her I was going to be. Worse yet was her mother's continuing satisfaction, humiliating to both of us, that she had done as well as could be expected under all the circumstances.

The arrival of our fathers did not make matters any easier. Mr. Hyde plainly resented being dragged across the Atlantic for so trivial a thing as a daughter's wedding, and my own poor father, for all his effort to please everybody, struck me for the first time as an almost tinny figure in a Hyde midst, the least little bit like a hand-rubbing floorwalker in a department store. He was not pleased with the match, but, unlike Mr. Hyde, he became almost unctuous in his anxiety to conceal his real feelings, and Angelica, professing to see in him the essence of the world into which she was marrying, drew back in alarm.

"Darling, now that we have each other, we don't need to worry about parents any more," I tried to assure her. "All that's in the past."

But her brooding look of doubt confirmed my own suspicion of how wrong I was. In the deepest part of my nature I loved the Primes; in the deepest part of hers she worshipped the Hydes.

Rex came over to Paris, to be my best man. It was wonderful for me, after a year and a half of the condescension of Europe and Europeanized Americans (granting that I had sought it!) to be again with a friend who, for all his criticisms, still cared about me. He was delightful in his enthusiasm; success, of which he was already having a taste, had softened him. He amused Mrs. Hyde with tales of the business world, of which she knew little, and delighted her husband with market tips. He listened affably now to Father's social anecdotes, and he won Angelica by telling her about his Lucy Ames and how they hoped soon to be in a position to marry. In fact he gave a dignity to the whole life that Angelica and I were about to live without which I believe at the last moment she might have broken off.

Angelica had no attendants, and I had only Rex. But at my bachelor's dinner at the Travellers' Club I had both fathers, all the Hyde brothers, old Mr. Baylies, our host of "The Loon," and Giulio de Medici. The latter, I may say by way of conclusion, was the gayest of all.

11.

WHAT REAL happiness could be expected of a marriage so flawed in its advent? What true union could emerge from the collision of two such illusions? I had hoped to find in Europe and in Angelica something better than the ratrace for commercial success in which Rex had outstripped me, and she had dreamed of discovering in New York a refuge from the wear and tear of aestheticism and the domination of an unbeatable mother. We both misjudged ourselves. Basically, I was born for a Yankee business life, and Angelica for the world of arts. Basically, I was always my father's child and she her mother's.

From the start, she was ashamed of me. That was the gist of it. She tried to be a good wife in the early years, but in a tepid, passive sort of way. She did most of the things that I expected of her (after a few terrible blow-ups) and adapted herself outwardly to the stock-market society in which I both wished and needed to live, but she was always a bit like a grand duchess in exile, making her noble best of an unfamiliar civilization of neon lights, and never quite coming alive. Sometimes I thought that her obedient conformity was a greater insult to my friends than the grossest insubordination would have been. "I'm not blaming you, any of you; really I'm not," her half-shrugging, mildly deprecatory air seemed to imply. "It's all my own fault, the whole thing; I've no illusions about that. What the devil am I doing *dans cette galère?*"

Of course, this is hindsight. In actual life the decay of our conjugal happiness was a gradual process. Our mutual attraction remained strong, at least until I went abroad in the first war; we had two children, who provided a naturally binding force, and there was always Angelica's Catholicism, stronger in

her than she would allow. Many couples have stayed together
with less in common. But after I returned from the army, and
the nineteen-twenties, so much my era and so little hers, began
their noisy course, our drift apart became a thing that we recognized and accepted. There was never any question of divorce.

I had regarded the war as a final opportunity to be something
other than Guy Prime, the stockbroker. I had fancied myself
becoming a hero, and if this should have happened, it would not
have mattered if I had been a dead one. I had gone eagerly to
the volunteer training camp at Plattsburg and thereafter to officers' school in Louisville, only to find myself kidnaped by General Devers and placed on staff duty near Paris for the duration.
Rex, on the other hand, who had been far too busy in de Grasse
Brothers to go to Plattsburg, far too indispensable a man of
affairs to go to Louisville, obtained a commission at the last minute by simple pull and went to France where he was awarded the
silver star for taking an enemy machine gun nest, one week before the Armistice. The gods had evidently closed their books
on any competition between him and me!

I came back from France, determined to enjoy life in what I
now deemed was the only way I could: I would make as much
money as possible and spend it as gaudily. I would ignore Rex's
hauteur and Angelica's moodiness. If there was not love enough
under my own roof, there would be plenty of it elsewhere. The
era, God knows, was propitious for all of this. It was the heyday
of the stockbroker, and my little firm did a bounding business.
In five years' time I had founded the Glenville Club, and Angelica had built Meadowview.

The latter was the price of "no questions asked." Angelica
forgave me my girl friends in return for a *carte blanche* for her
stables and kennels. It was never put so vulgarly, but that is
what it amounted to—a *modus vivendi*. To be queen of the
Glenville Hunt seemed to be all that she wanted, and the common gossip was that she had put romance behind her. "Does

anyone?" I used to retort with a wink. I was to regret my coarseness on the day I was proved right.

Rex, too, prospered in these years, rising rapidly to the position of managing partner of de Grasse, but his glory was shadowed by the increasing illness of his wife Lucy, who developed a crippling arthritis. It was very sad, yet I doubt if under the best of circumstances he would have enjoyed the 'twenties. Too many undeserving people were also making fortunes. Too many Guy Primes! And what made things much worse, much darker to this self-appointed judge of his brethren's morals, was that not only did the brethren pick up fortunes, so to speak, at the roulette wheel, but they had the time of their lives spending them. Shocking! The only job that Rex would have relished in a casino would have been handing out pistols to the departing bankrupt.

His time came with the depression, the odious depression. It was peculiarly a Rex thing. De Grasse not only survived with him at the tiller; it survived even more solidly than before. To Rex, shaking his head and puckering his brow, the crash on the big board came as a wonderful *Dies Irae*. He had not spent his money ostentatiously so it was difficult for the ordinary observer to tell how brilliantly he had avoided the general ruin, but Rex never minded the ordinary observer. He wanted to be judged only by his peers. A handful of the right people knew the full extent of his accomplishment in guiding his bank through those terrible times, and this was good enough for him. No cricket ever hummed more cozily on his warm hearth to see the snowbedraggled grasshoppers outside. As Rex's big dark car turned slowly into Wall Street in the early morning, the very spokes of its glittering wheels seemed to be saying to the apple vendors: "I told you so."

Whoa! my exhausted reader may cry. Do I realize, he demands, that I have covered the events between my marriage in 1912 and the bottom of the depression in 1933, a period of twenty-one years, greater than the age of most of my grandsons? Yes, I am well aware of it. But time is truly measured in intensity, which is why a brief youth seems so huge and vital a portion of a lifetime and a long old age so small and trivial a one. Consider how often a vessel must change its course in leaving a harbor, yet once on the high seas a single heading may bear it to its destination. So it may be with us. When I married Angelica and came back to New York to buy a seat on the Exchange my course was set. Only a major navigational hazard could make me change it.

In the first years of the depression I sustained my firm with a series of personal loans. I looked naturally first to my family, but by the end of 1933, even though I always paid punctually, my visitations to aunts and cousins were becoming less welcome. It was time to turn to Rex, whom I was seeing more frequently than usual, as he had taken to riding on weekends at Meadowview. This had been at my suggestion, when his doctor had prescribed regular exercise following a collapse from overwork. Angelica had even been teaching him to jump. Indeed, I had noticed with surprise and gratification that, despite the difference in their temperaments and interests, they seemed at last to be becoming the best of friends.

When I went one morning to Rex's bare cell of an office in de Grasse, with its single picture, a charcoal sketch of old Marcellus, on the wall behind his desk, and asked him for a loan of a hundred thousand dollars, he agreed after only a moment's hesitation, with a stare and not a sermon, with a grunt and not a growl, and with the odd flicker of something like shame in those gray-green eyes.

12.

It was my first hint of what was going on. I found out the truth of the old adage that the husband is the last to know. It is not that I would have begrudged Angelica a lover, other than Rex. I had always been uniquely free of jealousy. She could have had discreet affairs with the gentlemen of her hunting crowd, and I would have been careful to look the other way. But no, she had to choose the one man whom I could not tolerate as a "rival." For if Rex and Angelica came together, was it conceivable that the force which drove them was not directed at least in part to the destruction of Guy Prime? What did they have in common but me? How could the two people whom I had most loved and on whom I had built so many vain hopes and ambitions, love each other except at my expense?

It was not like Angelica to fall in love at all, let alone so violently. I was well aware that she had a reputation of frigidity in hunting circles. The very recklessness with which she jumped her fences was evidence of a compensatory motive. And if she settled on a man at last, in what should have been the common sense of her middle years, why should it have been a man who had nothing to do with sport or art or beautiful houses, a man who, if possible, was even less of a Hyde than myself? Why should it have been a man who cared exclusively for the downtown world that she had always professed to despise?

And Rex, what of his motives? Had he not always preferred women like Lucy, who placed their man's interests before all, or else pathetic lost souls like my cousin Alix? Had he not relegated women to the dullness of the home, to the dead peace of domestic chores? Had he not once told me that he loathed sophisticated, horsy females? What could he see now to admire in

Angelica who left her housekeeping to me and the butler, who
had never in her life made out a laundry list and who spent her
days in the saddle or at the kennels in defiance of the most ele-
mentary wifely duties?

Yet whatever the reasons or motives there was no possible
doubt that Angelica and Rex were carrying on a passionate
affair. For years she had paid me only a perfunctory attention,
ignoring my questions and opinions in the manner of many a
more happily married wife, but now I seemed not even to exist
for her. I had almost to shout my remarks to get an answer. She
would dream listlessly through meals and sometimes rise from
the table in the middle, even when we had company. It reached
a point where, if I met her walking across the hall, I had to step
out of her way to avoid physical collision. I learned the bitter
lesson of the Southern Negro who knows, when he passes a white
girl in the street, that he has become an invisible man.

Yet I dared not discuss it with her. I knew that if I did, she
would fling the truth brutally in my face. To have lived with
Angelica was to have learned to doubt if hypocrisy was necessarily a vice. Rex, on the other hand, took the greatest pains to
avoid a confrontation. He even found an excuse to cancel our bi-
weekly Monday lunches, a custom of twenty years' standing, by
writing me that his doctor had ordered him to stay in his office at
noon and take a nap. As if Rex ever took a nap! If I encountered him at Meadowview on weekends, riding with Angelica, if
I stopped my car to wave at them and chat, his constraint and
embarrassment were absurd to witness. Rex had learned only
one mask in his struggle up the business ladder: that of the stern
and magisterial money-lender. He was incapable, to save his
life, of assuming a casual pose. He had to be heavy about everything, including adultery.

For the first time in my life I was in the grip of an emotion
that I did not understand. Was my febrile agitation the agony
of humiliation or was it some strange species of ecstasy, a per-

verse satisfaction in watching the thing happen to those two people that I had always wanted to happen to myself? I felt as if the top of my head were expanding and rising in the air like a balloon. There were moments when I thought I was actually going mad.

Was I in love with Angelica again? Or was it simple male possessiveness that made me abhor her defection? Did I resent her conquering Rex's heart, which *I* could never conquer? Was it her taking Rex from me that I minded? Was I in love with Rex? Oh, in my desperation I knocked on every door!

The only thing which I could be sure of was that I was romantic again. I wanted to feel light rain on my fevered face; I wanted to peer through leafy hedges at a loved one bathing in a fountain who knew that I was looking at her; I wanted to kiss scented notes that accorded me secret rendezvous. I certainly did not want to be relegated to the Glenville Club while Meadowview throbbed with passion. Meadowview that Angelica had constructed as a temple to the chaste goddess of the hunt!

Maybe it was all hokum; maybe I was simply in love with love, their love. But it was still true that Angelica appeared to me with a freshness and a desirability that she had not manifested in twenty-two years. What was the key that Rex had found that I could not? And if he had awakened long dormant things in her, might not he be providing a forgiving husband with a second chance? As the weeks drew by, there seemed to be no alternative to my finding out.

13.

OUR TWENTY-SECOND wedding anniversary, in 1934, coincided with my annual dinner at Meadowview for the Glenville Club trustees, and we had guests for the weekend, including Angelica's mother. Mrs. Hyde, now widowed and old, was nonetheless as admirably brisk and decisive as when I had first met her. She had remained, in her own phrase, "the priestess of the life of reason." At Meadowview she found herself in the heart of Philistia and liked it. She had seen, after all, most of the beautiful things in the world, and she could afford to relax now and then in an easy atmosphere where comfort was more important than art, and food and wine considerably more important than talk.

"My friends will bore you to death," I warned her.

"Not over one weekend. Besides, they make themselves pleasant. You run a good house, Guy. That is an art which I by no means despise."

At Meadowview we always gave her the same room, overlooking the garden, and she spent most of her time in it, writing letters and reading. She would descend in the afternoon, crisply booted and buttoned for a solitary walk in the woods, and then she would not appear again until dinner time, at the end of the cocktail hour, in black velvet with a pearl choker. With her formal friendliness and her pleasant, incisive questions, she brought out the best in my friends.

I went to her room, dressed for dinner, on the evening of the Glenville Club party and found her sitting in a chair by the window. She looked up at me as if she had anticipated my need of communication.

"How nice, Guy. Are we to have a little chat before the festivities? I was just feeling the need of company. The evening's almost too nice for reading."

It was true. The windows were open, and her room was full of the mild spring air. Below, in the garden, the tulips were out.

"I'm worried about Angelica, Mrs. Hyde."

"Tell me why."

She listened gravely, without interruption, until I had finished the story of the affair with Rex. Then her voice betrayed neither surprise nor shock. "What do you want me to do about it?"

"I want you to keep Angelica from making a terrible mistake."

"You wouldn't say she's already done that?"

"I mean like leaving me and the children."

Mrs. Hyde shrugged. "Why should she do so? Doesn't she have everything a sane woman could want? A beautiful house, an assured position, plenty of money and a husband who does not begrudge her the company of Mr. Geer. In my day that would have been regarded as a kind of paradise."

"Well, I can't very well reproach her," I said, flushing at the uncomplimentary picture of myself in the background of Mrs. Hyde's bleak conversation piece. "My own record is not exactly stainless."

"Perhaps not, my dear, but a man's never has to be. However, far be it from me to deprecate tolerance in a husband. I have never considered jealousy a necessary attribute of virility."

"But I *am* jealous!" I exclaimed warmly. "I am hideously jealous. There are more ways of showing jealousy than murdering one's wife. I want her back. I want another chance with Angelica."

Mrs. Hyde really stared at this. "I thought all that was over between you two."

"Is 'all that' ever really over?"

"Between a husband and wife, it certainly can be."

"Well, let's put it that this thing with Rex has revived it."

"On the theory that we never really value a thing till we've lost it?"

"Or until someone else has taken it."

"Someone else, I suppose, whose taste and habits of acquisition we have always admired."

I did not flinch under that cool stare. If one went to Mrs.

Hyde for help, one had to be ready for the long reach of her speculations.

"Rex will never marry her," I said flatly. "He'll never leave his afflicted Lucy. So Angelica is bound to be hurt. That's where you come in. You must save her."

"But, my dear fellow, I repeat: why isn't the present arrangement tailor-made for their needs? Why must there be any question of marriage?"

"Because Angelica belongs to a marrying generation. As does Rex. They're not old-fashioned, like you and me. They won't be able to stand the guilt of their affair. And when they can't stand it any longer, they'll simply blow up."

Mrs. Hyde now seemed more interested. "Do you mean that they will do something violent to themselves? Or to each other?"

"Such things have been known. But people never anticipate them. Only when it's too late, then everyone says: 'Oh, if I'd only had the smallest suspicion!' "

But I had not, after all, convinced her. She weighed my argument for a silent moment, and in the end she shook her head. "Nothing of that kind is going to happen here."

"But you'll keep your eyes open?"

"I always keep my eyes open."

There was never any point pleading with Mrs. Hyde. Whatever one had got from her was all that one was going to get. It was almost time to go downstairs; the guests would be assembling. But I could not pass Angelica's door without saying something about our anniversary. I found her at her dressing table, in a splendid red evening gown that must have been new, in the process of putting on her diamond earrings. It occurred to me that she had never worn these for a Glenville Club evening. Was it conceivable that she was wearing them to please me? After all, Rex was not to be there.

"My dear, you look perfectly stunning!"

She looked up briefly at my reflection in her glass. "Ma said I was getting sloppy. She said it was high time I took some trouble about my appearance."

"Well, the trouble has certainly paid off. Twenty-two years, think of it! And you look younger now than you did then. You've been a good wife, Angelica."

There was another brief glance at my reflection, this time a quizzical one. "You don't have to say that, you know."

I decided that this meager opening was as good as I was going to get. "Listen, Angelica. Take your time about Rex. These things are short enough anyway. But when you and he touch earth next, try to remember that you have some ties here."

Angelica's face had congealed while I was talking. Now she rose menacingly to her feet and turned on me. "What ties?"

"The children and me."

"Leave the children out of this!" she cried, with sudden, shocking harshness.

"Very well, then. Me."

"What right have *you* to claim them?"

"Doesn't a husband have any rights today? Even in the horsy set of the north shore?"

"Oh, don't try to be funny!" she exclaimed brutally. "What has Rex taken that you have not freely accorded him? What has he taken that you have not sold?"

"Sold!"

"Have you not been borrowing enormous sums from him?" Angelica drew herself up now to a magnificent stance of contempt. "My only scruple, I can assure you, has been whether or not I was worth it!"

I think that my first reaction, before the humming in my ears became a roar, was simple astonishment that it had never occurred to me that this construction of my conduct might have occurred to them. I had too many relationships with Rex to see a necessary connection between the creditor and the betrayed husband. Besides, I did not regard my financial salvation as so personal to myself as to be inextricably tied up with honor. Guy Prime was an institution on which a small multitude of people depended: my old father, who lived, at almost ninety, like Anchises, on the vision of my glory, my partners and employees, my children and servants, even to some extent Rex himself and his sacred de Grasse partners. But now, oh yes, I saw it all, and now the noise in my ears became deafening. I raised my hand threateningly. But when Angelica simply continued to stare at me defiantly, I turned and stamped out of the room.

I drank many cocktails that night, but despite the glitter in my eye and the feverishness of my manner, on which Mrs. Hyde later commented, I think I was still at the height of my social form. Yet my mind, all the time, was hard at work on my problem. My mind has always worked best under pressure. It seems to have chambers that can be sealed off, like compartments in a vessel. I had wanted to save Angelica from violence. Now it was clear that I would have to drive her to it.

In the middle of dinner I rapped a spoon against the edge of my champagne glass and rose to announce that it was our wedding anniversary. I pride myself that no man, after twenty-two years of the most idyllic nuptial bliss, could have made a more moving address. I raised friendly laughter by saying that I had had to share my bride with the Meadowview Kennels and the Glenville Hunt. I charmed the wives present with the delicacy of my apology to Angelica for the distractions of my office work and the long hours which the troubles of a depression era had cut out of our shared lives. I made graceful allusions to my absent children and to my present mother-in-law. I delighted everybody by emphasizing how much a happy marriage always owed to friends, and particularly, in our case, to those there gathered about our board. I got a roar of laughter and a standing ovation by toasting future children as well as those in being.

Angelica behaved even worse than I had hoped. She refused

to respond to the toast at all, and after dinner she complained of a headache and went upstairs. Mounting guard by the window in the library where the men were smoking cigars and drinking brandy, I waited until I saw her figure in a coat flit across the turn-around towards the garage. Then I rang for Stride and told him to ask Mrs. Hyde to meet me in the hall. In the hilarious atmosphere of the library my preoccupation and disappearance were hardly noticed.

Mrs. Hyde needed no briefing. "Has she gone?" she asked at once.

"Oh, yes, she's gone to him."

"But isn't his wife there? How can she?"

"Lucy's in Arizona. She's been there all winter. I'll send for the car. Will you go after her?"

She eyed me grimly. "You expect a lot of an old woman, Guy."

"Do I expect too much?"

"Probably. But I'll give it a try. Why in the name of all that's holy did you have to make that toast?"

"So I could make you take this trip."

"You have your nerve!" she exclaimed sharply. "I think I shan't go, after all."

"Suppose Rex throws her out?"

"Ah, but he won't. You say his wife's away."

"Yes, but it's her house. Her home. Rex can be very terrible about such things. Angelica in that red dress on Lucy's sober hearth will strike him as the Whore of Babylon."

"Whom he loves!"

"And whom he must therefore expel from the premises. Think of it, Mrs. Hyde! Think what may happen when your desperate daughter is turned away from her lover's door!"

"Guy Prime, I believe you're a fiend!"

"But you forget. I love her too!"

"Love!" Mrs. Hyde's shrug was a vivid repudiation. "Thank God I was spared your kind of love!"

The formidable old lady was half-angry and half-amused, half-alarmed and half-intrigued. She and I had more in common than any of her family cared to recognize. We were both deeply involved with life, but at the same time understood the role of the looker-on. We could love and see ourselves loving. We could hate and laugh at ourselves hating. And we both resented the world for its audacity in feeling superior to us.

14.

MRS. HYDE BROUGHT Angelica back that night. Things happened essentially, although not precisely, as I had supposed they would. Rex did not bar his door to my errant wife, but he did send her home, and his doing so meant the rupture of their relationship. Angelica had her pride, at least enough not to go back to him after that. It helped, too, that Lucy Geer returned from Arizona in the following week. There was no further question of Rex riding at Meadowview. Mrs. Hyde, curiously enough, seemed to blame him for this. She was a thoroughly immoral old woman.

"What it boils down to is that Mr. Geer would rather have an easy conscience than an easy love," she told me bitingly. "But be gentle with Angelica. She doesn't suspect the subtle role you've played. That is just as well, believe me. Let it fall on my already despised shoulders."

Angelica's reaction was stronger than I had expected from so brief an affair. She was wan and listless, and for weeks she would not even ride. She would mope about the house, paying no attention to me or to the servants. She reminded me of Emily Brontë in a play that I had once seen, gaunt, proud and dying, roaming about Haworth Parsonage and pausing from time to time to gaze out a window at the moors.

Except Angelica was not dying. Her health was too rude to be destroyed by disappointed love. Never had she seemed more beautiful or romantic to my eyes. I stayed home every night and tried to devise things for her amusement.

Happily, as her mother had suggested, she seemed not to hold me in any way responsible for Rex's defection, and the ugly little scene in her bedroom before the Glenville Club dinner had apparently dropped from her mind. Or perhaps I was simply too unimportant to be resented. She sat impassively on the sofa while I read Trollope aloud and occasionally pulled herself together for a game of backgammon.

One evening she came out of herself enough to remark on the change in me. "Why are you so nice to me?" she asked bleakly. "What do you expect to get out of it?"

"Believe it or not, I feel sorry for you. Is that offensive?"

"No, but it's hardly necessary. I feel sorry enough for two."

"At least then we can be sharing something again. It's a start."

"To what?" she asked suspiciously.

"To a friendlier and more civilized relation," I replied simply.

For I was determined now to win my way back to the place in Angelica's heart that I had occupied a decade before. I was determined, no longer jealously but zealously, to be to her something of what Rex had been. I was perfectly willing to acknowledge the fact that for years—from the very beginning, if she insisted—I had treated her badly by demanding too arbitrarily that she be the kind of wife I fancied myself as needing and then, having driven her to rebellion, by casting her too completely upon her own devices. Maybe my friends *were* loud and dull; maybe I was loud and dull myself. But did I *have* to be? Had I not won Angelica originally by subtlety, and might I not win her back with a little of the same quality?

I gave up going to the Glenville Club; I even gave up golf and went riding on the weekends with Angelica. When the children were home, I warned them to be very gentle with their mother, going so far as to insinuate that she was traversing the nervous

tensions of a change of life. When Angelica learned this from a
talk with Evadne, she was touched and even amused. For the
first time since her break with Rex, I got a bit of her former
banter.

"I do think that was tactful of you, old boy. Troubles of the
heart are peculiarly undiscussable with children. For you to
have substituted another in their minds, equally undiscussable,
was sheer genius."

And, all of a sudden, Angelica and I were friends again. But I
was careful not to push her. Oh, so careful! Everything I had
learned in twenty-two years I now put to good use. I did not
talk about my usual subjects, but neither did I presume to talk
about hers. I steered our conversation as much as possible to
neutral territory where she could not have unfavorable precon-
ceptions of my opinions. These I could now adapt to fit the
image of the gentler, more liberal Guy that I was creating. Premeditated? Naturally! All courtship is premeditated. I was in
the ridiculous situation that French comic playwrights delighted
to explore: I had fallen in love with my wife!

"Of course, I see you have a plan," Angelica told me. "But
I'm darned if I see what it is."

"It couldn't be the very simplest?"

"The simplest?"

But we were riding, and she spurred her horse ahead to avoid
my answer. Obviously, she knew what it would have to be, and
I assumed that she did not want to have to repudiate it.

I wonder if Angelica today, so many years afterwards, would
still deny that something rather beautiful was happening to us.
Certainly at the time it was apparent to both that our reconciliation was going to be more than a handshake and a sharing of the
morning crossword puzzle. Angelica may not have wanted it to
be more, but she was like a person lost in indolence, floating
down a sluggish stream in a canoe. By simply dipping her paddle in the water she could have stopped it altogether, or at least

changed its direction, but the gentle movement had become habitual, almost pleasant. She was tired; she was humiliated; she was lovelorn. And there was I, her lawful, wedded husband.

I will not embarrass my reader with further details. I took Angelica off to my Caribbean island, wisely representing it as a business trip so that pleasure should not seem unduly to predominate to her embarrassed eyes, and there we had a second honeymoon, more wonderful, if briefer, than the first.

Angelica did not tell me when she became pregnant. I learned of it from her doctor who suggested that I persuade her to give up riding. She was forty-five and had not given birth for seventeen years. He warned me that she might not have too easy a time. Exuberant and exhilarated at his news, if not his warning, I rushed home from his office to embrace her and to be sharply repulsed.

"Please don't talk about it yet, please!" she cried in anguish.

"But, darling, why not?"

"It's so ridiculous at my age! How can I face Percy and Vad?"

"Why, they'll be tickled pink! Wait till I tell them. You'll see!"

"Don't tell them, Guy. *Don't*. I beg of you!"

I knew enough about the moods of early pregnancy to obey her and leave her alone. But, alas, I proved unable to be as discreet abroad as I was at home. I had now resumed my golf, and on a glorious Sunday morning, after I had gone around in seventy-four, I took my customary place at the men's bar with overflowing spirits. As luck would have it, one of my cronies was boasting that his newly born son, the fruit of his second marriage, was younger than a grandson, issue of the first.

"But you used two wives!" I burst forth. "Anyone can do *that*. The trick is to do it with one."

"Like whom?"

"Like me!" I turned to thunder at the bartender: "A round for all the gentlemen, Pierre. I may not have a grandson, but I have a boy at Harvard who is perfectly capable of giving me one. And in eight months' time that boy will have a baby brother or sister. A *full* brother or sister, gentlemen!"

I realized from the shout of congratulation that followed how grave my error had been, but what could I do but join in the toast and pray to be forgiven?

Angelica found out the very next day when the wife of one of my bar friends called up to "commiserate." Everyone assumed, of course, that the child was a "mistake." Angelica was angrier than I had ever seen her. I found her waiting for me that night in the hall when I came home.

"You couldn't wait, could you?" she hissed at me. "You couldn't wait to boast of your triumph in that sordid bar of yours! Like an old rooster going cock-a-doodle-doo before the other old roosters!"

"I'm sorry, dear."

"Sorry! Why should *you* be sorry? You're only being yourself. The same self you've been from the beginning. *I'm* the one who should be sorry. I learned once what you are, and I learned to live with it. And then I was fool enough to let myself get caught in the same old trap. Well, it won't happen again!"

Even after making every allowance that I could for her condition, I still could not explain away the near hate that I read in her eyes. "Angelica, please," I begged her, as the tears started into my own, "don't spoil the last two months!"

"Spoil them?" she retorted. "I think I can safely leave that little job to you!"

At this I lost all restraint. If the reader is astonished that our new happiness should have been so quickly dispelled, let him remember that it had been preceded by ten years of mere mutual toleration and, more immediately, by the affair with Rex. "It's because you don't want *him* to know, isn't it?" I shouted at her. "It's because you don't want him to know how soon you consoled yourself!"

Angelica, as she walked away, threw her retort over her shoulder in a voice of cold disdain. "You're not fit to discuss him. Not with me, anyway. I've told you that before."

A week later, in the big pasture, taking a four-foot fence she fell and miscarried. I was playing golf when word was brought to me. I drove home at a reckless pace and tore upstairs to the room where Angelica was lying in bed, her face a whitish blue, her eyes fixed on the ceiling. She turned to look at me, but she did not speak, and my heart overflowed with bitterness.

"You wouldn't have done it," I said with a sob, "if it had been Rex's child!"

Angelica simply turned her head away. The Hydes were intrepid people!

When she was well again, we went back to our old lives, she to her horses, I to my business and clubs. It was surprising how little animosity was apparent in our personal relations. But this was the period of my first embezzlement. I used bonds belonging to Aunt Amy as security for a private loan. In a month's time I had put them all back, and nobody was the wiser. Thereafter, I did the same thing in other accounts, perhaps half a dozen times. Each time, of course, it was a crime, punishable by jail. Yet I do not recall that I ever felt the faintest twinge of conscience.

Why? Why did a man brought up as I had been, a gentleman born and bred, after so many years of straight conduct, suddenly become a thief? And why did I feel no remorse? It was suggested at the time of my trial that I suffered from megalomania, that I was a kind of sun king of stockbrokers who recognized no distinction between his own accounts and those of his customers, that I strutted up and down between Trinity Church and the East River declaiming: "Wall Street, *c'est moi.*" But this was drivel. I would rather have people raise their hands about my morals than shrug their shoulders about my sanity. At all times I was perfectly aware of what I was doing and of the consequences of discovery.

What had happened was that I had lost my faith in the world as a place in which there was any point for me to live except as a rich man. Angelica and Rex, between them, had destroyed my faith in myself. He had scorned me as an equal in the man's world of business; she had scorned me as her master in the man's world of the home. So low had I fallen in my own esteem that I could no longer imagine that anyone in my family, in my office or in all my large circle of friends would be interested in seeing a poor Guy Prime. Like a prima donna who has lost her voice or a priest who has lost his faith, such a Guy Prime would have struck me as being without use or function. The world insisted on seeing me only in the role of king of the Glenville Club. Very well. It would never see me in any other. I would be that or I would be nothing.

I will say this much in extenuation of what I did. I never took a penny that its owner could not have spared. Not for me was the widow's mite, the orphan's pence. I "borrowed" from only three sources: from the profits that I had made for my rich friends and relatives, from the portfolio of the country club that I had founded and from a family trust that I had set up out of my own pocket. To keep up the position that the world expected of me, I borrowed the funds of that world. In a way, I still think it owed them to me.

15.

THE MORNING after the "Meadowview Pact" between Rex and myself in that fateful spring of 1936, when I bargained away my birthright to engage in business (my very manhood, by the standards of downtown) in return for a loan that was the merest pittance to him, I arrived in my office to find that, good to his dearly purchased word, he had already delivered the America City bonds from my loan account at de Grasse. By ten o'clock these had been delivered in turn to Jo Beal, Treasurer of the Glenville Club, and I was again a free man. Free, that is, to do nothing. Free to liquidate Prime King. Free to commit suicide and remove an unpleasant reminder from the high and mighty gaze of Reginald Geer!

But I had never for a minute intended to give him that satisfaction. I had already made my plans for the summer which, fortunately, proved to be a solitary one. Rex was in England, partly for pleasure, partly for business (de Grasse had a London branch), and Angelica had rented a cottage at the Cape where Evadne and Percy joined her. I gave up my apartment as a needless expense and took a room at the empty Schuyler Club. If I had changed my name I could not have removed myself more effectively from my Long Island world.

All during those hot months a part of me sat and watched Guy Prime struggle for his financial life. For instead of closing down my firm, I was using every last resource to place it once more among the first in Wall Street. Such was my real crime, if crime it was. As I saw it then and as I continue to see it today, my moral guilt turns on one question: what would have been Rex's damages had I succeeded? Should he not have been glad to have his son's future father-in-law a power again in Wall Street? And if I failed, where were these same damages? I would still be unable to repay his loan, that was all. It boiled down to this: Rex had stipulated that I cut my throat and leave his debt unpaid. I proposed to have my throat and pay him back. Was I bound to lose all for his pride?

I wanted to see no one from my old life. I was even glad that Evadne was away. I felt that the disgrace of being a small boy reprimanded by a stern headmaster had to be wiped clean before I figured again in the social world. However invisible the stain of this imagined shame, I would keep to myself until I

could appear, both inwardly and outwardly, as the old Guy
Prime. I would not so much as step across the threshold of the
Glenville Club so long as I was the creature of Rex Geer.

During the week I was busy enough, and on the weekends I
went to my sister Bertha in Westhampton, where she had a shingle cottage on the beach to which she invited her chattering old
maids and her crusty old bachelors. Poor Bertha, who had lived
with Father until he died, had developed with long delayed
freedom into the petty tyrant that she had hated him for being
to her. She had long straight sandy hair, tied in a knot in back, a
heavy countenance with chin thrust forward and watery pale
eyes. She lived, despite tweeds and walking sticks, and a considerable consumption of whiskey, on a gross mental diet of romantic art: of Verdi and Puccini and Saint-Gaudens and Rodin and
Greta Garbo.

She pretended to sneer at me and held me up to her friends as
Goliath himself, but she was really delighted to show me off. I
was the wind of the greenback prairies of the real world into
their closed interior, and I had come batting in—that was the
great thing!—not at their own timid solicitation but of my own
accord. I was the proof (or a little wishful thinking could make
me seem so) that the captains and the kings of earth, if they ever
listened for a moment to their hearts, would come down to the
beach and to Bertha Prime and sit on the veranda to talk of
death and beauty. Bertha had resented that Father and life had
loved me and scanted her, but she was all ready to forgive. Oh
so ready! A little scolding, and I was her big darling brother
again.

"I'm not surprised, Guy, after all that horsy set of Angelica's
and all those sports-coated golfers, that your soul should cry out
for a bit of companionship with those to whom the planet is
more than a field for organized sport. You're late in starting,
but you're not too late. After all, I can remember the dear dead
days when you and Rex read Browning aloud."

I was oddly content, in the suspended existence of those weekends, with Bertha and the gentle little group that obeyed her and liked obeying. We walked on the dunes; we read plays aloud; we listened to symphonies on the Gramophone, and we put away a lot of cocktails. Angelica, calling me from the Cape, thought I had taken leave of my senses, and of course I had. Waiting for things to happen, one did not want to feel the interlude.

From the beginning of September to the middle of October a series of disasters occurred, one after another, that proved, if proof were needed, that the gods were against me. No protagonist of ancient Greek drama was more buffeted and with less cause than I. Had I once spurned Aphrodite when she reached out her snowy arms to me? Had I enjoyed a nymph for whom jealous Zeus had lusted? Or was it a matter of inheritance, and did I, like my father, have to pay for the *hubris* of some Prime ancestor? An early fall hurricane wrecked my Caribbean resort so that its opening had to be postponed a year. An injunction in that almost settled title suit closed down the operation of Georgia Phosphates. And finally the government insisted on additional studies before authorizing the issuance of my little drug company's new pill to reduce apprehension. I could have swallowed our entire production.

All I needed was a little time to overcome my obstacles. As I have pointed out before, my ventures ultimately brought in millions—for others. Knowing that it was my last gamble, I now flung into my businesses everything I could lay my clutching hands on and borrowed from everyone I knew. Angelica was back at Meadowview, but I did not welcome her questions, or Evadne's, and I stayed in town. My days and nights were devoted to meeting friends in search of loans, to delaying creditors, to pumping heart into associates. But still I needed time.

When the idea occurred to me of using the securities in Angelica's trust, my first reaction was simply a mild surprise that it had not occurred to me before. I had set up this trust for Angelica and the children on Father's death, using all of my inheritance. I had wanted them to be independent, at least for necessities, of my own risky businesses. Standard Trust and I were the trustees, but because I was the donor of the fund and because the trust instrument had given me the widest powers of investment and discretion, the bank had tended to regard itself more as a depositary than a fiduciary, and had allowed me to buy and sell as I chose and to keep the securities in my office vault for months at a time. This may seem very relaxed to present-day readers, but we were in 1936, and my name on Wall Street was still a synonym for reliability. Ironically enough, I had done better with this trust than with my own things, and there were seven hundred thousand dollars of stocks and bonds in my possession on that autumn Monday morning when I decided to pledge the lot.

The curious thing about my mental state was that I *knew* it was too late. I was convinced, in superstitious fashion, that nothing now could save me. There simply seemed to be a bleak and necessary logic in hurling this last log upon a dying fire. I do not, however, mean to imply that I acted from suicidal motives. I acted to save myself and my firm. I had to put down the last trump; it was the only way to play the hand. But in playing it, as coolly as I knew how, there was no longer hope in my heart.

By the middle of October word of my multiple borrowings had penetrated even to the sleepy corner where Standard Trust Company, like the dragon Fafner, dozed over its hoards. It had been a great bank in its day, but, swollen with fat old trusts whose beneficiaries were now too numerous to be effective critics and under the presidency of my late Uncle Chauncey, who had always been off yachting with his rich wife, its claws had dulled and only a faint puff of smoke was from time to time emitted from its clenched jaws. Now there were stirrings. Twice my obliging friend Pete Bissell lunched with me and asked timidly if it wouldn't "look better" if the trust assets were kept in the custody of the corporate trustee.

"It certainly would," I agreed each time. "How would you look if your co-trustee made off with the corpus of the trust? I guess somebody at Standard would have *your* corpus!"

Pete laughed, chokingly, half reassured, half scandalized. In the soft compliant eye of the eternally reassuring trust officer there was a little yellow spark of panic. But no. Not the senior partner of Prime King? Not the nephew of Chauncey Prime!

"When will you send it over?"

"Next week."

And next week I would forget.

I might even have got away with it, miraculous as it now seems, had an article not appeared in the Sunday *Times* on the damage of hurricanes, with pictures of my battered resort and, alas, a picture of me. Fafner awoke at last, and on Monday evening, as I was about to leave my office, I heard his belated roar on the telephone.

"Mr. Prime? It's Howard Landers. I'm a trust officer at Standard Trust."

"What can I do for you, Mr. Landers?"

"It has come to my attention that some of the securities of Mrs. Prime's trust are actually in your custody."

"That has been our usual practice."

"It is most irregular, Mr. Prime. *Most* irregular."

"Look here Landers, this is not an ordinary trust, and I happen to be your co-trustee. Pete Bissell is the man over there I deal with. Have you cleared this call with him?"

"He's cleared it with *me*, Mr. Prime. I am taking over supervision of your wife's trust. The first thing that I shall do is to correct at once this unprecedented irregularity. I must insist that all assets of the trust be delivered to the bank no later than tomorrow morning."

"Tomorrow morning!"

"Is there any difficulty, Mr. Prime? Are the securities not physically in your office?"

"Of course they are. But I don't understand your tone. To call up a co-fiduciary, after years of allowing him to keep constantly traded securities in his office—a great convenience, incidentally to *both* trustees—and expect to reverse the procedure over night—well, it sounds as if you were suspicious of something!"

"I regret how it sounds, Mr. Prime. But our messenger will be over for the securities in the morning."

"Do you realize, Mr. Landers, that your attitude means that I shall never do business with Standard Trust again?"

"We have calculated the risks, Mr. Prime."

No, Mr. Geer was not in, his secretary told me when I called. Mr. Geer had left the office and was dining out—she did not know where—but was going to the opera later. I called Bertha who had Aunt Amy's box on Monday nights and asked her if she could spare a seat for me.

"Since when did you become an opera fan?"

"Be nice, Bertha," I sighed. "I've had a hard day."

"Well, if you sleep, don't snore. My friends are not the kind who go to the opera just to be seen."

I was late for *Traviata* and thought I would have to wait for the intermission to seek out Rex, but then I spotted him in a box only two away. I tiptoed out to the corridor and into the back of his box and stood for just a moment behind his chair before placing my hand on his shoulder. He looked up and, without even a word or a whisper, followed me from the box. He must have been prepared for the worst. No doubt to Rex my face had become the symbol of his personal doom. He would take it, as he took all things, like a man.

In a corner of the empty bar we sat at a small round table, and I looked about for a waiter.

"No, no," he muttered, "give it to me straight."

So I did, watching him as I spoke, seeing the too familiar process of his slow congealment. When I had finished there was a moment of silence, a moment of something almost like peace between us. What would have been the point of violence now?

"I realize that you may be the victim of an obsession," he said at last. "The rational part of me tells me that men like you may really not be responsible for their acts. But I wonder how much the concept of personal fault means to me. What seems important now—in fact, the only thing in the world that seems important now—is for me to recognize and learn to face the thing in you that is wicked. Maybe you can't help being wicked, any more than you can help the shape of your nose. But there it is, your nose and the wickedness. Before me. I see them." And he looked straight through me, as if at something strange and distant, but somehow no longer threatening. I had the distinct feeling that I was dead at last not only to Rex but to my whole world. There were many things in that feeling, but I wonder if relief may not have been one of them.

"Go ahead, Rex. Get it off your chest. I have it coming to me."

"We're beyond recriminations, you and I."

"Then let's not be beyond reason. Put up the money once more and I will sign over everything I own to you. You will hold it for Angelica and Evadne and Percy under any terms you wish. When my ship comes in—and it will come in—they will be rich. I will take myself away—to a Pacific island, anywhere— I'll never bother you again. All you will have to do is hold the securities and wait."

"How much will it take this time, Guy?" he asked wearily.

"Three quarters of a million. You see, I don't beat about the bush."

Rex continued to be inscrutable. "I'll have to go to my firm. I can't raise that much on such short notice. Your last loan cut me too low."

I stared. "But surely, Rex, you must be several times a millionaire!"

"It's all in trust for Lucy and George. I did what you did. Only I'm not an Indian giver. However, I can go to Marcellus de Grasse. Of course, I'll have to tell him."

"Of course," I murmured, without conviction. "But you *will* go to him?"

"Where will you be tonight?"

"In my room at the Schuyler Club."

"What will you do if the answer is no?"

"What can I do?"

Rex's gray-green eyes fixed me with a defiant glitter. The defiance was at my thinking that he would not say it. "Men have been known to kill themselves under these conditions."

"Well, I won't do that," I retorted with a grunt. "You can trust me to see the show out. I never could leave even a movie early. I like to know how things end."

"Very well." Rex rose. "Let this be good-by, then. Whatever happens, I don't think I want to see you again. I shall deal through George. George, too, will have to know all."

"Yes," I said, in the final flare-up of my bitterness, "he will have to know all, *your* all. Nobody will ever know mine!"

"Not even the creditor who shares your disgrace? Who is involved in your crime?"

"Oh, shucks, Rex, *you* won't have to go to jail."

"There are worse things than jail."

"That's the ultimate Rex!" I cried, in sudden, passionate anger. "That's the Rexest thing I ever heard! You've robbed me all my life, and now you want to steal the final iniquity of my punishment. And you call *me* the thief! When were you not picking my pockets? Father was on to you from the beginning. You envied me my popularity, my family, my whole bright little place in the sun. You hated those things because they weren't yours. You had to have them, not to enjoy them, but to destroy them. You grabbed the fortune that *I* should have made, and what have you ever done with it but build a big house that's as dreary as yourself and prate about morals while you practiced adultery? You made a world that's more sordid than the old Prime world that you sneered at, only yours isn't even gay. It's drab as a crow!"

Rex listened to all of this without the twitch of an eyelid. Then he rose.

"I'll send word to your club," he said in his stoniest voice, "when I've made up my mind."

He left the bar, and I returned to my seat in the back of Bertha's box. It was a strange place to review my life, with Bertha and her friends, at a performance of *Traviata*, yet it was there that I brought to its finest pitch the sense of detachment that I had cultivated all summer. It was the only thing that got me through my years in jail.

I saw that the common denominator of the little group in the box, other than myself, was that none of them had ever lived. The old bachelor colonel, a frustrated pederast, clutching the Republican principles of the Reconstruction era, lived only in his silly politenesses to spinsters and in the mutterings of his hate as he read of socialism in the newspapers at his club. The widow with the necklace of garnets and the turkey's neck lived in an imaginary past, the squeaky spinster twin sisters in an imaginary present, and Bertha, sleepy with her double potion of gin, beating time with her big foot to the music, dreamed of being a courtesan in the second empire, of giving up her house and jewels for a tiny villa in the country and a beautiful pale ardent young man.

Did I wish I were one of them? Did I wish I had stayed with Bertha, shared an apartment with her as a bachelor brother, gone to meetings of the Society of the Cincinnati and watched Armand and Violetta with moist eyes on Monday nights? Did I wish to be, like Bertha's friends, exempt?

No. Not even then. Not even with all the black void that loomed. I was happy that I had engaged with life, that I had married a beautiful woman and fathered healthy children and made and spent fortunes and founded a great club. New York would not soon forget Guy Prime. And if all ended hideously, New York would forget him even less.

When the big golden final curtain fell at last, on *Traviata* and on me, I knew that I would find a message at the Schuyler Club, that Rex had failed in his mission. I felt only numbness in my heart as I remained standing and applauding until the last curtain call. Then I followed Bertha to her car and talked about the singers until we reached my club. I slightly surprised her by kissing her goodnight on the lips.

The boy at the desk handed me the message for which I had already extended my hand. The next morning Prime King Dawson & King was suspended from trading, and by noon it was generally known in the street that we were bankrupt. The long Manhattan career of the Primes had ended in a hell as bright as any in the Bishop's sermons.

16.

ON TUESDAY afternoon, after my firm had closed its doors forever, I consulted with our aghast old lawyer, Horatio Carter, whose white cuffs fluttered like moths as I spoke, and told him that I meant to plead guilty to an indictment for embezzlement. I interrupted when he began to expostulate and requested him firmly to go to the District Attorney, who would be preparing a warrant for my arrest, and tell him that in the morning, after a night at Meadowview, I would be at his disposal. In the meantime, the Chief of Police of Glenville, an old friend, would guarantee my availability. When Carter had departed, his cuffs still aflight, I took my last drive to Long Island.

One more shock awaited me, and that was the inundation of sympathy in which I found Meadowview sopped. Limousines jammed the drive, the hall overflowed with flowers and, in the living room, a bewildered Angelica, still in riding habit, was serving coffee to solicitous friends. Something buckled in my resolution of detachment at the impact of so much affection and concern, and the tears boiled up in my eyes. But they evaporated soon enough at the realization that the love in that room was not for me. It was for Guy Prime, the bankrupt. They did not yet know of Guy Prime, the crook.

Standing in the doorway I raised my voice to dominate the assembly. "My friends, you are here under a misapprehension. You think that merely my firm has failed. That is the least of my concerns. Tomorrow I expect to be criminally indicted for the misappropriation of trust funds in my custody. I regret to inform you that I shall have to plead guilty to that indictment. I leave you now to offer your sympathies to my unfortunate family. This news is as much of a shock to them as to yourselves."

I have never known silence like the silence that followed this announcement. In the moment before I turned and strode to my study, it seemed that the very walls and floor must have been saturated with it, and the white looming faces of which I was conscious only in mass were no longer the faces of friends, but a composite expression of dread and horror. I had become a specter in my own home.

Angelica followed me to the study. She was very nervous and kept striking her leg with her riding crop. Rex, it appeared, had already telephoned and told her the worst. She seemed undecided as to what reaction was the most appropriate: indignation, sympathy or simply impatience at so bizarre an interruption of normal life.

"I know it is not the embezzlement that you will most mind," I said grimly. "It will be my letting Rex down after all that he's done."

"Well, I mind that, of course, I mind it terribly, but it's not Rex who's going to prison. Rex will survive. My concern, believe it or not, is for you, old boy. One can't be married to a man for twenty-five years and see him go off to jail with a dry eye. There must be some way I can help. What can I do, Guy?"

"Nothing, my dear. Nothing at all. In crime one is all alone. One never knows how much till it happens." I paused, making out the sudden warmer sympathy in her eyes. Poor Angelica! It was so like her to spurn participation in my success and then reach out to share my bread and water. Whatever else she was, she was a lady.

"I want you to know that I'm not being sentimental," she was saying. "I've thought it all out because I've seen it all coming. Not your going to jail, perhaps, but our being broke and under a cloud. I've had the summer for that. I think I'm even beginning to understand the role that our incompatibility has played. It occurs to me that this may be our golden last chance to make up to the children for our selfishness. Let's do the thing with style, Guy! Prison, poverty, the works! Let's show the world we know how to live on the bottom even if we didn't know how to live at the top!"

Did she mean it? Was it anything more than a handsome Hyde gesture, a bow to the code of behaving well? But whatever it was, it was too late. There had been too many years of laughs, too many shrugs, too many quips, too many sneers, too much of each seeing the worst in the other. No, we could never go back. What was there to go back *to?*

"That's very sweet of you, Angelica, but it's also very sentimental. Your feeling does you credit, but it's not a feeling to build on. It's too high class, too much the noble thing. My dishonesty has inspired you. But I have a better plan. I want to get out of your life, once and for all, and give you another chance. It's not too late." I paused, to give what was coming its full effect. "I want you to divorce me, Angelica. I want you to divorce me, and when Lucy Geer dies, which can't be too far off, I want you to marry Rex."

Angelica's dark eyes slowly hardened into two slate discs. "Did you have to become a crook, Guy, to get rid of me? Couldn't you have asked me for a divorce before?"

"Please. Angelica, don't make a drama of this. Try to understand."

"I'm trying! I've been trying for twenty-five years! Tell me what more I can do for you. Shall I get the divorce while you're in prison? Shall I go hunting tomorrow while you're being arrested? Shall I wear yellow when you're wearing a striped suit?"

"Angelica!" I exclaimed firmly. "You will do no such thing. The divorce can wait my release. It would look otherwise as if you were leaving a sinking ship. I'll be the rat, thank you, if there have to be rats. I'm getting out of your and the children's lives forever. And it will be very much to everyone's good that I do!"

"And my heart has bled for you all afternoon!" Angelica continued in a trembling voice. "You're right, Guy Prime. I'm an arrant sentimentalist. Why, you're having the time of your life!"

It was a terrible ending to a marriage unless one remembered that the marriage had really ended long before. The pain that Angelica's pain might ordinarily have caused me was reduced to a mere dull ache by the anaesthesia of my impending conviction. When one is going to jail, believe me, boys, nothing else is quite real. I remember thinking at that moment that I understood the style with which the victims of the French Terror went to their deaths. The same dope enabled me to get through the even harder scene with Evadne and Percy that immediately followed.

Everything that followed my conviction worked out as neatly as everything before it had ended messily. Once those gods had me in jail, they appeared to be satisfied. Standard Trust Company, sharing my negligence if not my crime, put seven hundred thousand dollars back into Angelica's trust without even a protest. At the same time Meadowview was condemned for a highway, and Angelica got a good price for it. In a smaller house she continued to hunt and to live well enough. Evadne married George and had no further money problems; Percy became a first-rate lawyer. Everyone survived the war, and everyone today is prosperous and happy.

When I was released from prison in 1941, where I had been allowed to work, not too unhappily, as a librarian, I went to Panama. Angelica, at my repeated request, divorced me in 1942. Lucy Geer survived until 1948, and Angelica and Rex, two elderly lovebirds, were finally wed. From all that I hear it has been a most happy union. The relationships that it created may seem a bit bizarre: Evadne and her husband became stepsister and step-brother, and Angelica became her own daughter's mother-in-law. However, in present-day New York such things probably no longer raise an eyebrow. Only the fundamentals count, and Rex has always been full of *them*.

Sometimes it seems to me that I was an Iphigenia, that the gods had simply demanded my neck as the price for according victory to the army of Agamemnon. Certainly as soon as I had detached my ill-fated self from the baggage train of the Geers and Primes, their progress became smoother. I was perfectly content for many years to philosophize to myself by the shores of the still Pacific and was proud to be above the need of self-justification. But now that a new generation is growing up that does not know me and that I do not know, I find that I do not want to exist for them only in newspaper accounts and in the smooth, no doubt charitable interpretations of my conduct offered by Angelica and Rex. I want, after all, to be heard. Please, Evadne, think twice before you tear this up.

Part II

Rex

1.

WHEN I HEARD of Guy Prime's death in Panama last January
(1962) of a stroke in the bar of the Rivoli Hotel, my first reaction was that I could not have wished him a more merciful or
appropriate end. My second was concern for the old sores and
sorrows that must now be reopened for Angelica and the children. My third was apprehension as to what last dirty trick he
might have in reserve for me.

As the weeks went by I began to be ashamed of this last reaction. Guy, as it turned out, had left his affairs in scrupulous
order. He had owned his house in Panama City free and clear,
and he had no debts. There was even enough money to support
his second wife, of whom I had always assumed I would have to
take care, and to provide small legacies for Evadne and Percy. I
began to wonder if the dreaded final trick might not simply turn
out to be a changing of card hands, a switching about that would
make us, the wronged, seem like Guy's persecutors, a *volte-face*
that would present his deserted and plundered family in the
guise of haughty and unforgiving patricians who had cast him
into outer darkness. Evadne, who had not seen her father in
twenty-five years, was assailed with terrible guilt feelings, and
Percy flew down to Panama to see what he could do for Carmela.

But no. I was wrong, or rather, I had been right in the first
place. There *was* a last trick, and just as dirty a one as I had
feared.

A month after his death Evadne, at once grave and flustered, strode into my office downtown and plunked on my desk the memoir that her father had written two years before and that his widow, acting on his posthumous instructions, had forwarded to her, unopened.

"I'm sorry but you'll have to read it, Uncle Rex. Every word of the wretched thing. When you and Mummie married, you became my real father. Now you'll have to see what the other one has done. Do I have to show this libel to my boys? He says the most ghastly things—really, you wouldn't believe it. I've simply got to have your advice. And Mummie's, too."

When she had left, I read the manuscript at a single sitting. Guy had had the consideration to have it typed. It was the last consideration that he had showed his survivors.

What he had to say about Angelica and myself was wormwood but I supposed that the grandchildren could take it. Youth had become extraordinarily tolerant about such matters, much too tolerant, I thought, but now was not the time to quibble about that. What was very much worse to an old man, what, in fact, turned my heart to black ice, was the prospect of having to show my three grandsons this baldly cynical account of their other grandfather's crime.

Obviously, Guy, to his dying day, had not believed that he had done anything really wrong. He had been the one to get caught; that was all. In the cartoon of his mind his judges wore striped suits beneath their ermine. There was no such thing as justice to be expected from such a bench, only cant. Wall Street became a kind of Nottingham, and Guy, Robin Hood.

Had he written the memoir at the time of his conviction, and had we been back in those days, I should not have so much feared its effect on young men. What disheartened me was the odious suspicion that time might have been on Guy's side, that perhaps young men today would *not* be so shocked at what he had done. Was it, as he implied, like being caught with a trot in school? Were rules and regulations more than penalties in sport? Was the whole sad business simply a game?

One thing, however, I was perfectly clear about. If we should decide that Guy's memoir had to be shown to his grandsons, they should not be allowed to read it without a rebuttal. Even if morals had gone out—which I still did not for a minute admit— I would insist on my right to argue that they had once existed.

I gave it to Angelica to read that night. She was much less upset than I. She professed to find it the kind of apologia that she would have expected of Guy, and she had even the detachment to be amused by parts of it that were not in the least amusing to me. She had no hesitation about showing it to her grandsons, and she made the telling point that Evadne might break down altogether if she were to tear up the manuscript and then, in a fit of remorse, decide that she had abandoned her father living and disobeyed him dead. Angelica pooh-poohed my plea that we at least suppress the chapters on Guy's courtship and on our affair.

"Certainly not. I never could bear the sanctimonious sort of person who takes an unfair advantage of survivorship to censor the dead. Let's either burn Guy up or keep him whole. Do you think Evadne's and Percy's children are going to be shocked that I had an affair with each of my husbands before I married them? Think of it, to have been twice made an honest woman! Anyway, it's nothing to what young people do nowadays. And, besides, they won't believe it because nobody really believes their parents or grandparents ever made love. My mother used to hint that she had had affairs, but I always thought she was boasting!"

I sighed at such evidence of my wife's intransigent honesty, but I knew there was nothing to be done about it. "You don't think the memoir contains some rather grave misrepresentations?"

"It depends what you call 'grave.' I certainly never found Guy's father the charmer he makes him out. Nor did I ever think Alix Prime had any looks. But I daresay that's *one* point on which both you old dogs might agree."

I coughed. "I was thinking of more fundamental things."

"Well, I'm sure your rebuttal will straighten the boys out on those. That is, if they can ever get through it. Don't be too heavy and bankerish, my dear. Remember, this is a job of persuasion. You have to write a short story, as Guy did. I doubt if you can write half as good a one!"

I could sense the defensiveness in Angelica's mood which always accompanied her suspicion that people were being too hard on Guy. Second husbands learn to recognize such things. "Why don't you write your own story?" I suggested. "We could bind the three together, as a kind of package deal, or time capsule, against mistakes."

"It's just what I've been thinking of!" Angelica responded, with an eagerness that surprised me. "Two men could not possibly tell all of a story like Guy's. And only one woman could have."

"Just so."

"Oh, I don't mean myself. I will do my best, but only as a supplement. I meant your Lucy. She knew everything."

"Ah, Lucy."

"But failing her, the three of us might have a fling at it."

Angelica went straight to work the very next day, but although she started at a great pace she was constantly revising and tearing up sheets of paper, and in the end the job took her six months. For a while, I was glad to have her occupied, for she had been restless ever since the doctor, on her seventieth birthday, had made her give up riding, but as the weeks passed I began to fear that there was something obsessional in her frantic scribbling and ripping. When I suggested that she give it up, things became a great deal worse.

"I'm not going to leave poor Guy to your tender mercies, thank you," she said tartly. "A lot I care for your bankers' codes and lofty rules. Guy had no more to do with all that—fundamentally speaking—than the man in the moon. He didn't live in your world, or in mine, for that matter. He tried to do right, by his own lights." She looked at me now with the dark, resentful eyes of Guy Prime's wife. "You're all so high and mighty about him. Evadne, particularly. I daresay her boys will be, too. Well, I've got to find a way to make them feel poor Guy. She paused, to speculate on her method, and seemed to forget for a moment that I was there. "I wonder if my mother didn't have the key to Guy. She had an extraordinary instinct about people. But if she did, why did she ever throw us together? Couldn't she have seen it wouldn't work?"

I knew by now when it was best to leave Angelica alone. Besides, I could not help her with her problem. I had a big enough one of my own. Out of my countless memories of Guy, which ones should I select to show the growth in him of the hate that led him to place his fingers on the jugular vein of the world that had nurtured him?

I decided that I could only tell the story in terms of the imprint upon myself of a growing awareness of his character and motives. When I had my thread, I was able to write the memoir in a week's time. I would have taken less had I not remembered Angelica's warning that I had to "persuade." For the boys' sake, may I succeed!

2.

To GIVE the reader some sense of the strong initial impact that Guy made upon me, I should explain the depression into which my spirits had fallen at the time of our first meeting at Harvard. He speaks sarcastically of the little book that I had privately printed for my son George about my "rectory boyhood," and it may be true that I made too much of the serenity of my parents' home. I wanted my descendants to know that a life of small means and high ideals could have its reward in this world as well as the next. But in the greater candor of my old age I will confess that it was not always so. My father, it is true, elevated by the three pillars of faith, naïveté and a habit of depending on others to take care of the practical problems of life, breathed a fine, clear air of which he was constantly urging his family to partake, but my poor mother, who had to market, cook, sew and clean for a family of ten and to be the lady of the parish as well, was too occupied for many such inhalations. It is a bitter truth that sheer hard work can dry up some of a mother's love, or at least the expression of it, and I am afraid that our home was a bit arid even for my austere tastes. As a natural defense, when in later years I encountered demonstrative affection between parent and child, I was inclined to regard it as stagey and insincere. I was often unjust.

At Cambridge my first two years were a terrible drudgery. I had a series of part-time jobs: in a laundry, in a bakery, in a tutoring agency. Working one's way through college was not then as systematized as it later became, and the odds were against the student. When Guy first thrust himself on my attention, I was virtually at the end of my rope. The illness of a younger sister had obliged my father to withdraw even the meager allowance that he had been making me, and although nobody at home ever suggested it, I had the uneasy feeling that I ought to leave college and help out. It can be imagined with what sullen eyes I witnessed the antics of my future friend, then in his golden prime.

I must be fair. I will admit that Guy, in our junior year, was as handsome as he himself claims. His was a glorious youthful presence, of high color and high spirits, and a charm that only a churl could resist. I was that churl. I could not imagine why he sought me out or what he wanted of me. It was not, as I first suspected, to do his term papers for him, for he had good enough marks of his own. It was not for my friends, for I had none. It was not even for my companionship, for I worked too hard to have much of that to offer. Was I, then, a kind of charity case, or did he wish to learn how the lower orders lived? If he sat next to me in class or followed me across the yard afterwards, bubbling with questions about Keats or Browning, I would be curt to the point of incivility. But nothing seemed to rebuff him. He was impervious to hints, and even I was not enough of a churl to go beyond them.

Then came the affair of the economics prize and Guy's intervention to obtain the early news of my winning it. Of course, I was overwhelmed. Who would not have been? Even today, half a century later, my heart still warms at the memory of his imaginative generosity. I was grateful then to accept his proffered friendship, and when I took time from work to discuss the world and its company in his rooms or to drink with him in Boston bars, my conscience was somewhat quieted by the thought that I was paying a debt of gratitude. Guy in those days was the best company imaginable: he seemed never to be in a bad mood, never to lose his fascination in the passing parade. It was before the day of popular psychiatry, and I did not pause to speculate what tensions might lurk under so persistently sunny a surface.

His conversation was intimate, but never unpleasant, mildly impertinent and extremely funny. He mocked my somber moods, my inhibitions, my small town prejudices, but affection always glowed in his raillery. I was too proud, too reserved, to give that much of myself in friendship, but his example taught me that this was a lack and not, as I had primly supposed, a virtue. Guy was an artist in living. In handball, in squash, in dining, in drinking, in reading, he was unaffectedly strenuous and enthusiastic. I can still see him lying in my window seat on a hot May day, one foot dangling out the open casement, reciting "Tamburlaine" in a stentorian voice that attracted a little crowd of students on the grass outside.

Is it not brave to be a king, Techelles?
Usumcasane and Theridamas,
Is it not passing brave to be a king
'And ride in triumph through Persepolis?'

How I hear that voice! The students may have laughed and even whistled, but not too much or too meanly. There was something disarming in Guy's spontaneity, and then, too, he had a quick temper and quicker fists. For all his colored vests and dandified airs he was very much of a man.

He was also very much of a ladies' man, both in the drawing room and at the stage door. His activities in this latter respect might have caused bad blood between us had he been less of a diplomat. I was inclined to be prudish and would have taken offense had Guy, like most college youths, boasted of his triumphs. But his charm never failed him. He won me to his side by professing to be ashamed of his fleshly weakness and to admire my chastity. I blush to think of the pompous sermons that I must have delivered to him, but I doubt if he laughed at me, even up his sleeve. He must have regarded me as a kind of talisman to protect him from becoming the frivolous creature he was afraid of becoming. Seeing him in the company of the sober and industrious Reginald Geer, would not people have to weigh their judgments? Might not some of that dark sobriety even rub off on him?

Guy was terribly keen to have me meet his family, and he finally prevailed upon me, with the help of a railway pass, to visit him in Bar Harbor the summer after junior year. I found his father even worse than I had feared, a boundless snob who could not be bothered to conceal his small opinion of his son's unprofitable new friend. Mrs. Prime, however, a soft sad gentle invalid, made up for his brusqueness in the sweetness of her welcome. It was almost as if she were looking for friends who would stand by and steady her son when she was gone. I was touched, too, by Guy's devotion to her. There was nothing put on about this. One had only to see the tears start to his eyes when she had one of her coughing spells to be convinced of his utter sincerity. Like many American men, Guy was at his finest as a son.

The great event of my visit was meeting Marcellus de Grasse, who owned the big hill on which the Primes' villa stood. Our first encounter was as disastrous as Guy relates. I went back to the Primes', thinking there was little to choose between my host and the crotchety "malefactor of great wealth" (I knew all the T.R. phrases), except that my host at least was a fine-looking older man while Mr. de Grasse, with alabaster skin and dyed auburn hair, hook nose and humped back, struck my youthful eye as an old woman. I was sure that nothing would induce me to accompany Guy on another visit to the top of the hill. If he enjoyed the company of such economic fossils, he could enjoy it alone.

Then came the beautifully bound copy of *Social Statics* with its handsome inscribed apology, and I was disarmed. At Guy's suggestion I went alone to thank Mr. de Grasse and received a second and even more gracious retraction.

"You must learn, my dear young man, the obligations of your generation to mine. You have to keep us from freezing. Everything in my life conspires against fluidity: my seniority in the office, my female household at home, my intellectual isolation in a money-grubbing era. Small wonder that I have become a petty tyrant! But what particularly distresses me about last Sunday lunch is that I put myself in the false position of defending economic monopolists. What, after all, have I to do with the Harrimans and the Hills of this world? My grandfather outfitted a frigate in the War of 1812 as a gift to the nation. I betray my essential self in taking sides between the cops of government and the robbers of business. I am an observer, Mr. Geer. Help me to preserve that detachment!"

And so a lifelong relationship with my future boss and partner began. I had been exposed to some great teachers at Harvard: Copeland and Santayana and William James, but only as a student. Never in my short life had I been in close contact with a mind as richly informed and as speculative as Mr. de Grasse's. Banking was only a small part of his interests which ranged from the excavations at Knossos to the possibility of life on Jupiter. The quality of detachment that he feared was shriveling within him seemed to me, on the contrary, his most enduring characteristic. Indeed, it was to increase with the years. Mr. de Grasse lived into his nineties. Let me record to his credit, although it worried me at the time, that he objected less to Franklin Roosevelt than he had to Theodore. In the end our roles were reversed. *He* was the one who tried to argue me out of a sullen conviction that the New Deal was pure iniquity.

When Mr. de Grasse wrote, in the fall of senior year, to invite me to come to work for him with Guy after our graduation, I went through a sharp emotional crisis. It suddenly seemed to me that it was all too slick and too easy, that I had betrayed the principles of my Puritan forebears and sold my birthright for a meretricious success. Did I even exist any more except as a little brother of the rich? And had it not, perhaps, been deliberate? Was all my churlishness of manner any better than a fawning coyness? Had I not pined for the Prime luxury from the beginning and set my snares to catch Guy's attention by the crude expedient of being the one member of our class to turn him a cold shoulder?

So at least his father had thought, as I learned from Guy's memoir. How surprised Percy Prime would have been had he known that I shared his suspicions of myself! For a week I tormented myself with doubts and questionings, and at last, unbeknownst to Guy, who regarded my attitude as simple hysteria, I wrote to Mr. de Grasse to ask for an interview and made the trip down to New York, which I could ill afford.

I think Mr. de Grasse thoroughly enjoyed that interview. I

remember how he rested back in his swivel chair before his huge mahogany table of a desk, littered with jade figures, with carved ivory junks and beasts of burden, with everything, it seemed, but ink and paper, and made a church and steeple with his long fingers.

"That question, my dear young man, is characteristic of your generation. You don't want anything that you haven't earned. But can you define earning? Do we ever really know what we're rewarded for in this life? Is it for our toil or our integrity or our family tree or simply for our *beaux yeux?*"

"Well, I admit, sir, there's chance in any career, but I hate to feel you're offering me a job only because of Guy's parents."

"Guy's parents? Bless my soul, I don't even like them! At least I don't like his father. He's the very worst sort of parasite, the kind that thinks himself a good citizen because his reputation is as unstained as his shirt front."

"Well, because of Guy, then," I muttered, embarrassed by so telling a description of a man in whose house I had been a guest.

"Because of Guy! You think, then, that I staff de Grasse Brothers at the behest of young men who happen to be summer neighbors?"

"I'm sorry, sir," I said, coming to my senses at last. "I see I've made a proper fool of myself. I shall be happy to accept your offer if you still want a greenhorn who wastes your time with silly questions."

"Impertinent ones, too. For don't you know, Rex, that I myself was the boss's son, and my father before me? We don't talk about pull and family influence at de Grasse Brothers. At least not in the office of the senior partner!"

I was so confused now that I could only rise and mumble a second incoherent apology. Mr. de Grasse, however, seemed to wax more ebullient with my embarrassment.

"Sit down, my dear fellow, sit down. I still haven't answered your question." When I was again seated, he stared at me with twinkling eyes. "You want to know why I offered you a job. I offered you a job because I think you have brains and character. Because I expect you to go far in de Grasse. I fully realize that this is not the kind of thing an employer is meant to say to a prospective employee. I should emphasize the magnitude of the task and your slender qualifications. But I know that as a true New Englander you are far too guilt-ridden to be carried away by compliments. If you could see how wretched you look now!"

"I am grateful for your confidence, sir," I stammered. "I shall work my hardest for you."

"Work for yourself, dear boy. Don't worry about me. And now I'm going to tell you a secret. It is not you who owe your job to Guy. Before I met you, I was thinking of suggesting to him that he might not, after all, be cut out for a banker. But when I saw that he had the intelligence to pick a friend of your caliber, I concluded that he must be more serious than I had thought."

"Oh, Guy can be very serious, sir."

Mr. de Grasse did not answer this. He continued to gaze at me quizzically, as if debating how much more to tell me about my friend. "I have never been entirely fair to Guy," he said. Then he picked up a small bronze Antinoüs, which I later learned was the work of Cellini, and gazed at it pensively for some seconds. "Guy is a very beautiful human being. He has not only beauty of body but beauty of heart. I have seldom known a more generous or outgiving nature. As you know, my home is full of women. When Guy presented himself, quite of his own accord, as a kind of summer son, the charm of the prospect was irresistible to me. He has an amazing way with older people. He doesn't seem to be even aware of the difference in years. I was able to teach him a good many things, but nothing to what he taught me."

"What could Guy teach *you*, Mr. de Grasse?"

"What I am." The long white hand fluttered for a moment

over the jades. "He taught me that I did not care about beautiful things as much as I thought I did. Or about beautiful people
or about beautiful hearts. He taught me, quite unwittingly,
that what I really care about is beautiful minds. And Guy does
not have one." He sighed and seemed to appeal to me for a
merciful judgment. "Guy bores me a bit, that's the trouble.
And it's my fault that he bores me. He's never pretended for a
moment to be anything he wasn't. But why must he fix his
affections where they can't be returned?"

From the silence that followed I understood that Mr. de
Grasse's question had not been entirely rhetorical. "Surely he
doesn't always, sir."

"But I suggest he does!" he snapped back in a voice that surprised me. "I suggest that Guy is a perverse little moth that will
always desert the rich linen closet of his natural inheritance for
the deadly heat of the candle."

I began to see that I was being sounded out. "Meaning that
you're a candle, sir?" I asked more boldly.

"And that you're one too, young man. And that candles get
blown out, if moths are big enough."

"Is that what moths want?"

"Moths don't *want*," he retorted. "Moths are moths. I'm an
old candle and can look after myself. But it takes some looking,
with Guy. He knows where to have one. He knows, for example, that I love to play the wise old Roman emperor to a wor-
shipping young tribune. He sees me seeing myself as Marcus
Aurelius, aloof, way up above the mob, reading books in my box
at the circus. Oh, he has my number!"

"And mine? He has that too, you imply."

"Ah, that's where he's really subtle." Mr. de Grasse chuckled,
with more than a touch of malice. "Subtle by knowing when to
be obvious. He sees that the son of a good country parson must
see the 'great world' as wickedness. As Sodom and Gomorrah.
And that he will be fascinated by what he most expects: a can-

vas of cupidity and vain sacrifices. A Hieronymous Bosch. Guy knows how to call a Baal a Baal!"

Being young, I thought that this was merely a sample of the kind of advice that older people felt compelled to give to younger and to which it was the bounden duty of the latter respectfully to listen. Indeed, I believed that the giving and receiving of such exhortations was of the essence of a proper relationship between the generations. But I never really considered that such warnings were meant to be acted upon. All the dragons that I feared were out in the open and had to be killed with spears. I had not yet met the kind of which Mr. de Grasse was speaking.

3.

GUY'S VERSION of what happened between me and his cousin Alix Prime is perhaps the most distorted portion of his narrative. I do not suppose that it was a deliberate misrepresentation of the facts, but rather a fantasy of what actually happened, nursed by his vanity and resentment in the lonely years at Panama.

His description of Alix as a doll has some physical truth. She had creamy, blemishless skin, an oval face, beautifully waved golden hair and large, blue eyes which, probably because of a slight thyroid deficiency, might have been described as "popping." She was pretty but, except when talking, curiously lacking in animation. Guy suggests that I fell in love with her looks. It was not so. What attracted me, quite against my better judgment, was something of which he as a cousin was totally unconscious. It was a sense of urgency under Alix's candy-box cover, a vivid hint of feeling in her giggle, an intensity behind her blue stare that made a man think the very things that may have put that near-panic in her eyes. Alix had great sex appeal, even if she had no idea what to do with it.

If her looks, by themselves, would not have attracted me, her conversation would have done so even less. On my first visit to her home I thought her the dizziest, most empty-headed creature I had ever met and the very prototype of what, in my bias, I considered the New York debutante to be. When I was invited, as I left, to come to tea the next day by her large, noisy and surprisingly friendly mother and when I heard myself actually accepting. I felt that I must have taken leaves of my senses. Was this how the devil of the big city caught one? It had never occurred to me that I would trot down the primrose path in full awareness that I was making an ass of myself.

The Chauncey Primes' house on Fifth Avenue was certainly the grandest I had ever been in. At last I could appreciate what Guy meant by the "poverty" of his branch of the family. It was a four story Louis XIII *hôtel,* of red and white brick with a steep mansard roof, like a segment of the *Place des Vosges,* handsomer than its Fifth Avenue neighbors, but with an interior made dreary by the gilded opulence of the era. I sat with Alix, away from the older people at the tea party, in a stiff little parlor that opened on the empty ballroom like a summer hotel porch on the ocean. She chattered on, nervously and pointlessly, about opera. I observed that I did not care for it.

"But why not?" she asked in astonishment. "I thought everybody liked opera."

I muttered something about silly plots and sad endings and received a spirited lecture.

"But operas are *supposed* to have tragic endings. If they didn't, they wouldn't be operas. They'd be musical comedies. In opera everything is just the opposite of the way things are in real life. The characters sing, to begin with. What would you think of me now if I suddenly jumped up and led Mamma's friends in a rousing chorus? That I was crazy, of course. In opera you let your emotion out; in real life you keep it in. At least, the people one knows do. And in the end the hero or heroine, or both of them, die, to show us the make-believe is over. Then we can get up and put on our wraps and go back to the real world."

"Is it a better one?"

"That depends on what you want." Oh, yes, she had thought it all out. "Things happen to characters in opera. Wonderful things and terrible things. But somebody has to die in the end. In real life nothing very much happens."

"But we all still die in the end."

"Yes, but it's different. It's not apt to be so violent."

"Which do you prefer?" I asked, beginning, in spite of myself, to be intrigued. "The opera or real life?"

"Oh, real life, of course. That's the right answer, isn't it? One is always supposed to prefer real life. Besides, who wants to die violently in the end?"

"Even for a handsome tenor?"

"Not I." She giggled suddenly. "I prefer bassos. Except they're usually fathers or villains. Do you prefer sopranos or contraltos?"

"I'm afraid I don't get much chance to tell. A decent seat to the opera is a bit stiff for a first year clerk in de Grasse, and I'm not enough of a fan for the peanut gallery."

"Oh, but I'm sure Mamma would be delighted to ask you to come in our box! We go to all the matinées."

The life that Alix led was considered a highly restricted one, even for those days. She took no courses, did no charity work and spent most of her time with her female Prime cousins. On Saturday afternoon after Saturday afternoon they overflowed the Chauncey Primes' opera box like violets in a red vase and scribbled their names in each other's programs with ecstatic comments. As no Prime ever threw anything away, I am sure that

there are still bundles of these in attics in Newport and Southampton with such finely flowing marginal comments as: "Sem-
brich magnificent! Ten curtain calls. Gladys—Manuela—Alix
—Mamma—Miss Pym."

How I see them again, those bright-eyed, gushing, over-
dressed Prime girls, so romantic, so earnest, so idealistic! One
might have thought that they were too soft and gentle for a hard
world, but that would have been because one did not know how
much of that world they owned. *They* did not forget it. Look at
them today. They may no longer have their looks or their figures, but they have still their fortunes and, more curiously, their
ideals. The American heiress is as tough as the heir is weak.

Except Alix. Alix was always the exception to every rule. She
was more childish, at nineteen, but she was also more sensitive.
She had a funny, intense way of going about all her small daily
occupations. She knew her opera plots, down to the last villain's
disguise and the last lady's maid's lament, and loved to talk
about them. I had not been to the Chauncey Primes' more than
twice before I realized that people treated Alix specially. They
listened to her in the patient way that people listen to a temper-
amental and difficult child. The surface of her calm was a brittle
one and covered a murky, perhaps even tumultuous adoles-
cence.

As I have already said, it was before the days of popular psychiatry, and young girls who suffered from what is now called
"manic depression" were simply sent to their rooms, or to country estates, until they were in a more presentable mood. Guy's
mother, who struck me as having "nerves" herself, was the one
who warned me about Alix.

"She's been different, ever since she was a child. First way up
and then way down. Gay as a lark and gloomy as an owl. People
talk about it, and of course my brother-in-law fancies that any
young man who looks at her is after her money."

"How horrible!"

"Well, I daresay some of them are."

"But Alix is an enchanting creature!" I protested warmly. "She doesn't need money to attract a man. Can't he see that? Can't her mother see it?"

"Oh, Amy sees things through her husband's eyes. Even when her heart tells her otherwise."

Guy's mother was right about this. Mrs. Chauncey Prime was not what she seemed. Everything about her appearance suggested a "no nonsense" attitude, a brusque but kindly straightforwardness, a large capacity for pulling aside confining drapery and letting in air. She was big and plain and hearty, and she used her parasol, like a terrible duchess in an English parlor comedy, to poke young people and summon them to her side. But what in reality was this paragon, this sweeping, feathered gorgon, this splendid despot, but a craven creature who trembled at the frown of the insignificant man whom she had made rich? I was to find New York society full of such paradoxes.

I went on three Saturday afternoons with Alix and Mrs. Prime to the opera before I was asked to meet their lord and master at Sunday lunch. Chauncey Prime was a smaller, dryer version of Guy's father, similarly immaculate, but instead of holding himself straight he hunched his shoulders and shook his head in endless exercise of an endless capacity for disapproval. He did not once evince the smallest interest at any topic of conversation at lunch.

"I hear you work for Marcellus de Grasse," he said to me gruffly. "I suppose you're a great admirer of his. All the young men seem to be."

"He has a great imagination, sir. In fact, I doubt if any man has a nobler concept of the role of capital in modern society."

Mr. Prime grunted. I should have guessed that enthusiasm was anathema to him. The man who had married his money could afford to admire only the bare fact of its possession.

"De Grasse may be all very well," he continued, "but he belongs to a bygone era. Men like Rockefeller and Carnegie could buy and sell him twenty times over today. He puts me in mind of a baronet in a powdered wig poking about in a steel foundry."

"But surely capital isn't only a question of quantity," I protested, perhaps too warmly. "Isn't the great thing to know where it's needed? A few dollars in the right place can still make industrial history. And I think de Grasse Brothers, with their flair for this kind of thing, will be around as long as your Rockefellers and Carnegies. Perhaps longer."

Mr. Prime gave another grunt and addressed no further remarks to me for the balance of our meal. If there was one thing he hated more than enthusiasm, it was an enthusiastic young man.

Alix walked in the park with me that afternoon. It was the fifth time I had seen her and the first that we had been alone. I was mortified to find that I trembled so that I could hardly speak. When I took her back to her house we had not exchanged a word that could not have been spoken in the presence of both her parents. Yet I was sure, from her own constraint and averted glances, that she was in trouble, too.

All my life I had fancied myself in charge of my destiny. One day, of course, I would marry, and my bride would be Lucy Ames, or a girl much like her. What I had never seen or wanted to see in my cards was an heiress. Yet here I was, choked to incoherence by my passion for a rich girl whom I did not even admire! Why in God's name was love called blind? I saw every fault in poor Alix and every disadvantage to me, by my peculiar lights, of her worldly advantages.

To do her justice, if she did not fit into my picture of what my life should be, she fitted even less into the Primes' picture of what *she* should be. Indeed, there seemed to be no pictures where she did fit. She dressed and talked more like someone playing a society girl on the stage than a society girl. At first I had suspected her of sarcasm, but better acquaintance routed this theory. Her nature was not rebellious. In fact, the very key to her character might have been in her absolute submission to the world in which she found herself. I doubt if it ever crossed her mind to question the validity of her father's rule or the point of her family's gilded vacuous existence. Yet this did not mean that she was lacking in character. Even her younger sisters, who were inclined to make fun of her, did not laugh when Alix's tone rose to shrillness. There were certain things she could not bear: she would clap her hands to her ears at any tale of physical brutality, of man's unkindness to man or to animals. Her greatest distress was that her sensitivity made her useless in any kind of hospital work. Sometimes it seemed to me that she clung to the world of the Primes only because it was so insulated from horror, that she picked her way across the carnage of the universe without daring to look down. But that was what distinguished her from the others. She *knew* that the carnage was there.

Something had to happen. I could not go on so. If I could not speak before Alix alone, I had to speak before others. One Saturday afternoon in that cold early spring, when I called at the house, I saw the tall maroon Daimler parked before the door and met Mrs. Prime and Alix coming out. They were going calling, and Mrs. Prime, in her usual friendly fashion, asked me to join them. She probably had not expected that I would accept, as calling was a ladies' pursuit, but I abruptly decided that this was my moment, and jumped into the car before she could change her mind.

We drove off. Mrs. Prime was dropping cards on the people with whom she had recently dined and on the people who had recently dropped cards on her, and in the smaller society of that day she could dispose of as many as five in a single street. She had a footman as well as a chauffeur, a not uncommon circumstance for the rich of that ostentatious era, and we sat in the back of the car, I on the *strapontin* and Alix and her mother on the cushioned seat, while the footman climbed the long stoops with the little envelopes. The lady of the house usually had the tact not to be "in," but occasionally she was, which would be signaled by a nod to the chauffeur, who would turn to alert Mrs. Prime, who would sigh and grumble and gather up her skirts to descend.

It was wonderful what the fashions of 1909 did to romanticize this simple bourgeois scene. Mrs. Prime's stalwart figure carried well the straight sweeping lines of silk, the puffed shoulders, the wide-brimmed hat with its ostrich feathers, while Alix, demure in a white blouse and plain black skirt seemed absurdly young and very sweetly filial. I think to this day of that street of cluttered brownstone stoops under a slatey April sky as the quintessence of romance.

While Mrs. Prime was making one of her calls, Alix must have felt the contagion of my mood, for she asked me: "What on earth can you be thinking about? You look as pleased as Daddy when someone asks him a genealogical question about old New York."

I burst out laughing. "I was just thinking that I'd like to go on doing just this, forever and ever!"

"Leaving cards?"

"Yes!"

"You must have taken leave of your senses. I should have thought it was purgatory for a man."

"Alix," I exclaimed with sudden gravity, leaning forward, "do you ever feel moods of wild, senseless, violent happiness?"

She studied my face curiously, and when she smiled, it was as if she had taken my hand on a beach, before a cold green ocean, and said: "I'll try it if you will." "I don't know that I do," was what she actually said. "I'm not even absolutely sure that I would want to. Are you feeling one now?"

"Yes! At this very moment! I love this street and this motorcar and that silly little black muff of yours."

"And is it fun to love such things?"

"Well, of course it's more fun to love people."

"People? How can one love 'people'?"

"Not people, then. You."

Alix drew quickly back. "Now you're going to be what Mamma calls 'silly.' "

"Silly? I've never made such sense in my life! Do you want me to sing it? Then it might be like one of your operas, where things happen. Do you remember?" I raised my voice to a chant. "Alix Prime, I love you!"

"Oh, good heavens, do you want the whole street to hear you?" She leaned hastily forward to place her fingers on my lips. "Please, Rex. Things happen in opera, but you forget what I told you. People *die* in opera."

"But they live first!"

"I suppose that's only fair. But hush. Here comes Mamma."

"Mrs. Prime," I exclaimed, as we drove off, in a loud, clear and I fear rather pompous tone, "I want to persuade you that I love your daughter and that I seek the honor of becoming her husband!"

"Alix, is the man out of his mind? We hardly know him!"

"I'm afraid he is, Mamma."

I was so exhilarated that I could only laugh again. Mrs. Prime, red and flustered, looked in bewilderment from me to Alix, and then picked up the voice tube and told her chauffeur to drive around the park.

"I don't know what to say to you, young man. If I had the brains I was born with I suppose I'd stop the car and put you out. Or even call a policeman. Imagine proposing to a young lady while she and her mother are dropping cards!"

"I'll do it any other time you say!"

"Well, at least you're open. Not all the young men who come to the house are. Indeed, some of them are very devious . . ."

"Mamma!"

"I know, I know, everyone thinks I'm much too frank, but

I'm simply trying to help you, my dear, that's all. Of course,
your father mustn't hear a word of this. It's much too early. We
must keep it strictly between the three of us."

"Keep *what,* Mamma?"

"Well, your engagement or whatever you call it."

"Mamma!" Alix cried in dismay for the third time and then
covered her face with her hands. "Really, this is all too mortify-
ing."

"Let me straighten things out, Mrs. Prime," I intervened.
"There is no engagement, of course, secret or otherwise. Alix
has not admitted any preference for me at all. She probably
can't abide me."

"Oh, Rex, I like you very much!"

This threw us all into greater confusion. "I mean any special
preference," I insisted. "All I want is for your mother to know
how I feel." I turned resolutely again to Mrs. Prime. "I cannot
come to your house any longer under false pretenses. I want
Alix's family to know that my intention is to urge her to become
Mrs. Reginald Geer. And I want to make it perfectly clear that
I'm not a fortune hunter. It may take me years before I can
properly support Alix, but I'd rather wait those years than live
off a single penny of her money."

"Please!" Alix cried with a despairing voice. "Must we talk
about money *already?*"

"It might be best," I continued, "if I went back to the house
now and had an interview with Mr. Prime."

"No!" both ladies cried in unison.

And then I discovered that for all Alix's seeming vagueness
and for all her mother's bustling confusion, they could be very
efficient when they acted together. There was no irresolution in
their joint attitude that whatever problem I might present, it
was one to be solved by the distaff side of the family. The female of the species is much less snobbish than the male. Mrs.
Prime and Alix did not really care a rap about the Prime social

standards, but, with the innate conservatism of their sex, they were perfectly willing to dress me up to look like something of which their old rooster would approve. They were even willing to regard the dressing process as a sacred duty. It was agreed before I got out of the car that afternoon that I was committed to Alix, that Alix was in no way committed to me, and that none of us should tell Papa anything. It served me jolly well right for putting myself in their hands.

Now I am sure it will have struck the reader, as it vividly strikes me in recalling these ancient events, that it was a very odd thing that I should not have told Guy of my love affair. After all, he was my landlord, my business associate, my closest friend and the cousin of my beloved. Insofar as I had a home in the city, he had provided it. Yet it is nonetheless certainly the case that not only did I tell him nothing, but that I took the utmost pains to conceal from him what was going on. I remember not being sure myself why I was so determined about this. It might have been the unconscious flowering of the seed of doubt that Mr. de Grasse had planted. It might have been my reluctance, being Guy's debtor for all my New York life, to owe him my romance as well. Or it might have been, more simply still, an old New England feeling that love was a weakness better kept to oneself. But whatever that instinct, it served me well. It was a pity that it should have ever been betrayed.

4.

Now COMMENCED a curious, unreal phase of my life that lasted only a few months but that was unlike anything that I had experienced before or was to experience after. I continued for the rest of the spring to call faithfully at the Louis XIII *hôtel*.

Sometimes I went driving with Mrs. Prime and Alix up River-side Drive to Grant's Tomb and back; sometimes Alix and I would walk in Central Park; sometimes we would simply sit in two chairs looking over the empty gilded ballroom and talk. Alix was alternately friendly and agitated, and she continued to forbid me to make love to her. It was horribly frustrating. I could not even kiss her.

"You keep saying that you have to establish yourself in business and that it may take years," she would protest in tears. "Then what is the hurry? Why can't we go on like this, being good friends? Why not, Rex?"

"Is that all you want?"

"It's all I want now."

"Why don't you come right out with it and tell me you don't give a damn about me?"

"Because it's not true! I like you very much, Rex. You know that."

"But do you think you can ever love me, Alix? That's the point."

"Yes, I think I might learn to love you, in my own way. Maybe I do now. But how can I be sure it's your way?"

"What's the difference?"

"But don't you see, that's just what I don't *know!*" she wailed. "And if I don't know, how is it fair to you?"

"Why not let me be the judge of that? Kiss me, Alix."

"Oh, Rex, there you go again. And you told me you wouldn't!"

"For God's sake, Alix! Have you no heart?"

It was about this time that Guy discovered my romance, much in the manner that he describes, except that the language which he used about Alix, and for which I knocked him down, was almost obscene. It is perfectly true, however, that he took up my cause after that and that the little houseparty at his parents' in Bar Harbor was of his own engineering. I had not seen my own poor family in a year's time, but I did not hesitate to chuck my plans for a vacation with them and hurry instead to the enchanted island of Mt. Desert to await the arrival of Alix and her mother. I felt a bit guilty about using Guy's hospitality solely to promote my courtship, but I swallowed these feelings as best I could. I was beyond such luxuries. I tried to make it up to him by doing all the things he liked: by playing tennis and climbing his favorite mountains and accompanying him without a murmur on his social calls. But all this broke up with the arrival of his aunt and cousins.

Mrs. Chauncey Prime was, to say the least, a discombobulating houseguest to her less affluent in-laws. She came with a motorcar, three daughters, a chauffeur and a maid, and another maid followed by rail with the trunks. She brought presents for all, which simply filled the Percy Primes' modest villa with tissue paper, and, as Guy put it, her very apologies seemed to contain further strains on his mother's limited household. But poor Guy's greatest disgust must have been having our strenuous tennis singles turned into a giggley foursome and our mountain hikes into chattering strolls before tea. I will have to admit that he behaved like a brick.

He was even nice to his sister Bertha, then a large, easily perspiring girl with the shrill temper of the sensitive adolescent. She had developed an unfortunate crush on me and was inclined to be grabby about my company when the four of us did things together. On our walks Guy would lead her ahead so that I might be alone with Alix, and in tennis doubles he always picked his sister for a partner. He even made the supreme sacrifice of looking after Bertha at dances so that I might be free to devote myself to Alix. I could appreciate the extent of his unselfishness in that he had once told me that to be seen dancing with a plain woman was a disgrace amounting to torment.

Yet nothing seemed to work with Alix. From the very beginning of her visit, which coincided with a spell of foggy weather, her spirits wilted. With each day she lost more of the chirping gaiety that had characterized her in New York. If I asked her what was wrong, she would only respond with a feverish cheerfulness that nothing was. And worse, despite all Guy's valiant efforts, I could never seem now to be alone with her. When he took Bertha ahead on a walk, Alix hurried to catch up with them. When we danced together she affected to be too intently following the music to pay attention to what I said. One evening I got her away from the others after supper and took her for a stroll in the small neat garden where Guy's mother occasionally puttered. When we were quite out of sight and earshot of the house I turned on her. "Would you rather I went away?"

The look of immediate distress in those bulging blue eyes would have silenced anyone but a lover. "Oh, Rex, how can you say that?"

"Because I'm obviously making you miserable."

"No!"

"What is it then? We were happy in New York. Why can't we be happy up here?"

"Oh, we *were* happy in New York, weren't we?" Alix clasped her hands, as if begging me to confirm something that she no longer quite dared to believe. "I wish New York could have gone on forever!"

"Well, we can always go back there. But what is it about Maine that changes things?" I seized her hands, and she was so troubled that she allowed it, but when I moved closer to kiss her, she jumped back. "What is it, dearest?" I implored. "What is it up here that changes everything?"

Her voice dropped to a whisper. "Guy."

"Guy!" Mine rose to a shout. "Has Guy been bothering you?"

"Oh, no, he's been kind, terribly kind. He's been darling, actually. That's the trouble."

A hideous suspicion lit up my darkness. "You don't mean he's been making love to you?"

Alix seemed even more distressed at this. "Oh, Rex, silly,

please stop imagining things, or I shan't be able to talk to you at all. Guy has been perfect with me. But he never was before, don't you see? He was always the jolly cousin who pulled my pigtails and made fun of me as a stupid little girl. And I adored that! We all adored Guy. And now he's so different, so serious, so *respectful*. I hate it!"

"Shall I tell him to leave you alone?"

"In his own house? How can you?"

"Oh, I can."

"But don't you see, Rex, he's right. He's absolutely right!"

I shook my head in confusion. "Right to be respectful?"

"No, no, no. Right to be serious. He thinks it's not fair for you to be engaged to me without my being engaged to you. And it's not!"

I breathed in relief. "Well, there's a very simple way out of that one."

"No!" Alix's tone was near panic. "That's what *he* says, don't you see? That's what I don't want! To be engaged!" In her fear she actually caught my arm. "I don't see how I can tell you this, but I don't want to be all those things that Guy says I ought to be. A woman and a wife and so on. Oh, Rex, help me! Rex, be my one friend!"

It was not the lowest moment of my life, but I think it was probably the lowest moment up until then. At last I began to have a suspicion of how ill the poor girl was. But I was young and in love, and it followed that I was hopeful. Could not Alix be led gently out of her shadowland by a man who loved her enough? Patience was what was needed, and I had plenty of time. Had I not promised myself that I would not marry until I could afford a bride? And even now, decades later, I do not know that a psychiatrist would say that my optimism was unreasonable. Alix and I, given time, might have found happiness. I am convinced that Guy's later supposition that she was in love with *him* was the merest fatuity. Even if she told him to stop

playing John Alden, I see no reason to infer that she meant anything but that Miles Standish should speak for himself. I doubt
that she had even read Longfellow. As a matter of fact, I doubt
that she had ever read anything but Gustav Kobbé's *The Complete Opera Book.*

I assured her now, as gently as I knew how, that she did not
have to become engaged before she wanted to, that she was perfectly free, if such was her choice, to live and die in single bliss.
When she seemed calm again we went back to the house, and
later that night, in our shared bedroom, I tried to persuade Guy
to alter his behavior towards her without telling him of her
psychic disturbance. I was not very successful.

"You mean I'm to pull her pigtails?" he asked in understandable bewilderment. "But she doesn't have them any more."

"All I mean is that she liked being treated the way you used to
treat her."

"Being kicked around?"

"If you want to put it that way."

"Look, pal, I don't want to put it any way. I only meant to oil
the wheels for you, and I seem to have been using glue. You say
Alix finds me too respectful?"

"Well, too courteous, perhaps."

"And she wants to turn back the clock to the days when I used
to pie her bed and drop ice down her neck?"

"Maybe not quite that far back."

"If you'll let me offer a word of advice, my friend, I think
you're going about it the wrong way. This idea of having to be
able to support Alix before you marry her is tommyrot. By the
time you're able to pay for a girl like that, she'll be an old maid.
And what's the point? Money isn't what she needs; she's up to
her neck in it. It's a husband she wants!"

"I wish you wouldn't talk about Alix's money," I protested.

"How can I help it? Can you think of a palm tree without
palms? Let's face it, old boy. You've got to supply the imagina-

tion that Uncle Chauncey lacks. He can't understand that you're just the son-in-law he wants, and he never will, until you *are* that son-in-law. He'll be tickled pink some day to see Alix married to the senior partner of de Grasse Brothers. But you have to put the cart before the horse."

"Really, Guy, you're too absurd."

"I tell you I know what I'm talking about! Alix's castle must be taken by storm."

"I think you'd better let me do things my own way."

"Very well then." Guy shrugged without the least show of bad temper. "You're on your own, boy. From now on I shall leave you and Alix strictly to your own devices."

Which I accepted. It seemed to me, all in all, probably the best course of action. In the days that followed, Guy abandoned our foursome and resumed his place as the shining center of the glittering youth at the Swimming Club. Bertha hung on to Alix and myself, but, as three could not play tennis, she had sullenly to spend some of her time on the big dark veranda where her mother and aunt knitted and chatted most of the day. When Guy came home he hardly spoke to Alix, beyond a few civil words. Indeed, he played his new role so well that his father criticized him for neglecting his houseguests.

Yet Alix's humor did not improve. Left more alone with me, she became even more uncommunicative. She must have understood that I had spoken to Guy, and this, I supposed, had made her wretchedly self-conscious. It reached the point in three days' time when she could not tolerate the least personal remark. She would raise her hands to her ears and repeat over and over again: "Let us please, *please* talk about the weather!" I finally welcomed Bertha's company. At least, Alix relaxed when she was with us.

I began at last to make out dimly what it was that she feared. It was not so much what Guy said or did as what she conceived him to be expecting of her. So long as he had treated her, however mockingly, as a child, it helped her to think of herself as a

child. But now, whether he talked to her or not, he still constituted an audience, and presumably an impatient one, sitting out
in front before the closed curtains. And what was the play but
the oldest of romances, the princess and the swineherd? When
the curtains parted, should the audience not see her, in a golden
robe and a golden coronet, ready to play her part in a golden
plot that led to a golden destiny? What was next to happen
must have come to Alix like the clapping and stamping of that
audience out front as she shivered behind the still-lowered curtain, knowing that she had no lines.

We were sitting late one afternoon on the porch, I reading
(yes, I could always read) while Alix, with her remarkable talent for doing nothing, was simply looking at the view, when
Guy joined us. For a few moments I was only vaguely conscious
of his sitting there, staring from one of us to the other.

"You two take the cake!" he exclaimed at last.

"What cake?" I asked.

"Here you are on a beautiful day in a beautiful place, young,
healthy and without a care in the world, and what do you make
of your opportunities? Sit here and mope! *Tempus fugit,* I tell
you."

"And what should we be doing?" I demanded, still thinking
that he was going to suggest a walk or a game of tennis.

"Why, anything else!" Guy threw up his hands. "I never saw
two people more in love who did less about it."

"Shut up!" I cried.

"What *should* we do about it?" Alix demanded now in a
high, strained voice. She was staring with a fixed horror at her
cousin.

"Elope, you dumbbells! Elope and wait for a 'come home, all
is forgiven' letter. I promise you'll get one, if I have to send it
myself!"

Alix gave a little cry and fled into the house. I turned hotly to
Guy who raised his hand immediately to silence me. "I know, I
know," he said coolly. "You're going to suggest I mind my own

business. But this *is* my business. You have made it my business. Don't worry. She'll come around. Someone had to do *something*."

Alix came down for dinner, seemingly collected, and our life resumed its usual if unsatisfactory flow. On the next to last day of my vacation, however, she complained of a migraine and retired to her room. That evening her mother showed me a wireless that she had received from her husband. "The Wandering Albatross" was en route to Bar Harbor.

"But isn't that a change of plans?" I exclaimed.

"Oh my, yes. They weren't planning to go further than Ilesboro."

"You meant they were *sent* for?"

"My dear boy, I don't *know!*"

I could see that she was agitated, even frightened, and I went to look for Guy. I found him in his room, smoking a pipe and reading, and the picture of his ease unreasonably provoked me.

"Your uncle and Commodore Thompson are coming to Bar Harbor!" I cried. "Do you suppose your father sent for them?"

"My dear fellow, why would he?"

"Because he suspects that a scheming pauper has designs on his niece!"

"My father is many things, Rex, but he is not obvious. Sending for Uncle Chauncey would be obvious."

His suavity at such a moment infuriated me. "Did *you,* then?"

Guy was on his feet in a moment. "Is that what you think of me?"

I turned away sullenly. "I don't know what I think of anybody," I muttered. "Why should you want a cousin of yours to marry anyone like me? It doesn't make sense."

"I'll try to remember you're under a strain," he said coldly, "and that you no longer realize what you're saying."

"Well, who did send for him, then?"

"Why did he have to be sent for? Couldn't he have come on his own? Daddy may have written him, quite innocently, that you were here. Couldn't he put two and two together?"

"You assume then," I asked wretchedly, "that he is coming because of Alix?"

Guy shrugged. "Why else would he come? He loathes Bar Harbor. That much we all know."

"And you assume too, I suppose, that she will pack her bags and jump on the yacht as soon as he gives her a nod?"

"Do you think she won't?"

"Oh, I'm not thinking any more. Except that it was a bad day when I first got mixed up with you Primes."

"Thanks, pal."

I did not fall asleep until the morning, and when I awoke it was past nine o'clock. With an immediate sense of disaster I looked over at Guy's bed and saw that it was empty. Jumping up and going out to the porch, I found him, in his pajamas, peering out at the harbor through a pair of binoculars. As both hillside and water were enveloped in fog I asked him irritably what he was looking at. He handed me the glasses and pointed. Out in the middle of the bay there was a large clearing, and framed in that clearing, like a marine print, long and low and as ominously white as Moby Dick, lay a great steam yacht.

" 'The Wandering Albatross.' "

"No kidding," I said grimly.

"Admit she's a beauty."

"As beautiful as death! Has your uncle come ashore?"

"Oh, no. Newport is the only dry land Uncle Chauncey ever touches in cruising. People go to Uncle Chauncey. He doesn't go to them."

"People?" When Guy simply shrugged I repeated harshly, "People? Meaning whom?"

"Meaning, if you must know, that I saw Alix leave the house

fifteen minutes ago. Aunt Amy's car took her off towards the village."

"Well, what's wrong with that? Isn't it perfectly natural for her to go to see her father?"

"At this hour in the morning? When even God has never seen Uncle Chauncey before ten? And why did she take two suitcases and her maid?"

In agony I rushed back to our room, flung on my clothes and dashed down to the dining room where, as I had dreaded, I found a pink envelope propped up at my place. "Dear Rex," her stiff little note ran,

> I am joining Papa and Uncle Sidney for the rest of their cruise. I have thought things over very carefully, and I am convinced it is best this way. At some rather later time, I hope that you will come to see me. Until then, please accept my gratitude for your kind opinion of me, as ever,
>
> ALIX PRIME.

Guy's memory is correct about my rowing out to the yacht, but it is wrong about my being refused permission to board. I was received at the gangway with perfect good manners and told that Mr. Prime would see me in the lounge.

The fact that he did not own "The Wandering Albatross" and was aboard simply as his brother-in-law's guest, Alix's father managed, in the inimitable fashion of the Primes, to convert into evidence of his greater prestige. Commodore Thompson, a small, hirsute, bustling man, had been somehow reduced to the position of a chartered skipper who took his great boat up and down the coast for the delectation of Chauncey Prime and who had remained a bachelor only to swell the inheritance of Prime nieces. When he had led me down a spotless white corridor to the broad white lounge where Mr. Prime, in a blue blazer and gleaming white flannels, was seated, he was asked, like a privileged inferior, to remain.

"Please, Sidney, stay with us," Mr. Prime enjoined him. "I prefer to have a witness. Now, Mr. Geer, will you kindly state what is on your mind as briefly as possible? We are anxious to get under way."

I stammered out that I loved his daughter and wanted to marry her. I said that I fully realized that in my position I must appear presumptuous, but that I hoped to rise in the world. I told him that I did not ask for his approval, but simply that I might see Alix alone to say good-bye.

"But has my daughter not written you?" he interrupted testily.

"She has, sir. But under the circumstances I feel that her letter came more from you than from her."

"You imply that I used force?"

"Only strong influence."

"I must always be the villain, mustn't I, Sidney?" Mr. Prime demanded of his brother-in-law in a sneering tone. "I must always be made out as slamming the door on true love because I can't see that the swineherd is really Prince Charming in disguise. You saw the state Alix was in when she came abroad this vessel. Was it her ogre of a father who had caused it?"

"Hardly, Chauncey. You've been at sea with me for the past month."

"Exactly, Sidney, thank you. I've been at sea. And I'm *still* at sea, Mr. Geer," Mr. Prime continued wrathfully, turning on me, "as to what my good brother could have been thinking of to allow you to pester that poor child within an inch of her sanity. Look at *that*, if you please, Mr. Geer." And he thrust before my incredulous eyes a ship's form of wireless with the typed words: PLEASE, DADDY, COME AND GET ME. "I suppose *I* sent that to myself! No doubt, you may think so. But I cannot afford to have my conduct guided by your hallucinations. No, indeed, I will not permit you to see Alix, either now or later. So long as she chooses to make her home with me—and she still does, sir, and of her own free will—there will be no further visitations or harassments from you. Now, sir, will you please go ashore?"

"May I not even say good-bye to her? In front of you?"

"You may not."

"You're afraid of what she might say!"

"I'm afraid of what *you* might do."

"I beg of you, sir. Let me see her. For five minutes!"

"Never!"

"I insist!"

"Must I ask Commodore Thompson to have his crew put you forcibly off the yacht?"

It was then that the regrettable scene occurred that so much mortified Guy and his father. I left the yacht of my own accord, but I rowed around it, shouting Alix's name, hoping that she might at least appear at a porthole. She did not, and I was almost hysterical when I finally came back to the Percy Primes'. Guy's father told me with white-lipped disgust to pack my bag at once, and so my visit to Bar Harbor was concluded. Some sores always remain partially open, no matter how much time goes by. I have never gone back to the beautiful island that Champlain named, most appropriately to my way of thinking, for its "desert" hills.

Guy never knew that Alix, as well as his father, had sent a wireless to the yacht. I blush to record this in view of the accusation that in my anguish I had flung in his teeth. I should certainly have told him when I wrote my letter of apology, but I was too proud to confess that my beloved had had to send for her father to get away from me. I yearned for the satisfaction of seeing Alix and myself as a pair of star-crossed lovers. But what happens to "Romeo and Juliet" if the heroine rushes from the balcony to arouse old Capulet? And if Tybalt, her fiery cousin, is on Romeo's side?

Poor Tybalt! I did him a grave wrong. Guy had put himself wholeheartedly at my service; he had toiled as best he knew to make smooth my course of love. It was not really his fault if he had set Alix's and my romance in a gilded frame that was precisely the one to terrify her most and to paralyze my powers of courtship. Guy put gilded frames on everything. Mr. de Grasse had warned me of moths. But this moth had meant well, and I hurt him cruelly, first with my accusation and later with my refusal to take it back as completely as it was in my power to do. I should have eaten my silly pride and stayed on in the New York apartment that he and I had shared. But instead I allowed myself to harbor a grudge against him for being a Capulet, and that grudge was all the deeper for being both unuttered and unjust.

5.

I WENT BACK to New York and to a shabby boarding house, where I hugged my disappointment. I rejected all distractions and immersed myself in my job, day and night. Alix went abroad. She wrote me that her father had decided to spend the autumn in London. Her tone was distant, her news all of Windsor Castle and the Tower of London. There was no further reference to the bond that had existed between us. Alix had evidently accepted her father's veto, as Guy had predicted she would. What else could I do?

The humiliating part was that I found that I, too, could accept it. For a while there was a dim comfort in my hopeless love, a grim consolation in my sense of life's injustice. Over the dusky desert of that first year of unremitting toil the memory of Alix rose with the pale radiance of a Ryder moon. But my darkness could not last forever, and in the early morning of my renewed and youthful normality I was ashamed to discover that Alix was becoming a rather thin presence in my disloyal sky. I found that the Alix who had explained to me the incredible plot of *Il Trovatore* seemed hardly credible herself. Again and again I would invoke the scene in the motorcar on that April day when Mrs. Prime was leaving cards, but although I saw Alix's mother and the chauffeur and even the footman, I found it harder and harder to recapture the image of Alix herself. She began to seem as fanciful as a childhood game in the dry masculine world in which I was living. I had put her away without in the least wishing to.

And then, of course, there was Lucy Ames, who could have been defined in opposites to poor Alix. Lucy had come to New York to make a career as a secretary in a law firm; she was the best of the new type of young woman—independent, capable, inexpensively but smartly dressed, jolly, a good sport and glad to spend an evening at the theater in the top gallery or a Sunday afternoon in the Metropolitan Museum. Lucy was pretty without being beautiful, sensible without being dull, and, ultimately, loving without being cloying. She had been in love with me since she was a girl. I can admit that without fatuity because she always told our son George so. Lucy made me everything that I became in life, and if she caught me, as she used to relate, on the rebound, it was the rebound of waking up to life from a dream.

We were engaged a year later, when I went abroad to be Guy's best man. Alix was at the wedding, and when we talked, seated together at the bridal dinner, it was as if we had met for the first time. Had I once been in love with this tensely chattering, archly staring society girl with the high silly laugh? It was in another country, and besides the wench was dead.

Later, when Lucy and I were married, I took her to call on Alix in the Louis XIII *hôtel* on Fifth Avenue. As we came away I told her how odd it seemed to me that our hostess should have inspired such seeming depths of feeling. But Lucy shook her head.

"No, I can see it. There's something very appealing in her. She reminds me of that song about the bird in a gilded cage. You want to let her out, but what would happen if you did? Wouldn't she be pecked to death by street sparrows?"

"Like me?"

"Exactly! Oh, she loved you all right—she still loves you—a woman can sense that. But she's afraid of you. Afraid of what you might be like when you discovered what *she* was like. When you stopped seeing her through a misty lover's haze."

"But I didn't see her through a haze! I always saw her limitations. Basically, she didn't want love. Love was for opera. Basically, she was relieved when Papa came to rescue her and take her away from the bassos and tenors."

"Maybe. But couldn't she have wanted to be a soprano? Was it her fault that she had no voice? Or thought she had none? Which reminds me, when you were getting your hat, she asked us to the opera next week. It's *La Sonnambula*."

And, indeed, we went to the opera with Alix and her mother, not once but several times. Alix seemed determined to relabel me as a piece of candy and fit me back into her candy-box existence. Sitting behind her as the lights went up on the great gold curtain and sensing in the stiffening of her spine how much she gave herself to this warbling world of make-believe, I felt the last drops of my bitterness drain off to expose the dregs of my male egotism. For the sadness of what happened to me was nothing to the sadness of what had happened to Alix. The crisis of her life had been resolved against her. She was never to have another chance.

As she grew older she became less *fée* and more, like her sisters and cousins, encased in the mannered friendliness of the Prime women, a polite and seemingly democratic formality which blocked any kind of intimacy or real understanding. Alix made much of Lucy and myself and asked us to dinner parties at the Louis XIII *hôtel*, where her father would grudgingly accord me a "howdy-do, Geer" and her mother would seat me at her right, no longer, alas, because of her bibulousness, a very desirable place. We were asked to the opera and to visit at Newport; we were indeed Alix's "best friends," but all that this meant was that we were admitted to the babble of her seeming confidences, which were not confidences at all. Poor Alix had become at last what Guy had always claimed she was: a doll.

Yet behind her mask was the same susceptible heart. I had not, as it turned out, inspired a life-long passion. When Alix was twenty-nine she fell in love with Alfrederick Fowler, one of those morose, blocky young men of good but undistinguished New York families to whom our rich burghers love to entrust their daughters. Freddy Fowler's reluctance to ingratiate himself with the Primes was taken by them for integrity and his perennial boredom as immunity to the ordinary temptations. Besides, Alix was getting on, and even her father would not have cared to frustrate her twice. Fowler, whose worldly qualifications were little more than mine had been, was given, almost without the asking, the hand that had been so rudely torn from my loving grasp.

Even so, it might have worked out, had Freddy not developed the most insidious disease that can strike the husband of the American heiress: ambition. He decided that his pride required that he become as rich as his wife. But no man can make a fortune just because he wants one, and Freddy Fowler was doomed before he started. He lost his own money and all of his parents'. He did not lose Alix's because he never got his hands on it. A Griselda in everything else, she was her father's daughter when it came to the cash box.

She tried to help him in other ways, but she had no ideas beyond those supplied by Primes. What did Primes do? They entertained. Very well, she would entertain. She would fill her house with important people and make her husband look like an important man. Unhappily, she accomplished the very opposite of what she sought. Freddy felt the irony of playing a part at dinner that he could not play in the office, of watching his creditors sip his wife's champagne and having market tips tossed at him over the brandy that he could never have cadged in the day. It was a surprise to nobody but Alix when he shot himself in a downtown hotel.

She came near to losing her mind, but in the end the Prime discipline carried her through. In her middle years Alix turned back again, this time for good, to the companionship of her own sex; it was the opera box filled with cousins as I had originally seen it. She lunched on regular occasions with Lucy, but to me she came now only for business. It was to my care, after her father's death, that she consigned her fortune, and I was able at last to do something for her. I was able to turn her from a woman who was simply rich into a woman who was excessively rich. Had I made her a gift of a new book of opera plots, I could not have given her a more useless present.

6.

GUY MAKES OUT our relationship in that first year at de Grasse Brothers as that of grasshopper and cricket. He liked to fancy himself as a society will-o'-the-wisp, blown from hostess to hostess without motive or plan, and me, disappointed in love and unknown to the gay world, as a surly drudge whom it was charming of him to befriend. But one night I discovered the quantity of calculation in his social maneuvers. The surprising thing about his grasshopper was that, all the while it appeared to be lost in song, it should, like a very different insect, have been weaving a web.

It was a Saturday night, and he was dressed for one of his

grand dinners, but he always went first to a bar in the old Waldorf, near which he lived, for a Martini cocktail and a dish of oysters. He had persuaded me that evening to join him there, and leaning against the bar, beneath the huge Bouguereau of a satyr teased by naked nymphs, his evening cloak open to show his white shirt front and pearl studs, he seemed absurdly youthful and at the same time quaintly old, like a schoolboy in a charade, personifying the dandy of the Edwardian era.

"My father has a dream. Shall I tell you what it is?"

"To see you make the greatest of all the Prime matches."

Guy's smile approached condescension. "How little you two understand each other. No, Father has poetry in his nature that you would never suspect. But the dream, will you hear it?"

"I can hardly imagine that I play a role in it."

"That depends on *my* role in its realization. If I tell Father: Rex and Guy, it's a package deal, then a package deal it will be."

"But what is the deal?"

Guy raised his glass to the nymphs in the painting. "Our own firm. Geer & Prime. Our own office. Our own seat on the Exchange. Say the word, and Father's ready. He has the capital already pledged."

All my life I have suffered from an unwillingness to express appreciation. It must go back to an infantile sense that gratitude is somehow self-betrayal. I had no interest in Guy's father's dream, but it would not have killed me to thank him for including me in it. Yet what did I say? "Pledged? By all your uncles' wives, I suppose."

Guy's eyelids did not flicker, but for a moment his features assumed the peculiar blandness that meant that he had been hurt, or at least puzzled. His tone, however, was mild enough. "Does it matter where he gets the money? It's honest money."

"And what would be the business of Geer & Prime?"

"Well, I suppose we'd have brokerage for a base," Guy replied apologetically, for he knew how I felt about that. "It would be our bread and butter until we got on our feet. But I would take care of that; you wouldn't have to be bothered. I'd pick up enough accounts if I had to put on my white tie and dine in Yonkers!"

"Greater love hath no man. And what would I do?"

"All the rest."

"The rest?"

Guy described a wide half-circle with his left arm. "The whole point of the firm. The capital. The guts of Geer & Prime. That would be yours, my friend. To do what you wanted with. Investing. Loaning. Underwriting. You'd be a one-man de Grasse Brothers. Do you know that between us we could go to the top of the financial world?"

For a moment I was intrigued. I had to admit that his scheme was designed to make maximum use of both our talents. But what it left entirely out of consideration was my love of de Grasse Brothers. I could hardly believe that he seriously expected me to give up a career of my own making to become the tool of his aunts' fortunes.

"Your family would say that having missed Alix's money one way I was going after it another."

Guy stared. "Would you really care if anyone said anything so stupid?"

Oh, your youth, Rex Geer! Your bitter, grudging, miserly youth! The contrast between the dinners that awaited us that night, his with gold plate and champagne, mine with a piece of cold meat and a market report, was enough to blind me to his need for a little friendliness. And yet had I not chosen my dinner? And was not his a kind of toil? "You'd better go on to your party," I said gruffly. "I'd hate to be responsible for the least slip-up in so brilliant a social career."

And so ended, for the time being, the firm of Geer & Prime. Guy was to mention it to me only once again.

I was in an irritable mood at this time because Lucy would not agree to a formal engagement. I had made a clean breast of the whole business about Alix, and she had objected that my wound was still too green. I had always taken for granted Lucy's partiality, and it irked me to have her now stiffen in direct proportion to my availability. My irritation was not diminished, either, by the new and unexpected friendship that had sprung up between her and Guy.

He had met her, of course, in East Putnam when he had visited my family, and when she came to New York he insisted on taking us out to dinner at one of those swell French restaurants where he knew so well how to play the host. Lucy was nervous about the dinner, fearing to appear a very plain wren beside this brilliant bird of paradise, and indeed it seemed to me that she was just the opposite of the type of girl to attract Guy. She had no beauty, no silly banter, no interest in the New York social life, of which, quite naturally, she knew nothing at all. But when she saw that Guy was not trying to impress her with grand names and that he seemed genuinely interested in her experiences as a secretary in a law firm, she opened up with a rapidity that amazed me. By the end of our meal I had the disagreeable feeling that they had formed a humorous alliance against me.

"I always thought I was a committee of one to keep down the stuffiness of Rex Geer," Guy observed to her. "Now I see I'm only a Johnny-come-lately in a field where you have been a worthy pioneer."

"But if I'd been that worthy, there'd be no need for *you!*" Lucy exclaimed. "And here you've had to work Rex right through Harvard and New York!"

Guy nodded with mock gravity. "My friends call me Sisyphus."

I suppose we always like a person by whom we have expected to be snubbed. When Lucy told me, a week later, that Guy had

asked her to dine at his family's and that she had gone, she was
delighted that I was jealous.

"Why, you old silly, what would your fine-feathered friend be
doing with the likes of *me?* He wanted to look me over, that was
all. It's really touching how much he cares about you. I like
Guy. I like his good spirits. Though the house was rather fune-
real. You know, of course, his poor mother is dying."

This was indeed the sad case. Guy was not coming to the
office now, but spending his days at her bedside. When I called
at the house after work one evening he received me in the downstairs parlor, looking haggard and sleepless. Yet he brushed
aside my solicitous inquiries to express his enthusiasm about
Lucy.

"She's just the girl for you, old man! She's got everything
Alix didn't have. If you let her go, you're a bigger fool than I
take you for!"

This was all very well, and I was touched and pleased, for
Lucy in my second New York winter had become the only thing
in the world for me outside my work. But I certainly did not
like what seemed to be going on between her and Guy. When
she told me that he had taken her out alone to dinner at Sherry's, I blew up altogether.

"Guy's concept of friendship is a bit too broad for me if it
means sharing my girl friend!"

"You use the term as if you were speaking of a chattel. I'll
thank you to remember that I'll go out with whom I please,
when I please!"

"Then you may find that 'whom you please' doesn't include
me."

"You can suit yourself about that!"

"Ah, Lucy, how can you be so hard?"

"Because you're hard, Rex!" Lucy was immediately at her
most serious and most didactic. "You're very hard indeed. That
poor fellow is in desperate trouble. He adores his mother, and

he can't face the fact that he's losing her. If going out to dinner at an expensive restaurant and letting him talk is going to help him, I'm going to help him! I wish it were always so easy to help one's fellow man."

"So long as it's just that," I muttered.

I tried to accept it, but I found that I could not. The next time Lucy told me that she had been to Sherry's with Guy (she was entirely open about it), I asked her if she could assure me that he had said nothing that could be construed, even by an old maid, as love making. When she laughed in my face and said that she hoped he was better company than that, I became very somber indeed.

"You admit then he's flirting with you?"

"I admit nothing!"

Whereupon we had the most serious quarrel in our lives, and when I went home, it was without kissing her good night or even arranging for a next meeting. For a week I brooded, and then, in a cold dry despair, I called at the Percy Primes'. The doctor was upstairs with Mrs. Prime, and I found Guy alone in the library. He seemed vague and preoccupied, and I should have sensed a crisis in his mother's condition, but my jealousy had driven everything but Lucy from my mind.

"I want an explanation."

"An explanation?"

"Of your intentions towards Lucy."

For a moment he looked utterly bewildered. "But I haven't any intentions towards Lucy."

"You've been acting as if you had."

Guy shook his head ruefully. "You're not really jealous, are you? It's too ridiculous. I suppose Lucy told you of our dinners. That's so like her. But she's been nothing but a Good Samaritan, you know. She's got such a big brimming heart that I thought you could spare me a few drops of it."

"Lucy and I are not engaged, you know," I said in my gravest tone. "If you and she want to go out together, of course, you're at liberty to do so. I simply want to know where I stand."

"Shut up, you silly ass, and don't go on like that," Guy interrupted me. "Lucy's crazy about you, and that's as it should be. I don't say if she hadn't been, I wouldn't have fallen for her. Hell, I probably *have* fallen a bit for her. What's the harm? But don't worry, I promise never again to see her without you. Does that satisfy you?"

"If you're serious."

"Of course, I'm serious. Listen, Rex. When it's all over upstairs, I want to go off for a bit. To the Pacific, to the Orient, I don't know. Would you like to come with me? Before you're bogged down in marriage and swamped with babies? It may be your last chance to live a little. What about it?"

"And my job?"

"Haven't I offered you a better one?"

Had it not been for the business about Lucy, I might have managed, with his mother dying upstairs, at least to give him a civil answer. But I was still too bitter. "De Grasse is the place for me, Guy. I'm not going to leave it now. Maybe your father's dream is right for you."

Guy's eyes narrowed in a rare expression of resentment. "Meaning that I may not make the grade in de Grasse?"

"Meaning that you may not be the type to be a banker." I shrugged to lighten the effect of it. "Is that so terrible? Does one have to be a banker?"

"*You* do."

He continued to stare at me, when I did not answer this, with a funny little smile that might have been the prelude to a much uglier scene had we not both become aware that someone was standing in the doorway.

"If your friend can spare you, Guy," Mr. Prime said in his most frigid tone, "I think your mother needs you."

I remained alone, in what discomfort can be imagined, while

the sound of feet above me and on the stairway gave me a horrid sense of the deepening crisis of Mrs. Prime's condition. I can see to this day that dismal downstairs library with the bronze stags pursued by wolves, the loudly ticking, violently striking, oversized grandfather clock that seemed, with its preliminary whirrings and rumblings, to shriek for my eviction on the quarter hour. It was a maid, weeping no doubt as much for excitement as for sorrow, who told me that Mrs. Prime was dead, and I fled, leaving a scrawl of sympathy for her son.

I saw Guy next on the day of the funeral. When I say that he looked very well in raven black I do not mean to imply that he was not grief-stricken. He and his father received the friends in the vestibule of the church after the service, and when I shook his hand he asked me to wait. I did so, until most of the crowd had gone, and then he took me aside.

"I'm chucking de Grasse," he said gravely. "I'm going abroad for a year. Everything points to a semicolon in my life, and I may as well acquire a bit of international polish."

"I hope it has nothing to do with what I said the other day."

"Of course, it has everything to do with it. How could it not? Are you going to tell me that you didn't mean it? Are you going to tell me that you don't want me to leave de Grasse?"

"But, Guy," I protested, appalled, "what I said had nothing to with what I *wanted*. All I meant was that you weren't necessarily cut out to be a banker."

"I don't understand that at all. If I like somebody, I want him with me. You and I went into de Grasse together. It was planned that way. I thought we were a team, to stay there or leave together. If you've changed your mind about it now, it's because you don't want me there."

I have always been very Yankee about the emotions. I have thought of "love" as something related only to a man's family,

and friendship more in terms of trust than affection. No doubt
this has been because of my Puritan association of sex with the
least warmth between two human beings. But at that moment,
in the dark sanctuary of the church vestibule, through which the
ushers were already carrying the huge floral offerings (trust the
Prime sisters-in-law!) that were to accompany the casket to its
last resting place, I had a glimpse of a different world as Guy
conceived it. Guy did not shut the heart up in boxes with labels
of "wife" or "mother"; he did not worry about Puritans, and he
did not worry about sex. Love was the color scheme of his landscape, and it made mine seem suddenly very bare and dry.

"You couldn't imagine I might be thinking of your best interests?"

Guy shook his head. "No, I couldn't. And with that in mind,
will you look me in the eye and tell me you didn't mean what
you said?"

It is hard to recall just how conscious were all my cerebra-
tions, but I am sure that somewhere in the bottom of my mind
was an awareness of the romantic fallacy that underlay Guy's
philosophy of friendship. If he identified himself with a friend,
then what he did for a friend he did for himself. I seem also to
recall a pull in my heart, a pull of pity, perhaps even of remorse.
I know that I had a sudden vivid sense of disaster to come, as if I
could make out in that murky air, perfumed by the passing flowers, the presence of some draped warning figure. It was up to
me—that seemed to be the message that flooded my astonished
mind—to save this man.

But one did not "save" people in 1910. I could only conclude
that I was being sucked into the bogs of Guy's sentimentality. I
have been called a hard man, but that is because I know when I
must make up my mind.

"I'm afraid I did mean it, Guy."

He smiled dryly and shook my hand. "There you are, fella.
You see?"

And he turned to go to his father. I was not to see him again for a year and a half, until I went to Paris to be his best man.

7.

IN ANALYZING GUY's narrative, I am struck by the way it skips over the years between his marriage and the ultimate catastrophe: a period of more than a quarter of a century. I wonder if there may not be a peculiarly American significance in such an emphasis on youth. Was Guy at twenty-five already complete and fixed in his groove, so that the balance of his story was simply the inevitable slide down the tracks to disaster?

Consider the outline biography that one fills in for a college reunion questionnaire. Most of it is apt to be given over to school, college and trade school, to fraternities, academic honors and athletic teams, to military service, marriage and children, all matters occurring in youth, while the bulk of life, even in many cases the passion of life, is sloughed off with: "Employed by Buckley Carpets as assistant sales manager, 1912. Became President 1940." Anyone who has watched the sentimentality of a college reunion will have noticed how deeply old graduates love to indulge the dream that their finest hours occurred before they had to face the world.

In Guy's case this was particularly true. Even before his marriage to Angelica the small pilot light of his idealism had been snuffed out. I have tried to be candid in explaining my own role in its extinguishment. A defense could be made that so mild a blowing must have been evidence of a rather mild flame, but such as it was, that flame had irradiated Guy's younger years with the glow that had won him so many hearts. I am afraid that his character changed with his direction when he left his youth behind at de Grasse. Before then he had aspired, in simplest terms, to be everything in the world, regardless of incompatibilities: to be a poet and a millionaire, a Don Juan and a family man, a gallant soldier on the battlefield and a general at headquarters clinking with medals. Afterwards, the attainable universe seemed suddenly to have shrunk to what? To the brokerage house and the country club!

Now, you will say, how could that have happened? How could a man of Guy's parts have sunk so quickly from Shelley to Babbitt? I can only answer that life *is* that way, that man is perverse. Guy was so desperately afraid of being Babbitt (long before Lewis had even created the character) that what may strike us now as a series of mild disillusionments may have been enough to confirm his underlying despair. But unhappily for the rest of us, he never forgot what he had left behind. He must have passionately resented the extinguishment, by himself or by me or by fate, of that more glowing Guy, for out of the pieces of his resentment he was slowly to fabricate the engine that ultimately blew us up.

I first met Angelica Hyde in Paris, whither I journeyed to be Guy's best man, just after the time when Lucy had at last agreed to become engaged to me. To my horror and chagrin I experienced immediately the same violent attraction that had flared up in me on first meeting Alix Prime and that I had naïvely supposed to be safely channeled into the calmer waters of my devotion to Lucy. Of course, I was man enough by then to be in control of my words and actions, but all my thoughts and fantasies rioted about the image of this dark pale beautiful girl so intriguingly remote from her own nuptial festivities, like a Roman princess captured by Barbarians and forced to marry the big blond son of the Goth leader. Goth? Who was I to cast aspersions at Goths or Primes, I who had betrothed myself to a gallant girl back home for whom, despite all my respect and reverence, I felt no part of the terrible emotion that now shook me?

Angelica in later years used to pooh-pooh this. She accused

me of making it up to accord with a myth which I was construct-
ing that there had really been only one woman in my life. Why,
she would demand, if I had felt that way, had I not broken my
engagement to Lucy, who was always the soul of understanding?
Well, firstly, I could not bear to hurt Lucy, but, secondly, and
even more importantly, I had decided that the savage brute
within me must at all costs be put down. For what but a brute
in the course of a single year could have proposed to two women
and fallen in love with a third! I had no idea then what pro-
tracted continence could do to a man, and I concluded that I
was a lost soul whom Lucy alone could redeem. I even managed
to convince myself that Lucy might be better off not having to
cope with the kind of passion that Alix and Angelica had
aroused! Remember, reader, those were different days.

In New York, after Lucy and I were married, I took care to
see as little as possible of Angelica. This was not difficult, as she
and Guy were very social, and it was made even simpler by what
seemed to be Lucy's instinctive aversion to her.

"You'll have to accept it, darling," she told me. "I can't look
at a woman like Angelica Prime without wondering if you
wouldn't have done better with a more elegant wife. Now,
don't tell me that underneath the beautiful enamel Angelica
is the same shrinking violet I am. Maybe she is. But with
women, beautiful women anyway, I have to judge by externals.
That's the woman in *me!*"

There now followed, despite our inauspicious beginning, the
good years for Lucy and me. I worked desperately hard, frequently at night, and she was constantly left to her own devices,
but it was always clear that we were ascending the ladder of fame
and fortune. A great *esprit de corps* prevailed in de Grasse
Brothers that reached even to the wives, who rarely resented
their husbands' preoccupation with the "cause." Besides, our
son George, as a boy, was a delicate child and required much of
Lucy's attention. Life was full enough. Later, when the money

came, she regretted those days, for she never cared about wealth except for her charities. And with the money came the event that darkened our existence, the loss of our baby daughter, a Mongolian idiot, whom Lucy pathetically and unreasonably adored, and the advent (now believed to have been psychologically connected) of her long, terrible arthritis.

Guy always made a great deal of how desperately he had sought combat duty in the first war and how shabbily General Devers had treated him by tearing up his applications and insisting to Pershing himself that he was an indispensable staff officer. It may be true, but I could never quite overcome my prejudice, as a graduate of the trenches, against those who professed to regard our experience as the great ball of the century that it was their tragedy to have missed. If it was a ball, we had not *all* found it so hard to crash. The Guy, at any rate, who emerged from the ashes of world catastrophe, bustling and busy, with the whispered message from Jupiter, the wink that sealed the hidden pact, the hand that propelled one out of the crowded antechamber and through the back corridor to the inner citadel, the Guy who ran errands for Mars and dined with Venus, the Guy, in short, of so many splendid façades that one felt a churl even to inquire about interiors, was the Guy of the 'twenties and of their inescapable symbols: the speakeasy and the bull market.

He accuses me of wanting all the same things that he wanted, but of refusing to admit it. It would be truer to say that I was afraid of wanting them. From the beginning of our relationship I had resisted fiercely, and at times, ungraciously, the temptation of things Prime. Actually, I exaggerated the danger of that temptation. My weak spot, as the reader should now be aware, was more in the flesh than in the pocketbook. Guy sneers at my "big dreary house," but I would never have bought it if Mr. de Grasse had not absolutely insisted that Lucy and I raise our standard of living. So it was that, with little heart in it, we acquired the Tudor mansion on the north shore of Long Island and filled it with Jacobean furniture purchased at what we hoped were good auctions. Over the mantel in the living room we hung a Rembrandt portrait of a money-lender, a Shylockian character selected by Lucy, that turned out to be a fake. Mr. de Grasse, inspecting the premises, chuckled repeatedly and murmured "Perfect." Of course, he was making fun of us, but even my eye was good enough to detect that his chateau at Fontainebleau suggested more Nana in her prosperity than the dean of the New York banking world in his. Old New York, however cynical, had its vulgar side.

I am afraid that I became even more dry and austere at this period of my life. It was my way of adapting myself to Lucy's increasing invalidism. I was what is called "devoted," but my devotion must have seemed at times mechanical to her. Poor darling, it was her discipline to accept it as devotion. She knew that, like many healthy male animals, I instinctively "disapproved" of illness. She would have preferred, I am sure, to have had me less faithful and more spontaneous. When infidelity came at last, as I shall record in its place, she never complained. But for the most part she had to live before the spectacle of my rather grim solicitude. She accepted it as she accepted her illness, with the gallantry that never deserted her, even when she pretended that it had, in order not to weary us with the spectacle of it. At the risk of inviting Evadne's boys to accuse me of the reckless sentimentality of a guilty conscience, I will aver that Lucy was a saint.

I was particularly anxious, in this period that ended with the market collapse of 1929, to distinguish myself from Guy. The plainness of my house was meant to redeem itself in the contrast that it afforded to the beauty of his, as my dark suits were to find their merit in their difference from his gay tweeds. I did not want my George, who was first a friend and then a beau of Evadne's and a constant visitor at Meadowview, to confuse her father's meretricious success with what I had the egoism to regard as my own more substantial contribution to the economy. What it really boiled down to (and it hurts even now to admit it!) was that Guy's constant identification of our careers and aims bred occasional doubts in my own heart as to their variety. When I beheld him in all his glory at the Glenville Club, shouting at me to join him at the bar, when he passed me on the road in some glittering foreign car, even when he strode into my office, dazzling the staff with the remembered first names that he so freely distributed, I could not altogether down the ugly little suspicion that we *were* the same, two boys who had made good together, I with his connections and he with my "savvy," two smart youngsters who had got more than their share of the icing on the world's birthday cake. The only difference, his broad grin implied, was that *I* was a hypocrite.

The depression changed my world, but in no way more importantly than by bringing the event that to Guy's mind was forever to justify his insinuated charge.

8.

DURING THE first years of the depression I toiled as never before to keep the great galleon of de Grasse off the navigational hazards that strewed that terrible time, and by the summer of 1933, when I was beginning at last to see my way into the future, my body abruptly signified its protest. One morning I fainted at my desk, and my doctor prescribed total rest for a fortnight. There was nothing organically wrong, he assured me, but the engine needed oiling. When I confessed that I had taken no regular exercise since 1929, he was shocked.

"Very well," I told him glumly. "What shall I do?"

"I know that look of yours, Mr. Geer. You don't think anything will do you any good unless you hate it. You want me to
prescribe some repulsive kind of calisthenics. Didn't you used
to ride?"

"I used to ride with Lucy. Until she had to give it up."

"Did you like it?"

"Pretty well."

"Then ride!"

So I bought a mare and went riding every Saturday afternoon.
After a month I took jumping lessons at the Glenville Club,
and by fall I decided that I was good enough to join the hunt.
At my first meet Angelica Prime, very impressive in a black
habit and tall silk hat, rode up to me.

"Since when did you become a hunter?"

"Since this morning."

"Are you really up to it?"

"How can I tell till I've tried?"

She looked me up and down and shrugged. "Your seat's all
right, anyway. Follow me, and don't take any jumps that I
don't."

Of course, I had to show her how good I was, as though I had
been twenty-seven instead of forty-seven, and it served me right
that I went off at the very first one that she passed up and that I
attempted, knocking my wind out and spraining an ankle. Angelica, to my intense mortification, insisted on leaving the hunt
to drive me home. On the way she gave me a lecture.

"There's no reason you shouldn't be as good a rider as you are
a banker, but you can't do it overnight. I'll be your teacher.
Why not? You're the oldest and best friend Guy has and the
only one, if you ask me (which he doesn't) that we can really
count on. I'm the idlest woman in the world, with both children at school, so why shouldn't I turn you into a hunter? You
probably never want to see a horse again now, but next week
you'll be feeling differently. We'll go out together."

And so it started. Soon Angelica and I were riding on Sunday as well as Saturday and, at Guy's insistence, I moved my mare to the Meadowview stables. Guy professed to be delighted that Angelica was "taking me in hand," and Lucy, upset by my tumble at the hunt, expressed relief that I had so competent an instructor. In fact, both our spouses seemed to nod over our weekend expeditions as if we were two young creatures whose artless innocence made a charming tableau. But I knew perfectly well that I had no business seeing so much of Angelica.

I tried to persuade myself that it was ridiculous to suppose that the feelings which she had aroused in me twenty years before could be aroused so easily again. I mustered in my mind all the arguments against such an eventuality—my own greater age and presumably greater wisdom, the fact that Angelica herself was now a middle-aged matron with nearly adult children and, finally, the total disparity of our tastes and interests. What had I to fear from a woman who seemed to fling in my face her espousal of every principle that I despised, who embodied in her trimly clad frame the sporting life of what I considered total irresponsibility?

Obviously, everything. But by the time I realized this, idiot that I was, I was too committed to those weekends to give them up. I felt, somewhere deep within me, a new, shocking, surly defiance of the sense of duty that had always dominated me. "What have you really had for all your work?" the truculent inner voice kept snarling. "What have you had but money that you didn't want and a home that has become a hospital?" Oh, I would be loyal to that home! I swore in my odious guilt that I would be. But how would it help Lucy if I gave up my rides?

Never had I discussed my life so intimately with anyone as I did that spring with Angelica. She and I were well prepared for this new friendship as we already knew the important things about each other. I knew about Guy and his philanderings; she about Lucy and her arthritis. She knew my George as well as I knew her Evadne. We were each hilariously refreshed by the novelty of the other's point of view in areas which we had thought too familiar for further surprises.

Nor was the danger only for me. Angelica made little effort to conceal that she found me a welcome contrast to the society that Long Island had offered her in such heaping doses. She liked my indifference to her husband's adored Glenville Club; she liked my seriousness about things that had been simply funny to her; she even professed to like my stuffiness and what she called my "axeless" religiosity. "You carry out so scrupulously the mandates of a God in whom you don't really believe," she told me. "I find that stylish!" I suspected (and it was more than the wish being parent to the idea) that she had lived too long without love. There was a candor about the pleasure that she took in our rides which had a quaint and charming innocence to it. But what happened to innocence if there was no conscience? And did she not boast of being an epicurean?

So, obviously, we should not have gone riding together, but after only two weekends it was equally obvious that we were going right on with it. There was not even any further pretense that I was being trained for the hunt. Our talk was too important to us. Sometimes we would proceed at a walk for as much as an hour at a time while Angelica talked of her life, her children, her mother, her house—and Guy. She seemed to take it for granted that I would accept any confidences, as if, in all the years of our acquaintance, we had both known that our brief and rather formal communications were destined one day to flower into this equestrian understanding.

One morning as we left the stable, Guy came speeding down the driveway in his yellow Packard roadster with a very vivid blonde, one Mrs. Apsley, on the seat beside him. He jammed on his brakes, hailed us, wished us a good ride and roared on.

"Guy always wants me to have a good time," Angelica observed dryly. "He might do me the courtesy occasionally to

frown when he sees me with another man. Just for manners'
sake. But no. He never had a jealous bone in his body. Even in
the days when he cared."

"He never cares now?" My effort to make the question casual
was so clumsy that she smiled.

"Well, he cares for Evelyn Apsley, but that, of course, won't
last. What I mean is that Guy is totally without sexual jealousy.
Some animals are like that."

"Rather low forms of animals, I should say. Are you jealous
of Mrs. Apsley?"

"Not in the least. But then I'm not in love with Guy. I
haven't been for ten years. But before that I was jealous. Oh,
yes, passionately! I could have torn the eyes out of every girl he
looked at. But he was always willing to allow me the same lati-
tude he allowed himself."

"How contemptible!" I exclaimed and kicked my horse into
a trot. I was still sufficiently confused about my emotions to
hate to hear Angelica talk dispassionately about her husband.
She was my heroine, and I wanted my heroine to be very brave,
very noble and very wronged, and how could she be all those
things if she didn't care what he did? It might seem that I
should have been pleased at her conjugal indifference, that I had
nothing to gain if she still cared for Guy, but what did I want to
gain? Nothing that I would yet admit to myself!

Lucy had gone to Arizona for what was now her annual cure,
and George was at Harvard, so that I was without the sense of a
family at home to restrain me on the day that Angelica and I
had our crucial talk. Once again it started with her analyzing
Guy. Her curiosity about a husband whom she professed no
longer to love exasperated me unreasonably.

"I suppose the secret of Guy is that he's always content with
the status quo," she was speculating. "Any status quo. It can be
very undermining to those who live with him. One finds oneself
so constantly being used. And Guy uses one in such perfectly

good faith, that's the devilish thing! My house, my horses, my friends, my own mother, are always being converted into stage props for the glorification of Guy Prime. We end up looking as he wants us to look, as *he* thinks we are. And as, God help us, we may be! Do you know that if I didn't lock my door at night he'd probably come from the arms of Evelyn Apsley to make love to me? As if we were a blissfully happy married couple? Sometimes I wonder which is the dreamer? Guy or I?"

"He is the dreamer," I said firmly. "Your feet are on the ground." I glanced away from her, over the meadows, to the long purple façade of her beautiful house. "So don't unlock your door."

I sensed the embarrassment in her averted head, but I knew that she was not offended. Her remark had been wildly provocative. "Never fear. I shan't. All that is long over between Guy and me. Tell me one thing about Guy, and then I'll stop talking about him." She reined her horse to a stop and gave me a searching look. "Has he borrowed any money from you recently? I mean since we've been riding together?"

I flushed very red. "No."

"Thank goodness." Abruptly she trotted on. "That's all I wanted to know."

"Are you having money troubles?" I demanded anxiously.

"No more than usual. Never mind about them. I count on you for sympathy, not for cash."

"But cash means so little to me!" I protested, spurring ahead to catch up with her. When she did not turn, I let slip the last cable of my common sense. "Nothing means anything to me but you!"

Angelica turned now, smiling, and reached over to hit my shoulder with her riding crop. "Pupils are not supposed to make love to their riding instructors!"

"Angelica, I adore you!"

For answer she simply kicked her horse and galloped away. All the way back to the stable she kept ahead of me, and when she dismounted, the presence of the groom prevented further confidences. But I noted the high color in her normally pale cheeks.

"Thank you, Rex," she called to me cheerfully, "for a very pleasant ride!"

My car was parked at the stable, in full sight of the groom; there seemed no way to be alone with her. As she continued to smile, I walked over to the car and got in. She waved her riding crop, still smiling, as I drove off.

9.

ON OUR NEXT Monday lunch Guy looked very grave and told me that he had an important matter to discuss. For a terrible moment I thought it was going to be Angelica, but almost immediately my incredulous ears were hearing his plea for a loan of a hundred thousand dollars. With a trembling hand I wrote the check right there at the dining room table. The trembling was caused by a giddy combination of relief and anticipation. The bawd is only a loathsome figure to the satisfied lover. At that moment Guy seemed as benevolent as Santa Claus. He had given me back my good conscience.

Now I come to the part of my memoir where I can mince no words. Lucy was off for the winter in Arizona. Guy was "squared." The next time I went riding with Angelica I proposed, in a dry, businesslike tone, designed to strip my words of any cheap seductiveness, that we become lovers. In like manner, if with the slightest parody of it, she agreed. Thereafter, we met every other afternoon, for a period of four weeks, in an apartment that I rented on Riverside Drive. Then our relationship was brought to a sudden close.

Those four weeks jump out of my chronology as a period with

no true part in my story, a chapter of lurid fiction irreverently inserted in a sober Victorian two-volume "life and letters," a ballet stuck into a social problem play. It was dope or euphoria or ecstasy. It was the highest point or the nadir. It was not I—at least the "I" that I had been and was to become again. It was Rex Geer posing as somebody else, Rex Geer so terrified of what he was posing as that, in the hours outside that furnished apartment overlooking a wintry river, he plunged convulsively into work and, when there was no work, grabbed people, buttonholed people, went into people's offices and clubs, did anything, in short, to avoid being caught alone with his conscience. And when he came home at night he would take two sleeping pills, he, who had never taken a sedative in his life!

I staved off remorse for two of those four weeks, and then it exploded in me like a fire bomb. People at the office asked me if I was sick or in pain. Walking down the corridors of de Grasse I sometimes put my hand to my side as if to allay an agony that seemed to be physical. But I did not give up Angelica. There was never the remotest idea of that. If anything, my agony increased my pleasure in what caused it.

On a Saturday night at the end of those four weeks I happened to be alone, except for the caretaker and his wife, in my Long Island house. During Lucy's absence I had given the staff a vacation. I was in the library reading, when Angelica, in a red evening dress and mink stole, appeared suddenly and defiantly in the doorway. Her hair was blown, and she was panting.

"I've left him!" she cried. "I've left him, and you can't make me go back!"

"Did you leave your dinner party, too?" I asked, as casually as I could, to calm her, and walked over to take off her wrap. "Didn't you tell me you were entertaining the local gentry?"

"We were entertaining all the idiots on the board of his damn club. An annual affair. And right in the middle of dinner up he jumps, with a half a bun on, to make one of his incessant toasts. You know how he *loves* toasts. He could make one in an Automat!" Here she went to the fire to warm her hands, but in a moment she had whirled around at me. "You won't believe what he toasted tonight. *Us!*"

I gaped. "You and me?"

"Well, not quite, though he would have been capable of that, too." She laughed, a bit wildly. "He toasted him and me. Our marriage. He said, with *tears* in his eyes, mind you, that it was our twenty-second wedding anniversary and he wanted to drink to 'two point two decades of bliss.' And he meant it, that's what kills me. I could stand anything in the world but his meaning it!"

"Is that when you departed?"

"No, I waited till dinner was over. I did that much for him. I slipped away while the ladies were out. Ma will see that they join the gentlemen." Here she snorted at my concern for detail. "Ma is always sublime in a crisis. It brings out the Roman in her."

"Oh, your mother is there," I said, relieved.

"Yes, and she'll keep Guy in hand. I left her a note, telling her to persuade him that it would be useless to come after me."

"And will she?"

"I don't know, and I don't care!"

I busied myself now at the cupboard getting her a drink. For the first time in a month my mind was working clearly, however feverishly. "You propose to stay here?"

"If I may?" she exclaimed in surprise. "If you'll take a poor refugee in?"

But I rejected her lightness of tone. "When I bought this house, I put the title in Lucy's name. That was more than a legal technicality. I regard it as her home."

"Pardon *me*. I'll leave right now!"

"No, my dear. You will spend the night. In a guest room. Tomorrow we will figure out a plan."

"Oh, Rex, how can you be so cold?" Angelica's tone had changed abruptly to one of throbbing appeal. "I respect how you feel about Lucy. I respect your delicacy. You can lock your door tonight if you want. What do I care about this house? Let Lucy have it. Let her have all your money, too, if she wants. Not that she does, worse luck. That would be too easy. But, poor sick darling creature that she is, isn't it enough if she has the home and George and the sympathy of all the world? Can't she let you go? Can't you and I have a little something of what's left of our lives? Good God, it's ridiculous! Here we are living in an age of universal divorce and acting like two characters in *The Scarlet Letter*. If you put it up to Lucy, do you think she'd refuse us?"

How well I knew she wouldn't! I think that moment was the climax of my agony. For there was no escaping the fact now that I was cheating two women. Nor is there any telling how I would have got out of it had not Swain, my caretaker, appeared just then in the doorway, very embarrassed and apologetic, to announce that a Mrs. Hyde was asking for me. Angelica and I exchanged glances.

"Alone?" I asked.

"Well, she's alone in the hall, sir. But she came in a big yellow car with a chauffeur."

It was Angelica who answered for us. "Tell her to come in. And, oh, Swain," she called as he turned to go. "Mrs. Hyde is my mother. I asked her to pick me up here tonight."

"Yes, Ma'am."

"Have I saved your reputation?" she demanded sarcastically, when Swain had gone. "Let me ask, in return, that you not desert me while Ma is here."

Mrs. Hyde, then in her seventies, with unwrinkled skin and white hair, dressed in black velvet with no jewelry but a small antique necklace, was more effectively feminine, more persuasively authoritative than when I had first met her. She came into the room as if she were making a simple after-dinner family call. She was carrying a knitting bag and paused before the portrait of the money-lender, which she examined with a tranquil attentiveness.

"I'm afraid it's a fake," I murmured.

"Ah, but one forgives it for making such an effort," she answered pleasantly. "I've never seen a picture trying harder to be a Rembrandt."

"Won't you sit by the fire?" I urged her. "And can I get you something? A liqueur?"

"No, thank you. At the Primes' one dines very well. We had everything a body could want." Here she sat down and at once took out her needlepoint. As she prepared to work, she cast an oblique glance in Angelica's direction. "Except perhaps a hostess. Although in *her* mood, there's some question as to how much one wanted her."

Angelica strode back to the fireplace and, putting her hands on the mantel, kicked a log back. "I'm not going home tonight, Mother. You may as well save your breath."

"That's what I assumed. That's why I've brought a night bag."

"Do you really think I need a chaperone at my age?"

"Certainly not. After the lives that you and Guy have led, it would be a ridiculous formality. I'm thinking of Mr. Geer. From what I understand, *he* still has some shred of reputation left."

"So that's your line tonight!" Angelica swung around angrily from the fire to face her. "Well, you're very resourceful, I will admit. My mother's a great diplomat, Rex," she continued, turning to me. "She knows just where to apply her pressure. If there's a bit of religion left in you, she can put on her tiara and preside over the Vatican like Lucrezia Borgia! Or if it's society you're afraid of, she can frown like Queen Victoria. Watch out, poor man!"

The old lady never flinched. "Poor man?" she queried. "I had thought he was an exceedingly rich one. I wonder if you have discovered already with your own offspring, Mr. Geer, that children think of parents as natural hypocrites. Angelica takes it for granted that I'm trying to reach her through you. It's very vain of her, really. Why shouldn't I be capable of wanting to reach *you* through her?"

"Because you hardly know him!" Angelica intervened indignantly. "You haven't seen him half a dozen times in your life. What can he possibly be to you?"

"Your victim, dear." Mrs. Hyde spoke with ominous mildness, and Angelica flushed.

"And why should you be concerned with *my* victims?" she demanded with a childish rudeness. "Haven't you enough of your own?

"Because if I bear the responsibility for my own, I must bear some for you. Surely, I should have given you a better orientation in how to live and love."

"Love?" Angelica asked sneeringly. "What could you have taught me about love?"

"More than you think, my girl," retorted her mother, whose tone became cooler as Angelica's became more petulant. "You aren't the only woman who's had to conform to a pattern in which she didn't believe or to give the appearance of loving where she didn't love. But in my day we didn't think it was necessarily a high honesty to capsize the boat and drown the crew!"

"And whom, pray, am I drowning? Could anyone as buoyant as Guy go under?"

"I thought we had decided that Guy, like yourself, was immune to the perils of your social adventurousness. It is Mr. Geer who is in danger of death by water."

How awesome is the power of a mother, particularly the power of a mother capable of such devastating detachment! I

shuddered with sympathy for Angelica, standing before her terrible parent with tear-stained eyes and trembling lip, a small
pouting girl again. But I said nothing, no, not even then. I was
as much in the old lady's grip as she. I knew that the drastic
therapy which she was meting out was our only salvation.

"Rex, tell her it's not so!"

"Yes, Rex, if I may call you that, tell her it's not so!" Mrs.
Hyde had dropped all pretense of banter now. She knew when
to drive home her points, and she was not in the least bit shy of
emphasis. She struck the handle of her work bag with the top of
her long needle as she summed up the situation. "Tell her and
tell *me* if you want to crown your career with the legalization of
a double adultery. And tell us, too, if you want to add a final
chapter to the charming little book that you wrote about your
rectory boyhood and call it 'How I married my best friend's
wife'!"

"My God, Mother, you monster!" Angelica groaned. "Rex,
don't listen to her!"

How can I describe my feelings at that moment? All I remember is suspecting that there would be little of me left to
come out of the vise formed by the opposed wills of these two
powerful women. Can I convince a modern reader that I adored
Angelica and was at the same time passionately relieved by her
mother's interference? No, that's hardly romantic, is it? I was a
very long way from believing that the world was well lost for
love. The vision of Lucy's pain-ridden eyes was an icy hell in
which the greatest heaven that Angelica could offer fizzled out
like a burning coal. I yearned for it all to be over, and, like a
coward, I clung to Mrs. Hyde's skirts.

"I'm waiting for an answer," the inexorable old woman continued.

"Yes, Rex, answer her!"

"Angelica, my dear, she's right. You know she's right."

Angelica became alabaster. "You mean I'm to go back?"

"What else have I to offer you?"

With a little cry she turned and fled from the room. When I was going to follow her, Mrs. Hyde called me sharply back.

"Rex! I think I'd like that glass of brandy now. The one you were kind enough to offer when I came in."

"But Angelica may do something to herself!"

"Don't flatter yourself. Or me. She'll be down in a minute and ready to go home. Believe me," she said, even more firmly as I hesitated, "I know her better than you do."

Quelled by that bleak, remotely twinkling stare I went to the cupboard and poured her a brandy, which she consumed in three quick sips. It was her only sign that the preceding scene had been a strain.

"It is not easy to talk to you, Mrs. Hyde," I said. "You must feel I have done you a great wrong."

"Not at all. In my generation, these things were blamed on the women, and not much on them unless they made fools of themselves. As Angelica did tonight."

"That is the European point of view?"

"I should prefer to call it the civilized point of view. An affair is one thing. Breaking up a marriage, or two of them, is quite another."

"It humiliates me to have to admit that your Catholic faith comes out of all of this better than my Protestant. I hang my head in shame, Mrs. Hyde."

"That will get neither of us anywhere," she replied briskly. "Besides, my Catholic faith has very little to do with it. I am indeed a Catholic, and I believe in the teachings of my church. But I would continue to believe in its rules even if I lost my faith in its teachings." She held out her glass. "One more tiny drop, please, and I'll tell you something. Because I think I like you, Rex." I poured her the drop, and she contemplated the glass as she contemplated her speech. "I may as well relieve your conscientious mind. Why, after all, should you labor under a debt of gratitude to me? I didn't come here tonight to save your marriage. It wasn't in danger. I didn't even come here to save you. *You* weren't in danger. I came here to save Angelica."

"From me?"

"Well, more precisely, to save her from the humiliation of slipping between two stools. To save her from discovering that you wouldn't leave your wife at a time when it might be too late for her to go back to Guy. For it's not too late now. Guy will overlook this episode. He is very tolerant. But even Guy has his limits."

"And what sort of a life will she have with Guy when she goes back?"

"The same she's always had. The life she chose. Don't stare at me that way, Rex. It isn't as if he beat her. Personally, I've always liked Guy. He's a good-humored man, which, as Dr. Johnson said, is a rare thing. Angelica's always picking on him for being vulgar. Yet all he's really doing is dabbing a badly needed spot of rouge on the poor old skeleton of our universe." She rose now and crossed the room to the door nearest the hall stairs. "Angelica!" she called up in a voice as casual as if they had been late for a dinner engagement. "Are you coming?"

And Angelica came.

She swept down the stairs and passed me like a queen evacuating her palace and making her proud quick way through the jeering rebel mob. I was that mob. I followed her and her mother out to the porte-cochère, where the Prime Hispano and chauffeur were waiting. So even that was a bluff! Mrs. Hyde had never expected to spend the night. She had had too much confidence in her own diplomacy to dismiss the car.

I did not see Angelica for six months, nor did we correspond. When we met at last, it was accidentally, in New York at her mother's, where I now regularly called. We came away together, and I walked with her to the door of the Colony Club.

"I've gotten over my hate of you," she said in her old brusque way. "I might even go so far as to say that you and Ma were right. But if you so much as *look* 'I told you so,' I shall take a small, pearl-handled revolver from my purse and shoot you straight through the heart. Isn't that what Joan Crawford would do?"

"I don't go to the movies."

"Then take it from me," she said, more grimly than her seeming joke implied, "that's what she'd do."

"There wouldn't be much to shoot. I've been pretty much in pieces."

"And to think I did that to the great Reginald Geer! I shall have it engraved on my tombstone. To the scandalization of the Prime mausoleum!"

If that was the note she wanted to strike, I would not be the one to jangle her tune. If I suspected that a passionate resentment was still seething beneath it, I would not be the one to let it out. Humbly, gratefully, a bit shame-facedly, I picked up my cue, and from then on I continued to see Angelica, as I had seen her before our intimacy, in groups, at her own house and at the houses of friends. I do not think that, while Lucy was living and while Guy remained Angelica's husband, we had a conversation that either Lucy or he would have begrudged us. Curiously enough, these social meetings, which might have seemed impossibly frustrating, were of immense comfort to me. On the threshold of fifty innocence was preferable to ecstasy.

The reaction of each of our spouses to Angelica's flight from the dinner party was characteristic. When Lucy returned from Arizona, I made a clean breast of the whole sorry business. She listened patiently, without a single comment, until I had finished.

"You must think me very obtuse," she said at last, "if you suppose I didn't know about you and Angelica. I do not blame you, not in my mind, anyway. My mind tells me that a healthy man needs love. My heart can't help being bitter about it. Nor can it resist a certain unworthy glee in knowing what purgatory your conscience must have made it for you. That is *my* sin, you see. We're *in pari delicto*. And the best we can both do is to make a pledge not to talk about your lady loves. It's this chatter that I find hardest of all."

"There will be no more lady loves to chatter about. I swear it, Lucy."

"Oh, my dearest, don't make a pledge like that. I know you're quite capable of keeping it. Don't, for God's sake, put me in the position of having to *urge* you to go and get what I can't give you. It's beyond flesh and blood!"

"Lucy, my darling, listen." I got down on my knees by her chair. "I am going to be faithful because I *want* to be faithful. Because it makes me happy to be faithful. I am making the pledge to myself, not to you. Does that make it any better?"

"Oh much better, my love. Except that it makes me want to die!"

I kept my pledge, and I can only pray that I did not hurt Lucy more that way than I would have by breaking it. She only let down her guard on a single other occasion when, years later, as she lay dying, she took my hand and murmured: "I'm sorry you're so old!" And immediately the pain flooded her eyes at the realization of what, poor selfless creature, she must have considered an unforgivable self-indulgence.

Guy met me for our Monday lunch as usual after the weekend of Angelica's departure and return, but he made no reference to these events. Instead, he talked about his phosphate mine, in which the de Grasse loans had given me a controlling interest. Discussion of business and little more was the characteristic of this stage in our relationship, the penultimate and, in retrospect, the most offensive to me. For I was always conscious now of a leer behind what I had once considered the simple friendliness of his eyes, and when we walked together back to our offices

I half expected to receive a sly poke in the ribs or some such tacit signal that we were fellows in the red plush school of deceit and adultery. I hated it, but I hated it in silence. There was nothing between us that would not have been made viler by discussion.

And so I conclude this chapter that has been the hardest thing to write that I have ever written. It was made necessary by Guy's decision to strut posthumously before his grandsons in the role of Othello. It is nobody's fault but his own that I have been obliged to uncover his closer resemblance to Iago, who pretended that his plotting against the Moor had been motivated by the latter's affair with his wife.

10.

WHEN GUY CAME to me in the summer of 1936 with the shameful story of the Glenville Club's bonds, I assumed, despite his protestations, that this must have been the climax of a long course of embezzlements. I could only comprehend it as having begun accidentally, in an office sloppily run by golfing partners, with the pledging of a bond thought to belong to one of them and subsequently discovered to be the property of a Prime aunt. How quickly it must have been put back in her account! But the memory would have lingered of so simple and painless a way of raising funds in a pinch. And then, with the depression and tight money, another aunt's bonds would have been used and replaced, always replaced, of course, and then another's, until at last, with the passage of years and the hardening of habit, Guy had calmly appropriated three hundred and fifty thousand dollars out of a country club's building account. Why not? Wasn't it good business? Didn't perhaps everyone do it secretly? Even holy old Rex himself?

But that was not, after all, the way it happened. Guy says that he first converted securities from a customer's account in 1934, only two years before the episode of the Glenville Club's bonds, and that he did it then, not accidentally but with a cold calculation. I have talked to his partners and gone over the accounts of his firm, and I have not been able to disprove this. Everything, on the contrary, tends to confirm the bracketing of his initial crime with the failure of his attempted marital reconciliation, and obviously I cannot evade the further bracketing of this same failure with what had happened between myself and Angelica.

Guy must have hated me as deeply as one man can hate another. To his inflamed imagination I had robbed him of the career that was his birthright and tossed his wife on top of the pile of my loot. The fact that he had played the role of the complacent husband had simply crowned my iniquities: it was as if by pushing him into this position I had tried to rob him of his resentment as well. In the two years that elapsed between my giving up Angelica and the collapse of his firm, the same years of his embezzlements, he treated me with a graveled heartiness that was an almost insulting parody of our former friendship. Yet there was never anything approaching an explanation between us. We knew each other too well.

The peculiar hardness and boldness of Guy in this era, which was so to strike and shock the public at his trial, was much more than a melodramatic defiance of fate. Old Mr. de Grasse put his finger on it when he suggested to me during the Congressional hearings that Guy was *enjoying* himself. He was. He believed that he had brought me down at last and with me de Grasse Brothers and with de Grasse the whole world of serious men who had denied him the leadership that he had so long and so almost crazily claimed. Oh, yes, he was a fiddling Nero, only a more dangerous one. Rome could be rebuilt. My Wall Street never was.

I do not mean that Guy intended to go bankrupt, but that sometime in that period he embarked on a course of action that could have only two possible endings, both heady personal triumphs for him. Either he would become the richest man in Wall Street or he would destroy Wall Street. Either he would be monarch of that famous thoroughfare or he would turn it over, with grass growing in its streets, to the jackals of the New Deal. As it began to look as if the second eventuality would be the one to produce his "cloudy trophies," Guy moved to enmesh me in his fall. It was essential to his plan that I should become his creditor, with full knowledge of his embezzlement. It was vital that I should become his accessory.

He was sure, of course, that he had me in his hands. He was de Grasse's broker and my friend and affiliate; a scandal was bound to spatter my walls. He was well aware (who better?) of my feeling for Angelica; he assumed that I would be anxious to spare her the humiliation of her husband's disgrace. And then, most potently of all, my only son was engaged to his daughter. Surely all he had to do was tell his tale of woe and pocket my incriminating money.

Yet there was a stubborn side of my nature that might have prevailed over all these things. Indeed, Guy's very cocksureness that he had me where he wanted me might have been enough to turn me against the loan. I have always hated to be taken for granted. But fortunately for his plans and unhappily for me, my stubbornness was aroused that day by another person.

The reader will remember that I told Guy on the telephone that I would give him my answer to his desperate appeal that night at Meadowview. After some hours of frenetic self-examination I decided to lay the case before Lucy. I left my office and drove to Glen Cove, where I found her on the flagstone terrace in her wheel chair, enjoying the early spring weather. By her side was the little table on which her necessaries were always laid: her books, her writing board, her field glasses (she loved birds), her journal, and the little radio which brought her the appalling soap operas to which invalids grow so attached.

She listened intently, but without seeming surprise, as I told my grim tale.

"Are you going to give him the money?" was all she asked when I had finished. It was like her to waste no time in ejaculations and laments.

"Don't you think I have to? For Evadne's sake, if no one else's?"

"Forgive me if I say that's tosh, my dear. Evadne and George can survive Guy's disgrace. If they can't, there's no stuff in them, and I think they have stuff. As for Angelica, she's been looking for challenges all her life. Why deprive her of one as real as this? Let's get down to brass tacks. You're thinking of de Grasse Brothers. Or you think you're thinking of it."

"I'm thinking of Guy."

"*Are* you?" Lucy's stare was intent. "I should have thought you would have been remorseless in a case like this. Is there a single extenuating circumstance? You haven't mentioned one."

"You forget how far back Guy goes into my past."

"I don't forget how much you dislike him. Isn't it time you faced that? And how much it motivates you? You're afraid of letting Guy go to jail because you *want* him to go to jail. You're ashamed of this, so you fall back on the other motive of saving de Grasse from being publicly associated with a swindler."

I breathed heavily. I never liked it when Lucy was coldly analytical, and, of course, she was particularly apt to be so where the Primes were concerned. Unfortunately for me, unfortunately for everyone, I ascribed her detachment that evening to a continued jealousy of Angelica. I believed that Lucy believed that I wanted to save Guy for Angelica's sake. "Well, of course, it's true that the tie-in between Guy and de Grasse has always been close," I said. "Some of that mud would be bound to stick."

"Not as much as if it were found out that you were covering up for him."

Oh, had I listened to her! "Then there's the question of his innocent partners. They'll be ruined, too."

"What do you care about Guy's partners, Rex? Can't you be honest about yourself for once in your life?"

There was something so icy about Lucy on this occasion that it virtually resolved me in Guy's favor. That is the tragedy of the closest relationships of life. At the most crucial moments irritation often occupies the center of the stage. Lucy did not believe that I was really concerned about Guy, and her distaste for what she considered my hypocrisy made her put her excellent advice in unpalatable form. I, in turn, believed that she would not face in her own heart a hostility for Angelica that made her welcome the prospect of disaster for the Primes.

"I am sorry to give the impression of so little feeling," I said dryly, and I went to my room to dress for dinner at Meadowview. It was while shaving that I conceived my plan of making Guy give up his business in return for my loan. Fatuously, I congratulated my image in the mirror on its brilliance. It seemed to me that this way I saved everybody and that I protected society into the bargain by chaining Guy up with his promise to retire. Of course, I was taking the law into my own hands, but in my conceit I never doubted that this was where it belonged. Who else, indeed, could rescue the innocent and restrict the guilty? The law would have punished both.

My resolution faltered a bit that night at Meadowview when I had to sit at Guy's table, in the presence of his family and my son (all, of course, ignorant of the impending crisis), and listen to him bandy cheap jokes about the suicide of Count Landi, whose position had been morally the twin of his own. This performance should have convinced me that the man whose promise to retire from business I was about to take (or rather to exact) had become totally depraved. But my heart went out instead to his wife and children, sitting there listening to his chatter and not knowing how close they were to a similar disgrace.

Why then, my reader will ask, did I not watch Guy, in the summer that followed, to make sure that he carried out his part of our bargain? I was in England, to be sure, but that was no excuse. I could still have had him properly supervised. The answer is that the very thought of Guy had become so nauseating to me that I weakly (and I hope uncharacteristically) tried to put him out of my mind. To explain this, I can only relate a conversation that I had with Angelica after what Guy calls the "Meadowview Pact" and before my departure for England.

She asked me to lunch with her alone. She said that she wanted to learn more precisely just what it was that Guy had done and why it was so wrong. I was pleased at her interest, for I had been upset at how casually she had taken the news of Guy's defalcations. But I soon found that she had other things on her mind. Women simply do not care as men care about the morals of the marketplace.

"How far back do you think these 'defalcations' as you call them, go?" she asked me. "As far back as 1934?"

"But that's only two years." Then I flushed as I thought I followed her thinking. "You mean you think there might be a connection between what he did and *us?*"

"Oh no. Between what he did and my miscarriage."

"Miscarriage? *What* miscarriage?"

"Didn't you know I had a miscarriage that fall?" Angelica took in my look of consternation and suddenly burst out laughing. "Oh no, you old silly, it wasn't *you*. It was Guy all right; the baby was only a few weeks on. But Guy seemed to mind it all so desperately, I wondered if it didn't have something to do with turning him bad."

He minded it! I think *I* minded it more than the discovery of his embezzlements. How had I missed it? Lucy must have deliberately kept it from me, with heroic delicacy, to spare my feelings. Or else she may have thought that it was my child and that I must have known. Heaven and earth! I do not recall what further conversation I had with Angelica at that lunch, but I know that I allowed nothing more to be said of the miscarriage and that I tramped all the way back from Fourteenth Street to my office afterwards. Dearest Angelica, you never knew what torture you put me through!

Of course, I forgave it. Of course, I blamed it all on Guy. It seemed to me, that dismal afternoon, that he had smeared everything he had ever touched and everything that I had ever loved. Had he not cheapened his cousin Alix by making me see her only as an heiress and myself as a fortune hunter? Had he not cheapened the whole trade of banking until I had had to drive him out of de Grasse? Oh, yes, I had driven him out—I saw that now! Had he not debased Angelica by winking at our love? And had he not now cheapened her again, hideously, unbearably? I could think of no nook or cranny of my life that had not been degraded by Guy Prime.

My trip to England was like a flight from a burning city. I did not want to think about Guy or hear his name mentioned. Before I left I told George the story of the embezzlements and asked him to be my watchdog. Poor George! Asked to watch his beloved's father! Besides, he was too young, too inexperienced. He did not even move in the world where he would have learned of Guy's borrowings. I had left a puppy to guard my fox.

When Lucy and I returned from England, we did not see the Primes, but George informed me that there had been rumors of Guy's borrowing. He said that he had reported this to Angelica and that she had told him that Guy was renegotiating an old loan that had fallen due.

"An old loan!" I exclaimed. "But surely he has dozens of those! He should have come to us. He knows that I want to settle this whole business, once and for all."

George flushed and said nothing, and I saw that he was as unsatisfied as I. What did I expect? How could he question his future mother-in-law's estimate of her husband's affairs? Angelica, who didn't know a stock from a bond!

And so it was, as Guy reports, that the moment I felt his heavy hand on my shoulder at the opera, I knew that my silly game was up.

Mr. de Grasse, fortunately, was in New York—he never went to France before the cold weather—and I repaired straight from the opera house to his red brick Federal mansion on Washington Square. It had belonged to his father and grandfather before him (an almost inconceivable rarity in New York), and I wondered if the Duncan Phyfe chairs and the Paul Revere tankards would not blush at the nature of my revelations. I had telephoned from a booth of the gravity of my mission, and Albert Simmons, senior partner of Simmons, Bly & Slater, our counsel, was there ahead of me. In the library, by a fire into which Mr. de Grasse pensively gazed, the three of us held our grim conference.

I had never much cared for Simmons, and that night I came near to hating him. He was an unctuous, soft little man with a mellifluous, never-ceasing voice, and he clasped and unclasped his fat little hands as he talked and shook his head so that the *pince-nez* on the thin bridge of his bulging nose was always aquiver. In a bonnet and cape he would have looked like a dear old granny, and it was perhaps to counter this image that he asserted his opinions so aggressively. Oh, of course, he was a brilliant lawyer, but I did not need a brilliant lawyer to tell me that to cover up for Guy Prime would be compounding a felony. Had I not already done it once?

"Thank you, Albert," Mr. de Grasse said when he had finished, or at least paused. "That seems to be perfectly clear, doesn't it? Let me beg your forgiveness for an interrupted evening. My car will take you home."

When Simmons had gone, obviously surprised and put out by his abrupt dismissal, having expected, no doubt, to linger luxuriously over the corpse of Guy Prime, savoring the scandal, deploring the crime, rejoicing in his sense of being the first to know, Mr. de Grasse looked up at me with an enigmatic little smile.

"So much for the law, Rex. Now for you and me. De Grasse Brothers obviously can do nothing. But Marcellus de Grasse is another matter. Draw on me for what you need."

With sudden, burning tears in my eyes I took his thin cold hand in mine. "God bless you, sir. Of course, I can't accept it. Guy must go under. And I must resign from de Grasse."

"Nonsense!" The old man had risen to clasp my shoulder. "A de Grasse partnership means more than a business association. Surely you have learned that in all these years. We stand together to the end."

"But if I've hurt the firm, sir?"

"If you've *killed* the firm, we stand by you. But, of course, it won't come to that. There will be a bit of a blow, and we may ship some water, but hang on, and we'll come through."

"I still think, sir . . ."

"Oh, go home and go to bed, Rex. You know you'd feel the same way if it was one of the other partners."

It was the memory of this scene that sustained me through the agonizing days that followed. When I consider what I have been to Lucy, to Angelica, to Guy and even to my poor over-indoctrinated, over-lectured son George, I cannot help wondering if my relationship with this cool, cynical old man was not the one successful relationship of my life. We asked very little of each other, gave less and fully appreciated what we received.

In the Congressional hearing that followed Guy's conviction, Mr. de Grasse continued his kindness. He knew that this would be the hardest part of all for me, harder than the newspapers, harder than George's misery, harder than all the terrible letters. He sat by me throughout the hearing and endeavored to lighten it by whispering joking comments about the witnesses and making fun of the zealous chief counsel for the Committee. When I stepped down after my ordeal in the witness box, he muttered:

"Cohen's a cad, that's all there is to it. A gentleman can't take that kind of thing too much to heart."

Perhaps not. But since when had I been a gentleman?

My ultimate revelation came with Guy's testimony. It was not in what he said, for that, of course, was well-traveled territory, but in the way he said it. Guy was what is called a good witness: grave, courteous, patient, simple and clear. It was as if he had been called as an expert on the history of Prime King Dawson & King and was testifying with perfect detachment. It was difficult for most observers in that chamber to realize that this calm, dignified, almost magisterial gentleman would, when the hearing was over, return to the penitentiary to serve out his three-year term.

Towards his partners, his associates, his friends and creditors in that crowded room his conduct was perfect. They might have been total strangers. He spoke to nobody and caught nobody's eye. When he and I passed in the corridor he looked neither through me nor away. He simply appeared not to recognize me. Nobody would ever have the opportunity to cut Guy Prime.

As the hearing went on, as he blandly and specifically uncovered for our benevolently despotic government every last detail of his peculations, I began to understand the motives that I have outlined at the beginning of this chapter. I saw that I had been Guy's tool from the beginning, first in de Grasse and later, when he set up his own firm, as a forwarder of business. Angelica had helped, his father and his uncles had helped, even his unhappy cousin Alix, by marrying me, was meant to have helped. Everything and everyone that Guy touched, even the country club that was his dream child, had had to be molded into instruments to bring about his greater glorification. If he had spent half the energy trying to achieve success directly that he had striving for it indirectly, he might have been one of the big names of finance. But his bigness, such as it was, was to be in his failure. He had to bring us all down with him, to soil the revered name of de Grasse, to disgrace the Stock Exchange, and to give the New Deal the ammunition, which until then it had lacked, to legislate out of existence the free economy in which *he* had failed. To save the name of Guy Prime from ignominy he had to make his era ignominious. He had hoped that in the future men would admiringly say: "Guy Prime? Bad? But he was the symbol of his time, wasn't he? It may have been a buccaneer age, but you'll have to admit he was a glorious buccaneer!"

Some of his motivation may have been deep below the surface; some of it may have been even subconscious. But the point is that it was *there*. Guy had to destroy a world—a world that I still believe was fundamentally a good one—because he could not dominate it. To my dying day I will hate him for that. Now the reader may say that he was a neurotic, a child; the reader may argue that he could not help what he was doing. Very well. But so am I a neurotic, a child. I cannot help hating a man who did what he did.

Part III

Angelica

1.

WHEN REX HANDED ME his memoir, I had still not written a line of my own—at least not a line that I had kept—and I doubt if I would have ever completed it had he not given me the impetus of his straight, honest, Rex-like approach to the mystery of Guy. I suppose that this approach has a kind of truth in that it is utterly sincere and that the sincerity of its author had an important function in Guy's history. But it is still misleading. Rex never understood anyone's sincerity but his own.

He certainly never understood Guy's. He never even understood how much Guy worshiped him. I realize that Guy in his own memoir makes a great deal of his supposed hatred of Rex, but this must have come later, as hindsight, while he was brooding over the past in the rains and bars of Panama. In my early married years Rex was invariably held up to me as the model of all that a man should be. Guy had an ideal of friendship, as he did of everything else. He and Rex had to be Damon and Pythias.

Guy never lost the dangerous capacity for convincing himself that his own shimmering vision of life was the true one. It only made things worse that he was able to convince others in the same way. He could convince Rex, for example, in areas where Rex was not a specialist. He got Rex to swallow, hook, line and sinker, his whole fantastic conception of the social position of the Primes.

I loathe everything about "society" and always have. I know

that this is a frequent pose of society people, but it is no pose with me. However, as Guy and Rex seem consistently to agree on the "splendor" of the Prime family, I may as well start by exposing that particular myth. One cannot possibly comprehend the temple of illusion in which Guy maintained his nervous existence without a long, hard look at its foundation.

He knew well enough that his family were worldly and snobbish, but he reconciled himself to these unlovable characteristics by endeavoring to see them as mere details in a canvas refulgent with gold and silver tones. It is easier for an English historian to accept the streak of cruelty in the Virgin Queen if he thinks of her in her ruff collar, decked out in a thousand diamonds. But how does she look naked, without her wig, her rouge, her gems? And suppose she had never had such accoutrements? Guy saw his family as the readers of tabloids saw them, in tiaras and opera boxes. Like many people in the social world he preferred the account of a party in a gossip column to his own recollection of it.

To put it bluntly, the Primes were a shabby lot, and were so regarded, when I was a girl, by most of the people whom they sought to impress. I do not deny that they were an "old" family, as New York families go, but they were utterly undistinguished. There was no Prime patriot or statesman or judge or man of letters; there was not even a Prime fortune. The old bishop, Guy's grandfather, was famous for his unctuosity even in that unctuous age. His fawning, mellifluous tone with the rich was laughed at by people whose own bowing and scraping would be regarded as comic today. The joke on which we all used to be brought up was that, en route between two fashionable resorts, Bishop Prime was asked to stop in a humble village to confirm a class of children. When he asked impatiently if an hour would be enough, the indignant local minister was supposed to have retorted: "Let me bring the children down to the station, Bishop, and you can wave your blessing as the train goes through."

That three of Guy's uncles married great fortunes there is no disputing, but they were three very new and peculiarly odoriferous ones. And let me note here an odd social phenomenon. It was presumably the function of the Prime men (being good for nothing else that I could ever see) that they would teach their more humbly born wives the social graces. Yet precisely the opposite happened. They lost their own! Guy's uncles, and even his father, seemed instinctively to prefer the vocabulary of the parvenu to that of the gentleman born. They would always say "wealthy" instead of "rich," "estate" instead of "country place," "socially prominent" instead of "snappy." Their talk, like their over-pressed clothes, smacked of a musical comedy about Newport or Bar Harbor. I have always suspected that there was something innately vulgar in even the oldest New York society that half a dozen generations could not breed out. Guy's newly rich aunts, on the other hand, pursued a different course. They all ended up as ladies.

Aunt Amy was the one I cared for most, mother of the unhappy Alix and a most unhappy woman herself, but who, when she had not been drinking or when she was not deferring to her odious husband, was capable of the greatest affection and understanding. For all her heavy features and heavy breathing, and, alas, occasionally heavy breath, she had more natural distinction than any Prime. I remember a party at her house when she walked serenely out of the dining room in her stocking feet, having kicked her slippers off during dinner and never noticed it. But of such trivia, alas, was made up the talk of the town. If poor Aunt Amy had only had the courage of her convictions, she could have been a great woman. As it was, she was only admirable to her intimates.

It was to her that I owed most of my knowledge of the Primes. Her outward submission to Uncle Chauncey did not encompass any loyalty to his blood, and she regarded a sympathetic niece-in-law as a natural confidante. She and I might have been girls at boarding school, smoking up the chimney and running down the faculty. She told me that Uncle Reginald Prime had been suspected of cheating at cards at the Knickerbocker Club and that the Bishop, as a senile widower, had made a fool of himself by proposing to every rich widow in Newport. But most fascinating of all she told me the true story of Percy Prime's courtship of Eunice Fearing.

Guy, of course, had built this up into the romance of the ages. Yet apparently his father, far from flouting the family tradition of good matches, had simply miscalculated the quantity of the Fearing fortune. He had fallen into the habit of denigrating the success of his younger brothers in the newer social fields by telling everyone that there was more money in old New York than people suspected, and he had ended by convincing himself. Mr. Fearing had not had to promise a penny to get an ailing and aging daughter off his hands, and when death had at last uncovered the modesty of his means, his crestfallen son-in-law had no one but himself to blame.

"Poor Percy," Aunt Amy would say, shaking her head, "I almost found it in my heart to feel sorry for him. Eunice would have been a sore trial to a rich husband, let alone a poor one. He might have learned to put up with her hypochondria, but not with the constant farce that she was being brave. Eunice always insisted that illness was boring and that she could not bear to talk about her own, but I would have defied you to get a word out of her on any other subject. When I used to call, after each of her 'attacks,' she would give me a dimply smile and exclaim: 'Oh, Amy, I'm afraid I've been silly again!' Now in my experience, dearie, people who say they've been 'silly' when they've been ill, are inevitably soaked in self-pity. What a strain for Guy and Bertha! To have to live in a house pretending there was illness when there wasn't any, and pretending that they weren't talking about the illness that wasn't when they were, and pretending that poor Mamma was being *so* brave about it when the very air was infected with her panic! At least, my girls only had to put up with a bit of gin on my breath."

"But, Aunt Amy," I can remember pointing out, "you say there was no illness, but she died when Guy was only twenty-two."

"And when she was fifty-seven. She was no spring chicken, you know, when she married. That was one of the reasons Percy went after her. He was never much of a hand with the ladies. Still, I grant you, fifty-seven is young to die." Aunt Amy at the time was well into her eighties. "But I doubt if there was anything really wrong with her until the last couple of years. I think she must have frightened herself at last into a fatal illness. Eunice played sick so long that she finally fooled the gods, and they whisked her off!"

Aunt Amy's theories about her sister-in-law were echoed by Bertha Prime. Guy's sister and I always got on surprisingly well considering how different we were. All my real friends were men, and all hers were women. I do not know if Bertha was ever a practicing Lesbian—her background may have too much inhibited her—but she had all the earmarks of one: the stocky figure, the straight hair, the mannish stride. Only in her gushing sentimentality over the arts was she feminine, whereas Mother's training had taught me to approach beauty dry-eyed. Bertha felt superior to what she called my "horsy set," but she respected my directness, and she always needed an ally against the combination of her father and Guy. Her early life must have been horribly lonely.

Guy, she admitted, had always been adequately nice to her, but not so her parents. All of her father's affection and as much of her mother's as she could spare from herself had gone to the handsome boy who was supposed to make up for what life had scanted them.

"I used to think that Guy had all the breaks at home," Bertha told me, "but time proved otherwise. Poor boy, he was quite taken in. All Mummie's and Daddy's false metal rang true to his ears. But I, being neglected, learned the hard way. I learned to see through people. When I was twenty-one I had my own job and my own apartment. Daddy expected me to stay at home and keep house for him. Well, he expected in vain!"

She used to relate a terrible story about Guy and St. Andrew's School. His mother had never considered herself well enough to make the trip to Massachusetts, but in his sixth-form year, when he was captain of the football team, she at last consented to come to the St. Paul's game, the great event of the school year. The day before, however, she had a "relapse" and sent Bertha in her stead with Mr. Prime. Poor Guy, after his victory, had the humiliation of sitting at the headmaster's table at supper with his stout dumpy pig-tailed sister. And, worse still, Mr. Prime, flushed with his son's triumph and egged on by sixth formers whom Bertha saw nudging each other, held forth, like a Yankee Major Pendennis, on the glories of social life in the 'nineties and the famous Vanderbilt fancy dress ball in which he had gone as Suleiman the Magnificent. Guy must have had to work his imagination night and day to eradicate from the background of his Titianesque portrait of Papa the smirks of his merciless contemporaries!

"But didn't he resent his mother's not coming up?" I asked Bertha.

"He would have if she hadn't been so clever. You see, she knew enough to make a hubbub about how hard it was on her to have to miss her big boy's big victory. She always did this whenever Guy won any sort of game or prize. Sometimes she would even bring on a small fit to recapture the family limelight. I believe, when she was first married, that she used to do the same thing to Papa when they entertained or went out together. She would faint or burst into tears or go mysteriously upstairs—anything to ruin his pleasure in the one thing that he was good at: parties. But with Papa she had a limited amount of goodwill to run through. When that was exhausted, he left her home and dined out *en garçon*. Mother was quick to catch on when she was wasting her time—she knew that I, like Papa, was on to her

—and she turned her attention to the richer field of an only son."

"And he never caught on?"

"I thought he might be going to when she died. But all was lost in the general horror of her leavetaking. Her panic blinded him to everything she didn't ask, everything she didn't say. And then the whole family extolled him as a perfect son. How could he really be that unless he had a perfect mother? Don't those things go best in pairs?"

I suppose it was natural for Bertha to sneer at Guy for being taken in (as she believed anyway) by his mother. Gullibility is always ridiculous. One of the first things a child learns is to disguise his ignorance. But when I think of that handsome sunny-natured boy making the best he could out of a bad deal in parents, my heart is more touched than it is by Bertha's vindictiveness. How easy it is to tear a mother to bits! I should know. I did a pretty good job on my own. Maybe it's the function of parents to let themselves be so used. Maybe a mother or father is a teething ring on which the little darlings should sharpen their molars. But when one of them chooses generosity, should we shake our heads? Should we not at least weep?

Guy took that ring out of his teeth and wore it over his heart. He took the shabby home of his actuality and converted it to a glittering palace. He made of his empty fop of a father a Thackerayan gentleman, of his whining hypochondriacal mother a saint and a martyr, of his scheming uncles the titans of a splendid society. He infused his imagined world, not only with glory and elegance but with love and goodwill. He inherited a Daumier lithograph and turned it into a lace valentine.

All right, sneer, my readers. Call me dotty, senile, what you will. I realize (who better?) that all Guy accomplished in the long run by his wishful thinking was to shift the burden that should have been borne by his parents to the shoulders of his wife and children. But just now I don't care. Just now it gives me a nostalgic pleasure to remember that Guy's vision of his world, although not a particularly fine one, was a good deal finer than its reality. And perhaps it is important for me to remember it, too, for I seem to be the only person living (except perhaps for the little widow down in Panama) who has still a kindly feeling for Guy. The others think he blackened our world. Perhaps so. But only after years of trying to give it a spot of color.

2.

So MUCH FOR Guy's background. What about my own? He and Rex have already said enough to make it clear that I too had a mother problem. What self-respecting girl does not? But since I have grown old (and I am now nearing the age that Mother was when she died) I have learned to see these things more dispassionately. I have even learned to appreciate the possibility that Mother herself may have been afflicted with a female parent.

Yet still I envy her. Still it seems to me that she and all her lucky group were the last human beings to have had everything. Europe before 1914 was as yet unspoiled: they had the motorcar to flee up and down its highways and the steam yacht to scout its waters. A generation earlier, and travel was all dusty discomfort; one later and the world had fallen apart. But for the elect of Edwardian and early Georgian days, our little planet was a delectable oyster. The same long white hands clutched each other across the same Cunarder-crossed sea. In Washington one dined with Henry Adams and Bessie Lodge; in Boston with Mrs. "Jack"; in London with Ottoline Morrell and "Emerald," or else drove down to Rye to see poor old Henry James. In Paris

there was "Dear Edith," in Rapallo "Max"; in Florence "BB."
And, oh, the remorseless, insatiable thirst of Mother's friends
for the beautiful! In their talk and letters, roaming through
churches and palaces, looking at painting and statuary, sipping
wine, savoring food, even gossiping, there was hardly a minute
of the day or night when they relaxed their militant aestheticism. Yet for all their bustle and sincerity (it was true that in
time, like dope addicts, they could hardly subsist without
beauty) some of the indelible silliness of their era put its heavy
stamp upon them. Like Victorian paintings of classical scenes,
they betrayed their true date by a bright, naïve exactitude, by
an air of "dressing up," by an inner faith, peeping out like a slip
under a skirt, that all their quest of beauty was a mere charade
against the sober reality of their social snobbishness.

Many of the "elect" were critics or artists themselves—some of
them very considerable ones—but Mother was pure of the smallest foray into the world of participation. Not only did she never
compose a rhyme or paint a still life; she never purchased so
much as a watercolor or set finger to a musical instrument. She
maintained that, as art was only communication among the en-
lightened, he who received had to be the equal of he who gave.
Indeed, I suspect that Mother in her heart may have felt that
she played the superior role. After all, whereas the mere artist
had but one vision, his own, she had her own and his.

It is a pity that Mother did not take as much trouble commu-
nicating with her children as she did with her friends. There
were six of us, three boys and three girls, and until we were of an
age to accompany her on her European peregrinations we were
either left at home in Tuxedo Park with governesses, or the boys
were shipped off to boarding schools and the girls to convents.
Not that our education was neglected. We had the best of in-
struction in everything, and Mother quizzed us carefully herself
whenever she was home. But too much was left to discipline.
The best that I'll say for Mother was that, unlike Guy's mother,

she was never a hypocrite and never expected gratitude or ap-
plause.

My hardest time was the two years that followed my unspec-
tacular debut at a tea dance in the shabby brownstone that my
parents, who both hated New York, had reluctantly rented for
the season. I knew few young people in the city, and Father,
whose social ideas were of the eighteenth century ("Did you
speak to him?" was his only comment on hearing that I had sat
next to Jay Gould's grandson at dinner), absolutely forbade me
to go to college. *"Do?* What do you mean you have nothing to
do?" he would bellow at me. "Have you no needlework?" The
only alternative to spending the next two winters with him in
Tuxedo was to travel with Mother. Neither of them would have
heard of my getting my own apartment, and I had no money
except for a meager allowance. My only hope was that Mother
would stay long enough in one place for me to meet some men.

By twenty, I was in a really bad way. I had fallen in love
twice, but briefly and very unsatisfactorily: once with a big red
pig of a guards officer who was looking for a fortune and thought
all Americans must be rich, and again with Mother's Italian
courier whom even I had to disqualify as a suitor. Moody and
intractable, I derived my sole pleasure in sneering at the people
and things that Mother admired. I hated Europe, yet dreaded to
go home. I envied my New York contemporaries who had gone
unsensationally to Miss Chapin's or Brearley, made their debuts
at Sherry's and had now settled down in the suburbs with nice
young lawyers or stockbrokers. I must have been a trial to be
with. I doubt if it was entirely by accident that I left Mother's
precious inscribed copy of the privately printed *Education of
Henry Adams* on a train between Florence and Milan. It was
this episode, I think, more than anything else, that drove her at
last to action.

When she told me, one beautiful spring morning in Paris that
she had asked a "handsome young man" to go with us to Senlis, I

said abruptly that I wouldn't go. I assumed that it would be another of the twittering homosexuals whom she gathered about her as the Pied Piper did children. But Mother knew exactly what I was assuming.

"I wonder how Mr. Baylies will like him," she mused, referring to the moth-eaten old bachelor who was providing the limousine for our excursion. "Dear Henry is hardly used to football players."

Well, of course, she was being subtle, as they say, like a meat axe. But why should she have wasted anything subtler than a meat axe on me? The bait was quite enough. The next morning I was ready to go when the car came, and she was far too wise to make any reference to my change of mind.

Let nobody tell me that love at first sight is an invention of poets! Guy was waiting for us at the doorway of his hotel in a red blazer, and when he bounded towards the car sweeping off his straw hat, when I saw that crown of blond hair and those sky-blue eyes, I knew that I had never seen anything so beautiful in my life. I fell in love on the spot and remained in love for ten full years. When I emerged at the end of my amorous decade, the wife of a prosperous stockbroker and the mother of his two fine children, possessed of all the wonderful American things that I had thought I wanted, I found that it was a bit late to start my emotional life over from scratch.

The most amazing thing to me in Guy's memoir is his obvious unawareness, during the months of his courtship, of what was going on inside me. Although I naturally took the greatest pains to conceal it, I should have thought no young man could have helped but guess. The answer must have lain in Guy's uncanny talent for turning the world into a romantic stage. Looking back on our Mediterranean cruise aboard "The Loon," *I* may see a worldly mother who had lured a young man on board to get rid of a petulant daughter, but that is a set on which Guy would have promptly rung down the curtain. When he raised it again the mother would have become a benign and worldly-wise philosopher and the daughter a dark, brooding, sultry Electra. It would have been *Aeschylus* with a happy ending, where Orestes, the brother turned lover, by a valiant exercise of his brilliant personality would dissuade Electra from her morbid preoccupations and lead her to the altar with Clytemnestra smiling over an orchid in the front pew. What became of this magnificent mish-mash, of the *Oresteia* ending in *Pinafore*, if Electra simply collapsed in a heap at the first appearance of the hero from the wings?

I had some small sense of this, very early in our relationship, some faint suspicion of the role in which he had cast me and of the importance of my maintaining it, but that was only one of my reasons for resisting him with such apparent ferocity. Another was a virginal instinct of self-defense. Never had my senses been so violently assaulted, and I was appalled that a single ride in a motorcar from Paris to Senlis opposite a young man in a jump seat who directed all of his conversation, with an exasperating relish, to my vain old mother, should have reduced me to such a state of wanton submissiveness. As he and I roamed about the cathedral after Mother and Mr. Baylies, my thoughts were wildly inappropriate for a house of God. It was my first intimation that a respectable girl could be turned into a tart in an hour's time.

Worse still, much worse, he was Mother's candidate. *That* was what she thought of me. She had borne my tantrums with a maddening patience until I had lost her precious Henry Adams. That had marked the boundary of my permitted iniquities; clearly, it was time to turn on a young man. What kind of a young man? Oh, any bland young Yankee with a Charles Dana Gibson face and football shoulders, the kind one could find by the dozen, yawning through Europe, spending their days in cathedrals and their nights in bordellos, filling in the prescribed interregnum between the college years where they had left their

souls and the downtown office where they would lose their looks.
Just the kind of young man, too, that Mother most despised,
representing everything that had driven her to near expatri-
otism! But good enough for Angelica. Oh, yes, if anything, too
good for Angelica. Her total indifference to my chaperonage
aboard "The Loon" and on our shore excursions smacked of the
procuress. How could I reconcile myself to being so exactly
what she took me for?

Then there were my brothers. Unlike Mother, who never
wavered in her professed approval of Guy, they made constant
mock of him behind his back and even to his face. Poor Guy did
not recognize their sarcasms. They would pick up his banal
comments on any ruin that we visited and toss them back and
forth with ostensible admiration. I suffered obvious agonies,
which of course delighted them. It was the gentle, sympathetic
Giulio de Medici, one of Mother's epicine young men, whom
Guy so comically persisted in seeing as the object of my adora-
tion, who helped me with my brothers.

"Angelica, cara, do not trouble yourself about Teddy and
Lionel. They think they are superior to Guy because they know
Europe a tiny bit better. But it is a very tiny bit, believe me.
To us who belong here your Yankee young men are very much
alike. The difference is that we prefer the more genuine product. Look at Guy now." We were in a Sicilian village, and Guy,
in white flannels and a sun helmet, was bargaining in a bazaar, a
little crowd of successfully begging children at his heels. "He is
a generous man and a good one. Why should you be made to
feel ashamed for admiring so fine a product of your native land?
Let your brothers sneer if they want. I believe they're only envious of him, anyway."

I considered this for a hopeful moment before at last rejecting
it. "No," I said gloomily. "My family envy nobody."

"How very unwise of them," Giulio retorted. "I make a point
of envying many people. I envy Guy, for example, the pleasant

impression he makes. He thinks *I* make one on you. Which is quite all right." Giulio drooped his left eyebrow in what was as near as I ever saw him come to a wink. "Let him."

It was all too much. Guy wanted to marry me, and everyone, even my brothers, thought he was quite as good a match as I was likely to make. Guy and I, indeed, were the only persons on board "The Loon" who were not convinced that his courtship would succeed. I found myself in a shocking position, for in 1911 I was still, for all my petty revolts, very easily shocked. I wanted Guy for a lover, and I wasn't sure that I wanted him for a husband. There were moments when I thought I was going to explode into tiny pieces and be plastered from one end of the yacht to the other.

The final stage was shame. I was suddenly horribly ashamed of the whole farce. Here was a nice young man, a fine young man, as Giulio said, a young man whom any decent American girl should have been proud to marry, being taken in by a mean old woman and her two snotty sons, who were trying to pawn off a sulking, bad-tempered girl by taking advantage of his naïve faith in their supposed international sophistication! And what was the girl doing but pretending to be in love with a pansy in order to excite his passion? What a shoddy crew of expatriate adventurers! It was like a sordid parody of a Henry James tale. I had read Ibsen and Strindberg and Baudelaire and Zola. What business did *I* have acting like a coy debutante? Could I not rise once beyond the miasma of convention and live? If I wanted Guy, could I not have the simple honesty to tell him so?

So I went that night to his cabin, and the scene occurred that he has quite sufficiently related. I shall not attempt to embellish his lush paragraphs, but I will admit that he is correct in concluding that I had not realized how completely the act of love would deliver me into his power. After that night there was no further question of my not marrying Guy. Had he bade me apply a match to a fuse that would blow up "The Loon" and escape with him on a lifeboat I would have done so. In those last days of our cruise, if Teddy or Lionel dared to make a single joke about Guy, I was on them at once like a spitting cat. They soon learned to let me alone. I even tried to trap Mother into some remark that I could construe as derogatory to the Prime family so that I could jump on her, too, but she was too clever for me. She was entirely consistent in her attitude that Guy's family were all one could hope for as in-laws.

"None of the Primes were ever fat," she observed in her unexpected way. "That always seemed to me the worst thing about New York social life: the stoutness of the men and women. It may come from too little conversation and too long meals. But the Primes are civilized folk. They talk while they eat."

What could you do with a mother like that? Yet there was apt to be an uncanny relevance to everything she said. Some years later, when Guy started putting on weight, I remembered it.

Until we arrived in Paris Guy showed only his lover's side, and I lived in a state of drugged euphoria. With the announcement of our engagement, however, and preparations for the wedding, I saw a very different man emerge. Had I seen this Guy on our first meeting, he might not have exercised so strong an attraction. But it was far too late for any such considerations. Had he turned out to be the devil himself, Angelica Hyde would have been stuck.

Of course, I would have preferred the devil. I think the hardest thing that a healthy American girl can face is the discovery in her beloved of a rigid sense of the importance of social observances. Guy in Paris decided that it was time to bring me down from my cloud and to teach me to face what he considered the realities of life. What realities! The first thing I had to learn was the Prime family tree, on which he gave me, in all seriousness, a detailed lecture. The picture of such a silly topic on the lips of such a beautiful young man struck me as too ridiculous, and I interrupted him with shrieks of laughter. There was no answering mirth.

"I know it's fashionable to laugh at these things, dearest, and of course one has to in company. Nobody wants to seem stuffy. But all these social attitudes are only conventions, you know. Your friend Giulio bows to the rule that 'smart' Italian aristocrats must laugh at their ancestry, but if you ask him privately to explain his relationship to Catherine de Medici, he'll talk for an hour. Your trouble, sweetheart, is that your mother is so sincerely above these things, so genuinely intellectual, that you don't realize that underneath all the chatter most people know their family trees, if they have one, to the last twig."

This attitude was decidedly repellent to me. Not only did I reject his concept of the preoccupations of the "real" world, but I passionately rejected his concept of Mother. I told him angrily that I wasn't marrying his family tree and that I would be delighted to discover that he had been a foundling.

"Very well, I see you're in no mood for this today," he said in a mild enough tone, but with a sudden flicker of bronze in his blue stare that chilled me. "I'll come again when you are."

We had met in the sitting room of Mother's hotel suite, and now he rose. "Guy!" I exclaimed. "You don't mean you're leaving because I won't let you bore me with all those silly old Primes who are dead and buried?"

"No. I only care that you should learn about the living ones. For the most practical of reasons. When we get back to New York I expect to set up my own brokerage firm, and until I get my head above water I must depend on family business."

"You mean you want me to be a retriever!" I cried indignantly. "You want me to fawn on all your rich relations so we can get their business. I never heard anything so contemptible!"

For the first time I saw Guy really angry. His voice became deep and resonant. "You're nothing but a spoiled brat," he shouted at me. "You've taken for granted all your life that money comes out of taps. Just the way you take for granted that someone will make your bed and clean your bathroom. Well, I'm not marrying any little Miss Muffet, thank you very much.

When you've made up your mind that you want to be Mrs. Guy Prime—a very different thing, I can assure you, from being Miss Angelica Hyde—you can send a note to my hotel. Only I wouldn't wait too long if I were you."

And he walked out. He really walked out.

The next day I waited for him to send me a letter of apology, but I knew in my heart that it wouldn't come. Whatever else it might have been that I had hooked myself to, there was no question that it was a man. By evening I had worked myself into such a panic that I even appealed to Mother. As I might have known, she took Guy's side.

"There's always been a lot of that kind of back scratching in financial life," she told me. "Your father and I have been able to avoid it and see only the people we like because your father's mother had the good sense to be born a Bartelet in Brooklyn in the days when it meant something to be a Bartelet in Brooklyn. But I'm afraid your father has made rather a dent in his share of the Bartelet money. Your generation will have to go back to caring whom they ask for dinner. It's too bad, but it's the way most of the world lives."

"But, Mother," I protested, "you never could abide people who mixed business with social life! Don't you remember that man in Tuxedo who was always asking you and Daddy to dinner because he wanted Daddy to invest in his sugar company?"

"Yes, and it's a great pity we didn't," Mother said feelingly. "You and Guy could retire to Biarritz if we had. But he was such a vulgar man! I'm sure the relatives whom Guy wants you to be nice to can't be *that* bad."

"But is there no question of principle involved?"

"I should think none. The greatest luxury money can buy is choosing your own friends and snubbing the people you want to snub. Yet it's curious how few even of the old rich avail themselves of these privileges. Most of them are as cautious as the worst parvenus."

I thought Mother quite shockingly cynical, and I continued

to believe that there was something dishonorable about cultivating frumps for business reasons. As a matter of fact, I continued to feel this way right up to the time when, as an elderly woman, I married Rex. Then I discovered that the saintly Lucy, right through her lifetime, had entertained exclusively for the benefit of de Grasse Brothers. Because her dinners had been dull and stately, I had assumed that they had been disinterested. I was quite wrong.

But for all my disapproval, I still surrendered. There was never any real question about this. My little principles and prejudices were swept aside like crisp, disintegrating autumn leaves before the stiff stern broom of my aching need. Before the second day I had gone to Guy's hotel. It was true, to continue and no doubt to strain my metaphor, that those leaves were to form a compost heap that nurtured later dissensions, but at the time the issue was clear. I humbly begged his pardon.

He took it for granted, but he was still magnanimous. He took me out for a superb dinner, and we were very gay and jovial. No more was said about the Primes or even about our wedding preparations. But the very next day my lessons were resumed.

I had to write a letter to each of his aunts, and although he did not say so, it was perfectly evident that the length of each letter was governed by the size of the aunt's fortune. Grimly I determined, like a good little girl, to swallow without question whatever was placed on his inexorably extended spoon, and, after the first few gulps, I was rewarded by the taste of some sweeter elements in the ingredients of my medicine. Guy, I was relieved to discover, had more things in his mind than simple opportunism. Rich or poor, healthy or sick, weak or mighty, he never forgot a human being who had once entered his life.

Old servants of the family, old-maid cousins of his late mother living in shabby genteel retirement, old masters of St. Andrew's School, old tutors and nurses, all these had to be written to, as well. Guy could never let any part of his past go. Whether it was affection, or generosity, or simply the natural desire to strut, in the role of the young heir, before devoted retainers who tugged their forelocks as they called down blessings upon his golden head, I did not know or care. I was only too happy to make the most of each good point that I could find in my new master.

My worst blow was the arrival of his father. I took an immediate dislike to this sporty old fraud that I was never able to overcome in all the years that elapsed before his demise. Not that I really ever tried. But I did have to try to keep my feelings to myself. It was obvious even to a callow girl that Guy's passionate devotion and admiration for his progenitor were unbreakable. One had only to see them strolling down the Champs Elysée together, arm in arm, with matching gray trousers, gray coats and spats, lifting their tall hats in a uniform gesture of gallantry to a passing lady, to be convinced that one would never succeed in breaking through the clichés of a daddy who was "more of a pal than a parent" and a son who had no secrets, even of the boudoir, from his beloved mentor. Even Mother finally conceded that I had a problem with Mr. Prime.

"The thing to remember, my dear, is that men like that are never really a threat. As long as they're listened to, they won't interfere, and it's easy enough to listen. In time you can learn to think your own thoughts while they're talking."

In time I did, but in the meanwhile I had to listen to exhortations from the grandfather of my future children, of which the following may be a fair sample:

"Two attractive young people like you and Guy, my dear, should have all New York at your feet. Between you, you're related or connected to practically every family that counts, both old and new. For I am not one to neglect the new, Angelica. Some old fogies used even to suggest that we Primes had let down the bars a bit too much, but I don't think many people think that any more. To be young, to be healthy, to be hand-some—ah, my dear, what a gentle prospect for you and Guy! It may be a positive advantage for you both to have little money for a while. I won't conceal from you that I had always visual-ized Guy as marrying more of an heiress than yourself, but that was simply because the heiresses were always after him. Now I see it's even better this way. A Guy and an Angelica who had a fortune on top of everything else—perhaps it would be too much. People might be glutted by it and envious. This way, everyone will be able to *do* things for the young Primes. You'll find you're the pet couple of all the older people. Don't let it go to your head!"

As if I was apt to!

It was the arrival of Rex Geer, in the midst of all this, that helped save my day. He is gallant enough to write in his mem-oir that he was attracted to me from the beginning. I, too, found him attractive, but not in the same sense. I could see no man but Guy, and that was to remain the case, as I have already said, for a long time. What helped me in Rex's presence was to see that a man of obviously high character and ability, a man who was not in the least social, should be Guy's best friend and best man. One had only to talk to Rex for a very little while to realize that he was not in the least impressed by wealth or social pretension, that, on the contrary, he was very easily put off by these things. If he had picked Guy as a friend across the sea of snobbery in which Guy's father had sought to drown him, it must have been because he had seen that in his heart Guy was sound. And was it not equally to Guy's credit that he had picked out Rex? Did it not prove that he could substitute his own judgment for his father's when he saw fit?

And so we were married. Looking back at those first years of our shared life, I am struck at how they have run together and blurred in my mind. I was at once very happy and acutely, even agonizingly, apprehensive. To dull the latter feeling I tried

blindly in everything to adopt Guy's standards. I went so far as
to quarrel with my brothers when they sneered at our "perfect
little house" and "perfect little parties." I made it entirely clear
that I did not care to see anyone who would not accept Guy
on his own terms. But if I presented a loyal face to the world, I
often found that I could present none at all at home, and I
would turn away from Guy lest he perceive to what extent I was
not with him.

Passivity was my answer for that decade. All the people asked
to our house were Guy's friends; all the parties we attended
were given by people cultivated by him. It was Guy, the gour-
met and amateur chef, who planned the meals; it was Guy, with
his flair for color, who decided on the decoration of the living
room; it was Guy who chose the places we went in summer, the
schools for the children, my very clothes. The more vacuums
that I left the more speedily he filled them. Nor did he seem to
object to my listlessness. He adored running things. Our relationship was that of a strong, indulgent father and a pampered
child. I did as I was told and tried not to wonder too much
where, if anywhere, we were headed.

My readers may say that such a life is incredible, that I must
have "repressed," to use a psychological term, my memories of
our fights and arguments. But I do not think so. I even think
that my docility in those years was characteristic of many young
matrons of the period. It must be remembered that Guy and I
had a glorious sex life, that the birth of two children was an
absorbing experience and that there was nothing in my pre-
marital existence that I missed. Furthermore, Guy in those days
had great charm and gaiety and could be extremely amusing
when he chose. And, finally, with his passion for company, we
were rarely alone. Many of my contemporaries thought I had
everything a woman could want. Many of them would think so
today. I stilled my doubts as best I could by reminding myself
that I was what Guy had called me in Paris when he had first lost

his temper: a "spoiled brat." And who could have denied the truth of that?

But doubts stilled were not doubts smothered. There was a limit to the number of times that I could tell myself that Guy was just like anyone else's husband. There was something else about him, something that warned me, in the dusty little corner of my mind where reason still maintained its precarious existence, of a special failing. His estimates of people were always wrong. Now this might have seemed a small thing in another man, but in one so intensely gregarious and of such multiple enthusiasms, it struck me as alarming. Guy was a hero-worshiper who lived in a gallery of plaster-cast figures that he took for marble.

He was never, I will concede, wholly wrong. His "great" man of letters was always a competent writer, his great statesman an able politician, his great banker a successful accumulator. But they still looked pretentious in the golden frames in which he encased them. My mother, for example, was never quite the high priestess of the life of reason that Guy saw, nor was even Rex the Michelangelo of financiers that Guy imagined. It sometimes seemed to me that my husband's mind was turning into a private hall of fame and that the day might come when the last door that connected it to the avenue of life would be closed.

What I did not realize was that I would be the one to close it, and close it with a bang.

3.

I THINK REX is unfair when he implies that Guy may have deliberately avoided combat duty in the first war. Nobody could have prepared for it more assiduously, with all his training in the Seventh Regiment and at Plattsburg. It was hardly Guy's fault if he stuck out from the multitude as the perfect aide. General Devers could no more have missed him than could a collector of shells have missed a chambered nautilus on top of a heap of clams.

The army was Guy's idea of the true society. His astigmatism was corrected within the walls of its hierarchy. A world where power went according to rank and where it was constantly recognized by salutes and heel clicking was a world that made basic sense to him. He would have been equally happy at Versailles under Louis XIV or at Sans-Souci with Frederick the Great. Absolute authority does not repress or depress those who know how to live with it. On the contrary, they find it exhilarating.

For all his disappointment about not getting to the front, Guy's happiness in France was the greatest of his life. His letters were filled with it. He tried to make me think that I was missed and that he was saddened by the carnage from which his role exempted him, but it was no use. He was doing what he deemed vital, useful work, and he adored it. In the glitter of an international headquarters, Guy, who understood authority under every flag and insignia, knew just when to wheedle, when to cajole, when to whisper and when to shout. General Devers told me, some years later, that he had Guy's sergeant under secret orders to warn him of each move that Guy made for a transfer to combat duty. "I was not going to be left in a frog puddle without my tongue and one of my eyes."

The hardest time that Guy had in the war was when Rex visited him on leave. He wrote me a revealing letter about it which I here transcribe. I wish I had kept more of Guy's letters, for he wrote more frankly than he talked.

"Rex has come and gone. It was wonderful to have him, but terrible to see him go back to danger when the end may be so near. I did what I could to amuse him but the boys from the front live in another world. It is understandable that we at headquarters, in our nice clean uniforms, with our nice clean motorcars and all our good food and wine (not to speak of girls —for the unmarried officers, of course) should strike them as simply playing at war. And yet shall I confess it, dearest? I expected a tiny bit more from Rex. After all, he's not a raw kid, like most of them; he's thirty-one years old. He's seen enough of the world to know that it isn't the man laboring on the railroad or in the coal mine who makes the vital decisions of industry. It's that pot-bellied gentleman stroking his whiskers as he stares out the window of de Grasse Brothers. Why should war be different? And yet there is something about Rex that has always made me feel, not exactly inferior, but as if I somehow wasn't really there. At Harvard he managed to imply that I wasn't quite a student and at de Grasse not quite a banker. And now I'm not really a soldier! Sometimes I want to tweak that masterful nose of his and shout: 'Look here, old man, there are other ways of living than Rex Geer's!' "

My glimpses of such failures in Guy's self-confidence had been rare. I had seen him weep distractedly at the funerals of elderly relations whom I had not thought he had known that well, and I had heard him rave against imagined bosses in his sleep, but he had never told me that Rex made him feel like nothing. I wrote him at once, telling him that Rex was the worst kind of show-off, the silent type of stuffed shirt, but his next letter contained no further reference to Rex. It was full of the excitement of a visit of the Prince of Wales to the front. Guy's confidences were one-way streets. Sympathy only provoked collision.

I was terribly upset when he did not come home after the Armistice. He wrote me, rather pompously, that one of the liabilities of a non-combat officer was the moral obligation to stay on and help pick up the pieces, but I knew that ambition was his real motive. There was always the chance, as the great peace conference loomed and the eyes of the world turned to Paris, that an able young lieutenant-colonel with the proper connections might make his name.

Indeed, as it turned out, the one thing more suited to Guy than war was peace, or at least the making of peace. His letters began to read like the pages of Saint-Simon as the great ones of the planet filled up the City of Light. When Wilson arrived with the American Mission, Guy was assigned to it as a liaison officer and later attached to Judge Stedman, who needed an army assistant in his conferences with Italian and Balkan representatives on Dalmatian boundaries. With this Guy appeared to have reached his zenith.

"Entirely aside from the fascination of the work," he wrote me in rhapsody, "it is a privilege to live in such constant proximity to a man of the stature of Judge Stedman. I am keeping a notebook, and every night I write down the better things he has said during the day. Sometimes he is very fierce and sarcastic, but this, of course, is best! Last night he said the League of Nations should support itself by selling 'indulgences' for little wars. 'We have to have little wars,' he insisted. 'That's the trick. What we've just learned is that we can't afford big ones.' He thinks diplomacy would go out the window with war, as he thinks manners went out the window with dueling. But then, of course, it's impossible ever to tell what he really thinks. Is that a characteristic of great men?"

Mother was in New York, and fascinated by all the details of the peace treaty. For once I was the possessor of superior knowledge, and I read all of Guy's letters aloud to her.

"Why do we get it all second hand?" she demanded at last. "Why don't we go over? Get that sister of Guy's, what's her name, to move into your house and take care of the children, and you and I'll go over. Why not? I'll blow you to the trip!"

Once again I found myself back in Mother's competent hands, but oh, the difference! I was docile now and grateful as I watched her, with her customary competence, make all the arrangements—no easy feat in the winter of 1919. Only our accommodations in Paris did she leave to Guy. He had been staying in the big house by the Parc Monceau that Judge and Mrs.

Stedman had leased, but he cabled that he would secure hotel rooms and move in on our arrival. I had been apprehensive that he might feel that Mother and I were like teachers from school looming up unexpectedly in the midst of a carefree vacation, but there was no such note struck in his correspondence. He seemed perfectly enthusiastic about sharing his postwar Paris.

When I spotted him on the pier in Le Havre on the damp dark day when we arrived, his smiling face, with upturned searching eyes, was a beacon light of warmth. I burst into tears and waved my arms and made what Mother called a spectacle of myself. Guy responded superbly. He bounded over; he was the first to board the ship and he gave me a wonderful hug. Yet even in those first exciting moments, as he busied himself about our baggage, I had a quaint little feeling, distinctly unlike anything I had felt before, that we were playing a comedy for the staring people on deck, a French comedy, one from Musset. I was the *jeune fille,* just out of the convent, and Guy was the young officer whose suit was approved by my family, and Mamma was the wise old Countess who sees how pretty the young lovers are but knows how fast it all can change. Fortunately, when he and I were alone in our suite in Paris that night the stage quality of our reunion evaporated. *That* side of our relationship was all right to the very end. How I have laughed at people who claim that when a marriage fails, it fails in bed!

In the days that followed, the comedy kept coming back. Guy was very busy, but he managed to find the time to take Mother and me out to lunch or to drive us to places where he could catch a glimpse of the "big four" arriving or departing for conferences. Mother was tactful and tried to persuade him to leave her out, protesting that Paris was full of her own friends, whom it behooved her to see, but Guy always insisted that she come with us. At last I began to be afraid that he did not want to be alone with me, and with the subtlety of my generation, I blurted it all out to him. He shocked me with his look of sudden fatigue.

"Look, honey, take things easy, will you?" he begged me. "We've been away from each other for more than a year, and I've been through some pretty jarring times. Maybe I haven't been in the trenches, but that's not the only kind of hell a man can experience. Back home I took a lot of worry off your shoulders. Now it's your turn to take a little off mine. Just let things develop easily and naturally. All right?"

Well, what could have been more reasonable? I promptly assured him that I would bother him no longer with my doubts and suspicions, and I tried to assume that we were as close by day as we were by night. But I could not forget the happy note of his letters in the whole of his year abroad. If he had been so strained by worry, why had none of it appeared?

It also irked me that we had to see so much of the Stedmans, whom Guy treated as if they were Zeus and Hera. It was like the Prime aunts all over again, except that I could not see what earthly good they would do us once Guy was out of the army. However, as even Mother seemed to think that they had to be cultivated, I did my best. The old judge took a fancy to me, and I went driving with him in the afternoons. Unlike his assistants, he seemed to have a great deal of time on his hands.

"When you get to be my age," he explained, "you let the others mark up the drafts until they work their way back to the first one."

It did not take me long to discover that Judge Stedman was a very different man from Guy's hero. He was one of those dignified Southern intellectual gentlemen, tall, grave, courteous, snowy-haired, whom one associates with mint juleps, quotations from Catullus and the gentler sort of darky stories told in dialect, who, with the least bit of drawing out, could show a savage, almost anarchical cynicism and, I am sure, in male company, a fascination for obscenities. The distinctions that he had obtained in public life meant nothing to him; those that he had missed were constant sores. He had resigned from the Supreme Court of Virginia to run unsuccessfully for governor; he had given up the United States attorney-generalship to be defeated for the Senate. Of a naturally aristocratic and judicial tempera-ment, he yet hankered after success in popular politics. He was a Coriolanus who ran after the multitudes that he despised. Now, as an old man, he had come to Paris, simply another of many distinguished consultants, to help draft a peace, as he put it, "among jungle cats." He loved to orate on our drives.

"Wilson's idealism I found a bit trying until I met the people over here. When I heard every tailcoated monkey from the Bal-kans jabbering about how Mr. 'Weelson' didn't know a fig about practical politics, I began to think it was six of one and half a dozen of the other. Except 'Weelson,' bless him Jove, was at least trying. Sometimes I think he's the only one who is. Amer-ica is no longer Yankee Doodle, my dear. America is still young, but beginning to be a bit knowing, a bit paunchy. America is the tiniest bit like Guy, if you'll forgive me. Handsome, stal-wart in uniform, but *just* beginning to expand at the waist, *just* learning how to kiss the hand. And Europe—well, Europe is like my Lavinia, a bit too gay for her age, a bit too smart for her own good, fooling nobody with her make-up and convinced that it's perfectly proper to flirt with truth—even to jilt it—in the name of diplomacy."

Such detachment about a spouse told its own story. Lavinia Stedman, fifteen years younger than her husband, was still a good fifty. They had been married, he a widower and she twice widowed, ten years before—time enough for him to have learned more than he evidently wanted to know. The peace was to her a simple social oportunity. Independently wealthy, it was she who had rented the big house by the Parc Monceau and who gave the big pointless receptions. I say pointless because they accomplished nothing, even for her. Delegates simply ate and drank at them as at a cafeteria. Lavinia, swathed in veils like a contemporary movie star, dark-eyed, raven-haired, wide-hipped, smiled and blinked at everyone and went almost unnoticed. Looking back at her, I can see that she represented a bridge from *art nouveau* to the jazz era. It was as if Sarah Bernhardt had stepped down from one of her *Salome* posters to do the Charleston.

In short, she was an ass.

But an ass married to Judge Stedman, that was the point. What a fate! To write (and publish) lacquered love lyrics and know that he read them, to giggle and coo at dinner and know that he heard, to believe in one's stormy soul and be subject to the prick of his needle of dissection—it was not an enviable lot. Lavinia was one of those women who was so false that there was a kind of integrity to her very phoniness. One would have been shocked to find anything straight in her.

It was on the night of one of her parties that I was able at last to put my Paris interlude into focus. The great parlor of the house was a horrendous second empire; there was even a huge ottoman in the center with a forest of tropical plants on the back rest, and between the scarlet curtains on the windows were Bouguereaus and Cabanels of more than life-size nudes and cupids. It was a perfect background for Lavinia, had anyone noticed her. She took out some of her frustration on me, ordering me about with little whispered hints as if I were a daughter or niece in residence.

"Look, child, take a glass of punch to old Mr. White. Can't you see he's dry as a bone, poor dear? Land sakes, girlie, never mind the Arab delegation. They don't drink nohow. And where's that lummox of a husband of yours?"

That night I drank enough of her champagne to lose control of my manners. At eight o'clock I told Guy that I was ravenously hungry and insisted that he take me out for dinner. He responded curtly that we could not leave until Mrs. Stedman gave us permission. I told him boldly that I would go and ask her, at which point he took in my condition and decided that it might be better, after all, to get me out of there. He spoke to Mrs. Stedman, who looked very dark indeed, got Mother away from Mr. White, and we three went to Maxim's.

It was hardly a gay evening. I eased my heart of the stored-up venom of several weeks and told Guy that Mrs. Stedman was an old tramp. He was scandalized.

"Please, Mrs. Hyde, do something about your daughter. She's quite out of hand. Lavinia Stedman is one of the remarkable women of our time. Not only is she a poetess of merit . . ."

"You can't be serious!" I almost shouted.

"Not only is she a poetess of merit," Guy repeated angrily, trying to suppress me with a stare, "but she is a bit of a pioneer in her own right. When her first husband died and left her with a Texas ranch of seventeen hundred head of cattle, an alcoholic manager and no cash, she . . ."

"Spare us, please," I interrupted him. "Mamma and I don't want to hear the inventory of her wealth or of her charms. If you have to look for a mother in every old Southern tart that walks the boulevards, that's your affair. But don't extol her to the ladies of your family."

"Angelica, dear!" Mother protested. She had not seen me in such a mood since before I had been married. Indeed, I had not *been* in such a mood since before I had been married. Suddenly, the loneliness of my Paris visit and Guy's new strangeness was too much for me.

"A mother!" he exclaimed angrily. "Just because I had the misfortune to lose my mother early in life is no reason to make mock of me every time I make friends with a woman a few years my senior."

"A *few* years! Twenty!"

Guy looked so angry at this that I was a bit sobered. "All right, then, not your mother," I muttered with a shrug. "Call her your mistress if you like."

It so happened that I was looking at my mother as I spoke, and I caught a small involuntary sparkle of yellow in the iris of her eyes, almost as if she were trying, against her better discretion, to warn me. And then, in a moment, everything was clear. Lavinia Stedman *was* Guy's mistress. Incredible, revolting, it was still true. And everyone knew about it: Mother, the judge, everybody.

"I want to go home," I said in a dead voice.

Guy looked up quickly. "Home?"

"Back to the hotel."

I said not another word until he faced me in our hotel room, after bidding Mother good night, his back to the door he had just closed, a defiant half-smile on his lips. Guy, as the world was to learn one day, was always defiant when caught. He was a combination between Peck's bad boy and the George Washington who cut down the cherry tree.

"How *could* you?" I hissed. "With a woman that age? With Paris full of pretty girls? All right, so I grant a soldier with his wife across the ocean isn't going to be a saint, but does he have to give Granny a whirl?"

His smile faded into a rather ugly sneer. "You don't know anything about those things, little girl. Sex is not a matter of age, but experience. If you'd read your Benjamin Franklin . . ."

"I *have* read my Benjamin Franklin. But he didn't mean a woman *that* age! Honest to God, Guy, I think there's something wrong with you. I'm going to have it out with the Judge and get you transferred."

He became very white. "Do you want to kill him?"

"Kill him? Do you mean you think he doesn't *know?*"

When Guy reached out and slapped me brutally across the cheek, I think I must have been the most surprised woman alive in those surprising times.

"I ought to wash your mouth out with soap! Speaking of a great man that way! Do you know what the Judge has done for me? Why, he's educated me, that's all. He's simply educated me. He has taught me more about life and law, and men and God, than all my years at school and college put together! And you!"

I had it on my lips to suggest that if this was the case, Guy was requiting his mentor in shameful fashion, but I dared not risk another slap. Guy became more and more emotional as he ranted on about the Judge, and he finally got out a bottle of whiskey. We sat up late, I not saying a word, occasionally in wonderment stroking my bruised cheek, while he talked, in what seemed to me near hysteria, about his debt to the Judge and what it meant to have been the intimate of one of the great figures of American history. Neither of us had the bad taste to mention Lavinia Stedman again, and when we retired at last we made up our quarrel in the most conventional of fashions.

Guy went to sleep but not I. Through that long night I lay awake and considered, dry-eyed, what I had learned. I reflected that my husband had not deemed his affair with Lavinia of sufficient importance to apologize for it. He had simply assumed a furious offensive when I had, naturally enough, implied that the Judge was a *mari complaisant*. It was Judge Stedman, then, with whom Guy was in love, an old man, not an old woman, an old man in whose image he fancied he could make out the distinction that was always eluding him. Guy thought he could get close to Judge Stedman by sleeping with his wife!

These were not pretty things for a woman in love to learn. But I was no longer a woman in love. I had grown up in the course of a single night. I had had my first long clear look into Guy's soul and the frenzy of his need to identify himself with things braver and bigger than the Primes. I could never again see him as my master. He would have to be a man whom, at the best, it was my simple duty to help. My brothers, way back, had been right. Guy was ridiculous, and I was ridiculous to have married him.

The next morning, at breakfast, he acted as if nothing had happened, but I interrupted his cheerful discussion of the Stedmans' party.

"I want you to come home, Guy," I told him flatly. "I want you to resign from the army and come home with me. I've been away from the children long enough, and I most assuredly am not going to allow you to stay here and continue your intrigue with Mrs. Stedman. You needn't look at me like that. I'm not going to say a word against her to the Judge. I'm simply telling you that it is not fitting for things to continue this way, and I do not intend to put up with it. I repeat: it's time we went home."

Guy walked to the window and stared for a long time down at the Place Vendôme. When he spoke, his gentler tone seemed to recognize my new air of authority.

"It was all over anyway with Lavinia," he said. "You're right. It's time we went home."

4.

GUY AND REX BOTH speak of the little change brought by the middle years. How true! What happened to my life between 1919 and 1933? Nothing but a mystifying and relentless decline. Youth is said to pass fast enough, but middle age goes at a gallop, and one hears the refrain in the hoof beats :"Too late for this, too late for that." One learns to face the fact that all one's small ambitions are never going to be realized; that one is never going to perfect one's French or Italian, that one is never going to achieve that perfect game of bridge. One learns to accept the bitter knowledge that one is no better a parent than one's parents, and no better a spouse. One learns the humility of recognizing the sameness of human material.

When I had seen Guy once, as I had seen him in Paris, clearly and steadily, I found that I could not go back again to my old habit of blinking. I did not dislike him; I did not even disapprove of him, but I *saw* him, and what I saw I could smile at, I could even at times be fond of, but I could never love. What was worse was that Guy saw me looking at him. Sometimes I thought I could read in his eyes a desperate plea for help, but it was not uttered, and if it had been, I do not know what I should have done about it.

Why, my reader may want to know. Why could I not have reached out a helping hand? It was not as if there were other men in those years. There was never another man until Rex. What was the reason for this reluctance to do what I could for the one man who needed it?

I suppose it was my inability to forgive myself for having been such a fool. For a woman to have invested her ten best emotional years in a blind alley is a sorry state of affairs. I did not even have the satisfaction of being able to blame Guy, for he could not help being himself, and I *could* have helped seeing him as something other than what he was. It seemed to me that whichever way I turned I saw myself sneering at myself.

There was, of course, the remedy of divorce. My generation was the first to avail itself in large numbers of this new freedom and to make it as respectable for women as drinking hard liquor or smoking. But Guy never wanted it, and I was a Catholic, not a good one to be sure, but good enough to have qualms about such a step. I felt I had no business undoing a bargain that I had made when I was free and twenty-one. There was more of my mother in me than I usually cared to admit.

And so I built Meadowview and made it my refuge from the world. I turned not to men but to horses, and Guy, eager to make up for his increasingly flagrant infidelities, let me spend what I wanted. Even when the depression came, and he and I agreed to economize, I never cut down on Meadowview. I had a

Hyde feeling that money spent on horses and gardens and out-
door things was not extravagance. Because I bought few clothes
and no jewelry, because I rarely dined in a restaurant or went to
a play, because I did not gamble at cards, I was able to convince
myself that I was economical. My needs were "basic": plants,
live stock and a house whose beauty should edify the country-
side. Guy and I ruined ourselves expressing our natures in brick
and mortar: he with his country club and I with my home.

There were men who made up to me occasionally, usually
members of our hunt, but I had nothing to do with them. It was
as if, in those years, tearing across fields and through woods,
leaping ditches and fences, I was trying to forget my long sub-
jection to sex, yearning to recapture my virginity and escape
men forever in the guise of Diana. They were nervous, foolish
years, but they were not altogether unhappy ones.

Unhappiness came with Rex and with the return of love.
When we started riding together, I understood, almost at once,
that it was a serious involvement. This grave, deliberate, obviously powerful man impressed me as the very embodiment of
everything that Guy was not. I was adequately armed against
any man with anything of Guy in him, and for years there had
seemed to be none without. But now it was different. Now I
was faced with something I had ceased to believe in: a total man
who was also a total gentleman. I am afraid I acted like a teen-
ager on her first date with the captain of the high school football
team.

I certainly must have been obvious, for Rex knew right away
that I had my eye on him, and Rex, at that time, knew very little
about women. He has had occasion to learn more since. This
will make him angry, but he never knew, for example, and neither did Guy, what was the matter with Alix Prime. Alix fell in
love with *both* of them. That same summer, when her father
took her away, she fell in love with a sailor on "The Wandering
Albatross." Alix, in short, was a bit of a nymphomaniac, and her

subsequent goings-on had a good bit to do with Freddy Fowler's suicide. I have spared Rex's pride all these years, but now that we seem to be telling everything, he may as well know that, too.

Oh, the Primes buried it, of course. Trust them! The Primes were masters at the art of covering up. Aunt Amy's drinking, Uncle Reginald's slipperiness at the card table, the awful legend about the old bishop and the pretty choir boy—well, Alix's problem was relatively simple. Guy was never told about it, because Guy, for all his great popularity with the family, had a reputation (well deserved) for conversational indiscretion.

I had no qualms about my affair with Rex. It seemed to me to be nobody's business, even that (may He forgive me!) of my Catholic God. My children were almost of college age; Lucy Geer, poor creature, had become a wife in name only, and Guy had pledged his marital rights for an easy loan. Whom was I really hurting? Did not life owe me *one* piece of unsullied bliss? Of course, I can see now that I was hurting three people badly: Lucy, Rex and, most of all, Guy. Yes, most of all the person who had forfeited all right to feel hurt.

But I never despised Guy as a cooperative cuckold, as he seems to have thought. I was simply angry at the least interference with my affair and brutal to Guy when he offered any, even if it was only a social engagement to which we were both committed. His good nature about Rex was more disarming than contemptible. His attitude seemed to be one of congratulation on my good luck in finding love on this planet of disillusionment. Once he went so far as to say that if Rex should ever bring himself to seek a divorce, he would not stand in my way. Small wonder that I did not suspect that he was seething underneath! Knowing his long standing worship of Rex I wondered if he did not somehow view the possibility of my becoming Mrs. Geer as a personal triumph. This may sound fantastical, but had I not observed him trying to get closer to Judge Stedman by sleeping with his wife?

The parallel with Mrs. Stedman is reinforced by the fact that, after Guy and I had our first candid talk about the affair, his attitude began to change. He started to court me again. Perhaps in his fantasties I had actually become Rex's wife, and therefore he could revenge himself by making Rex the cuckold. Or did he rather wish to cement his intimacy with Rex by sharing Rex's mistress? In any case he was always now looking at me slyly, sidling up behind me to slip a hand around my waist, blowing kisses at me over the dining room table. It was his rather fatuous theory that any woman could be broken down by enough of this. I felt that I was being treated like a tramp and became very indignant. At last, after his revolting sentimentality at the Glenville Club dinner and his coarseness in alluding to the possibility of our future issue, I fled the house to take refuge at Rex's. Little did I dream that in six months' time I would be pregnant, and by my lawful husband!

I returned to Meadowview that night, crushed in defeat, with hate in my heart, led, as if on a leash, by my triumphant mother. Like Hermione in *Andromaque* I would have been capable of urging Guy to slaughter my smugly virtuous lover. But Guy had no such murderous intentions. He was entirely concerned with our reconciliation and treated me as a nurse might treat a hurt child, which was as good a way as any to treat me. It was not long before he obtained what he wanted. How could it have been otherwise? He was my husband; he was gentle; he was *there*. And I was wild with anger and humiliation and the need to hurt Rex for preferring his peace of mind to my caresses.

Guy interpreted my response to his love-making as proof of his own irresistibility. But, far more than that, it was evidence of my own passion to do something for any human being who needed me (even my own husband!), to fill in the terrible vacuum left by Rex's holy departure. If I had once felt in that period that Guy really loved me, it is possible that our reconciliation would have been the beginning of a new life. But Guy did not love women. He conquered them. His idea of the act of love was a kind of rape, and of a man's greatest triumph in the seduction of a woman who sincerely loved another. His heart was always a virgin.

Maybe he was afraid that a woman who really loved him might have pitied him. Or maybe, having deep down so low an opinion of himself, he despised her for her bad choice. At any rate, he never encouraged me to love him as I interpreted love, and he was entirely satisfied with what to me was the cheap carnival of our briefly renewed intimacy. After my miscarriage we never made love again.

Guy charges me with inducing this event. If I did, it was not consciously. It is perfectly true that I went riding, and even jumping, against what he claimed was the doctor's advice, but he never stopped to consider how essential this exercise had become to my mental and physical well being. In my other pregnancies I had ridden almost to the last month. When I realized that my renewed intimacy with Guy was not going to do anything for either of us, that I had betrayed my and Rex's love for nothing of value, I had to go back to my horses to prevent a complete nervous collapse. In that state, I am sure, I would have as surely lost the baby.

As to his accusation that I did not want to have my pregnancy known because I did not want Rex to know of it, just the opposite was true. In my fury against Rex I would have been delighted to fling it in his teeth! As it turned out, anyway, Rex did not learn of it until I mentioned it to him, quite casually and thinking he knew, two years later. By then my rancor was gone, and I was merely distressed to find that I had hurt him.

My rancor, indeed, disappeared with the convalescence that followed my miscarriage. During the slow, dull days, lying in bed too listless to read, I did a lot of thinking. The most important result of it was that I forgave Rex. I comprehended at last the torture that adultery had been to him, and I even suffered at my new understanding of his suffering. Months later, when I met him by chance at Mother's, I was able to be jocose, if a bit metallic. He was relieved, and he was hurt. That was as it should have been. My life was under my own control again. I went back to my hunting and Guy to his deals and his girls, each a bit more reckless, each a bit more frantic, and so we remained until the final debacle.

5.

I ASSOCIATE THE disastrous summer of 1936 with beaches, at the Cape and on Long Island. Whenever I left my adored Meadowview, I used to seek out surroundings that were as opposite to it as possible. Guy had told me that he would not be able to get away that summer, occupied as he ostensibly was in liquidating his firm, in accordance with his promise to Rex, so I took a cottage at Cape Cod where Evadne and I would be able to sit on the sand and look at the sea and enjoy the long talks that mothers and about-to-be-married daughters were traditionally supposed to enjoy.

Evadne, however, was just as self-contained engaged as she had been free, and I found that I had all the time I should have needed to plan how Guy and I would live when he retired. I would walk miles down the beach and sit by myself, a lone speck of humanity under wheeling gulls, and speculate idly on where we would go if we had to give up Meadowview. And then my thoughts would drift into a sun-beaten, sleepy incoherence, and I would abandon myself to the negative delights of passivity. I might have been a clam on that seashore for all that I accomplished. But the real reason that I could not think about this particular future was that I did not believe it would happen. And it didn't.

George Geer used to come up on the weekends, and one Saturday morning, when I was sitting under my usual dune, I made out, way down the beach, his white-trousered figure approaching. It was not like him to leave Evadne to seek me out, and I had a vague feeling of apprehension. He greeted me cheerfully enough, but his eyes avoided me. George, happily for one of Evadne's strong character, was less formidable than his father, but he was no better an actor. He sat down in front of me and scooped sand with both hands.

"Have you and Vad had a quarrel?"

"No. Why?"

"Where is she, then?"

"Back at the house. No, it's not Vad that's bothering me. I'm terribly sorry to say this, Mrs. Prime, but I'm afraid your husband's not sincere about retiring. Instead of going out of business, he seems to be going a great deal further in. He's borrowing again."

I could see why Evadne loved this boy. He was so earnest and good that one wanted at such moments to hug him. Those sad brown eyes betrayed a heart that, unlike most hearts, really suffered at the prospect of others suffering. I was touched that he should assume that I cared as much as he did about what Guy was up to. Of course, I cared, but it did not surprise *me* that Guy should double-cross a friend.

"Can't my husband change his mind about retiring?" I asked.

"He gave Dad his word of honor."

"Did your father tell you why?"

Now, at last, those eyes, like Rex's, confronted me. "He told me everything, Mrs. Prime. My father trusts me. And he told me that *you* would see that the agreement was carried out."

"Did you tell Evadne?"

"Oh, Mrs. Prime, what do you think of me? How could you imagine that I'd destroy Evadne's faith in her father? This whole business has driven me almost frantic. If it ever becomes public, I think it will kill Evadne!"

I looked at him musingly. "It won't kill Evadne," I said, with a touch of grimness. "But I'm beginning to wonder what it will do to *you*. I suppose I'd better go and see Guy."

"But he's all the way down in Westhampton with Miss Prime!"

I rose now to my feet and smiled at him. "Then I suppose I'll have to go all the way down to Westhampton to Miss Prime's!"

It was eleven the next day, a Sunday, when a taxi from the station set me down at my sister-in-law's old shingle beach house. Bertha was standing on the front steps, as I drove up, peering down in her cross way to see who her uninvited visitor might be.

"Why, Angelica! Is anything wrong?"

"Perhaps I should ask that of you. Have I come too unexpectedly? Has Guy got one of his girls here?"

Bertha became crimson. "What do you think I keep here? A disorderly house?"

At this point her little group of guests, except for Guy, came out of the house, all dressed for church. What a crew! Guy has described them, and I will not repeat him, except to say that he was charitable. I was told that he was walking on the dunes, and I went to the porch in back to wait. As I sat there, once again looking at the sea, I tried to imagine wherein lay the charm for such a man in Bertha and her collection of lame ducks. It was certainly a side of him I had not seen before.

"So you couldn't stay away from me, is that it?"

I had slept badly on the train the night before, and I must have dozed off, for I awoke with a start to find Guy standing over me, smiling broadly but somehow impersonally. He was dressed in white, wearing a Panama hat and smoking a cigar. With his bull neck and big shoulders, his thick curly hair and wide girth, he might have been a magnificent overseer, stopping by, whip in hand, to look over a new slave. The impression, anyway, was enough to put me on the offensive.

"I hear you've been borrowing again."

"Who told you that?"

"George."

"When the old watchdog's away, he leaves the puppy to guard me, is that it?"

"The boy's only doing his duty."

"Boy!" He snorted loudly. "I suppose Rex told him the whole pretty story. He would." Then he seemed abruptly to weary of George. He walked over to a wicker chair and sat heavily down. "Very well, Angelica, I've been borrowing. What's it to you?"

"Do you forget that you and I promised Rex that you would close the firm? Is borrowing necessary for that?"

"It could be. It so happens that it's not."

"Then you admit you're breaking your promise?"

"A promise given under duress is not valid."

"Duress? After what Rex did for us?"

"Rex never did anything except for himself."

"Oh, Guy!"

"Oh, Angelica!" His tone mocked me.

"You give me no alternative," I said angrily. "I shall have to cable him."

"What can he do about it?"

"You're not so grand, my dear, that a word from Rex can't shut off your credit!"

"But what would he gain by saying that word? Three hundred and fifty thousand dollars is a pretty stiff sum to lose, even for the pleasure of seeing *me* in a bankruptcy court!"

"The money means nothing to Rex. It's a matter of honor."

"Oh, honor." Guy shrugged and took a deep pull at his cigar. Then he turned away to contemplate the sea. "Well, you honorable people had better do what your honor dictates. But don't talk to me about it. I have nothing to do with such things."

He sat absolutely still now except for the mechanical gesture of lifting his cigar to his lips. For several minutes I watched him watching the sea. I had a curious feeling that he was no longer conscious that I was there. There was an extraordinary power of rejection in that stocky white motionless figure.

As we continued to sit, watcher and watched, on the big veranda of that crazy old shingle house, I wondered again why he was there. There was nothing in the house or in its weatherbeaten furniture, or in its mild, sweet, faintly nutty occupants that had anything in common with Guy. Nothing except Bertha, and she, I suppose, represented childhood. Was Guy trying to return to his childhood? Was he rejecting all that had happened since?

I felt a thickening in my throat as I pictured, behind that humped, seated figure, my beautiful bridegroom of a quarter century before. How he had seemed to bound at life! How he had grasped at all its good things: friendship, romance, success! It struck me that they had all rejected him, that they had sent him back to Bertha. And now he was through. Now, a sullen child, he was signing off.

"Guy," I pleaded, "we're not all against you, you know."

"Which of you is not?"

"*I'm* not."

"Yet you're about to cable Rex. You're about to let your former lover put your husband out of business."

His tone was extraordinary. It was devoid of the least anger or bitterness. It was detached, remote, factual, bored.

"But I'm not!"

"You mean George will do it for you?"

"No, because I'll tell George . . . oh, I don't know what I'll tell George!" I got to my feet in astonishment at my own commitment. But I knew now that I could not join the pack against this broken man. "Tell me what to tell George, Guy!"

He eyed me curiously, I suppose to assess the staying power of my reaction. "Tell him I've been borrowing to pay off an old debt." His voice was level, but I thought I could nonetheless detect a throb of eagerness in it. "Tell him I'll be out of business by Labor Day."

"And if everything goes to rack and ruin, it will all be my fault?"

Guy actually chuckled. "That's it, my girl. If everything goes to rack and ruin, it will be *your* fault." He rose and crossed the porch to put his hands on my shoulders. "But stick by the old man, and he won't let you down." I stared into the blue expressionlessness of his eyes and wondered if anyone had ever known this man.

"Suppose you call me a taxi," I proposed.

"Are you going back to the Cape?"

"No, I'm going to Southampton. I'm going to my brother Lionel's. I think I'll stay there awhile. Then I won't have to face George. I can be more convincing by letter, don't you think?"

Guy nodded as he considered this. "Let me write it out for you," he suggested. "That will be best. You can copy it when you get to Lionel's."

Together we went into the library, and the letter to George was drafted. It was my first intrusion into Guy's business life, but I admitted a very large steer into that porcelain cabinet. I have never been properly ashamed of this, as no doubt I should have been. Had Rex been home, I might have consulted him. But I could not side with young George against my poor old husband. There are loyalties that may be senseless, but there they are.

Reading Guy's trial in the newspaper, I learned that it was *after* my visit to Westhampton that he plundered the family trust. Had I cabled Rex as I had threatened and had he put a stop to Guy's activities, I might have saved him from jail. But I do not believe that Guy would have thanked me. He was perfectly content with the progress of the events that he had set in motion.

If I had had any doubts about this, they would have been dispelled by his behavior on the fatal day when his firm was suspended from trading. Rex had telephoned me in the morning and told me the whole story. I was obviously not too surprised, but I was dazed. Typically, I went out for a long ride and returned to find the house full of friends calling to offer their sympathy. Of course, they had heard only of the failure of the firm, not of the reason for it. Then Guy himself strode in and made the speech in which he announced his pending indictment.

What most struck me about that little oration was how carefully rehearsed it must have been. No man could have been at once so concise and so effectively dramatic had he not planned it that way. The same eerie conviction came over me that I had experienced at Bertha's in Westhampton: Guy was delivering a long-planned valediction.

The offer that I made him, when the friends had gone, to share disaster as we had never shared prosperity, was perfectly sincere. Not only did I feel a responsibility in not having acted to interrupt his downward course, but I did not see that I was any use to anybody else. Lucy Geer was right when she told Rex that this was the challenge I had waited for. I never had a moment's doubt as to where my duty lay. This sick man, this sinner, this compulsive escapist was my husband. Where else did I belong but at his side?

His rejection of me was calculated and complete. He told me how I should live until Lucy Prime should die. I remember falling on the living room sofa, sobbing with uncontrollable anger and humiliation, and when I got up, he was gone. I never laid eyes on him again. In prison he refused to see me, although he saw Percy, and when he came out he hired a lawyer who wrote to tell me that his client was seeking a divorce. By then, however, I was ready for it, and our marriage was dissolved very

simply and without undue publicity by a Reno decree. I had
learned the futility of trying to stand between Guy and his imagined liberty. Nothing was going to keep him from the particular suicide that he had planned so long.

6.

NOT EVEN PERCY could break through the barrier that Guy
erected. He visited his father once a month during the whole of
his prison term and reported that he found him affable and
friendly, but that it was like talking to a stranger. Guy would
listen to Percy's account of his problems and enthusiasms as a
law student and make polite answers. Poor Percy was upset by
his inability to narrow the gap.

"I'm sure that Dad's convinced himself that he is only a liability to us and that the sooner we forget him the better," he told
me. "If only I could make him see that it would help *me* to be
close to him!"

Percy never succeeded in this, but I was proud of him for trying. Of all of us, he came out of our tragedy the best. He
seemed to mature overnight, and having started Harvard Law
School as a playboy, he ended as an editor of the Review.

Evadne's problem was harder. She married George, when he
at last convinced her that she would not disgrace him, and they
are very happy together, but neither he nor I were ever able to
persuade her to see her father. She was altogether inexorable in
her condemnation.

"It is not the embezzlement," she kept repeating to us. "If he
were ten times a thief, he would still be Daddy. But when
George's father stuck out his neck for him, and Daddy broke his
word, that, to me, was unforgivable. Mr. Geer has suffered far

more in all of this than anyone else. Daddy told me to be a Roman and adopt my husband's family. Very well, I'm doing so. I'm all Geer now."

There was a point in Evadne's argument that I could not entirely deny. Certainly, George and his father had been badly treated. But I do not for a minute believe what Rex believed: that Guy deliberately embroiled him in his disgrace. That was not the way Guy's mind worked. I am sure that he had no conception of how great the scandal of his trial would be. He intended to bow quietly out of society as simply another of the numberless embezzlers of financial history and start a new life for himself. He intended to leave all of us better off by his departure, even Rex, who, if he lost the money that he had put up, was to be compensated with me. Guy was a testator who planned to survive the probate of his own will and to watch from afar his legatees enjoying their bequests. But what he was going to enjoy most of all was his own liberation into a new life: a life that would be just like the old with one all-important exception. He would not disappoint anybody in it, including himself, because nobody in it would have expected anything else of him, including himself. This life he was to find in Panama.

In support of my supposition that Guy was seeking extinction and not revenge, I submit here the letters that he wrote to our children on that last night at Meadowview, before he was placed under arrest. The first is to Evadne.

"My own darling daughter: from your face today and from your paucity of words, I see you are all Geer and no longer Prime. That is as it should be. In ancient Rome a wife was adopted by her husband's family and ceased to be a member of her own, even for purposes of inheritance. This was a wise system and avoided many complications. Your mother would never become a Prime. Profit by her error and cease to be one.

"You told me that you were ashamed now to marry George. Forgive me, dearest, if I say this is drivel. The scandal of my conviction will be blown away in five years' time. And if the sins of the fathers are visited on the sons, I never heard that they were visited on the daughters. Because I have made George suffer, must you? Surely you will see that it is rather your duty to make up to him for my misdeeds by becoming a good wife.

"And now I am going to give you a piece of advice that will not be agreeable. Do not desert me too openly. People will be very critical if you do. Come to visit me in the pentitentiary. I will make it very easy—you will not even have to see me. But you will win golden opinions from the multitude. I would suggest further, if it doesn't sound too cynical, that you take, for a couple of months anyway, a job as a secretary or receptionist. By the time you become Mrs. George Geer you will be so admired for your fortitude in adversity that you will bring more luster to old Rex than you would have in the greatest days of Meadowview!

"That is how to play the hand I have dealt you. That is what I expect of my girl. Farewell."

But Evadne was not to be persuaded by any such arguments as these. She refused to take the smallest advantage of her situation to win the approval of a sentimental public. It was her idea of integrity to fling in the face of our world her repudiation of her father, and our world made her suffer for it. People said terrible things about Evadne. They said that she was ashamed of her father. They said that she had made a rich marriage to get rid of her old name and her new poverty. It was a great pity that her engagement to George had not been announced in the newspapers before Guy's disgrace. But Evadne was able to stand up to sneers. The only thing I worried about was the possibility of her subsequent remorse, a worry that has now been to some extent justified. As for Guy, I knew that Evadne's scorn would not reach him. He had immunized himself from more than his family.

Guy's letter to Percy was even more matter of fact.

"My own dear boy: this is not a time to mince words. You have never had the highest opinion of me, and events have amply borne you out. But you have always been a good son, and now you are exempted from further duties. You will find that you will do better in life on your own than as a child of privilege. Like many fathers, I have been obtuse about such things. My fall may give you the jolt you have needed. That, anyway, must be my consolation. But to the point.

"There is one important service that you can render your mother. Standard Trust Company will be bound by law to restore the money I took from the Prime trust. They were obviously negligent in allowing me, even as a co-trustee, to have possession of the securities for so long a time. Even if your mother should want to let them off the hook, it would still be beyond her power to do so, because unborn Primes and collaterals have a contingent interest in the money. What I want you to do, therefore, is to persuade your mother to accept the income and rebut any of her grand ideas of renunciation. If you will all only do as I tell you, everything can still be all right!"

Percy and I were simply surprised that Guy knew us so little as to suppose that we would ever touch a penny of the money that the bank was forced to restore because of *his* peculation. Ultimately an arrangement was worked out whereby the trust income was accumulated, and on my death it will go, with the principal, to Percy's and Evadne's children. As they were not living when the moral question arose, I assume they will feel that they can take it with impunity. I hope so, for if not, it will go to old Bertha who, I am sure, will survive us all!

When I had time to consider my own position, I found that,

except for Meadowview, I was penniless, and Meadowview was condemned that same year by the state. One of Mr. Moses' favorite highways was run through the house itself. It seemed an appropriate finale to the saga of the Primes. The wicked were jailed and destroyed, and a beneficent government would not, even after a law suit, give me more than a hundred and fifty thousand dollars for the place (remember, it was 1937). When I had given Percy enough to complete his law school education and paid all my expenses I found that I had three thousand a year to live on. This was not starvation in those days, but it was penury for one who had lived as I had lived.

I was planning to set myself up as a riding instructor when Lucy Geer sent for me. There was a vacant superintendent's cottage on their place, a charming old Long Island farm house, that would be at my disposal, with water, gas, heat and electricity thrown in and service from the gardeners and maids at the big house. Add Lucy's open invitation to all meals and I could pretty well spend my little income on clothes!

"Now before you refuse it pointblank in a glorious gesture of pride," Lucy warned me, "let me tell you something. I am not asking you to take it for your own sake or for Rex's. I am asking you to take it for *mine*. I am a sick woman, and I need a lot of attention. Believe me, Angelica, you will more than earn your keep."

It was so big of Lucy to put it that way that I burst into tears and, after making a sloppy scene, I accepted. For the ten years that she survived I lived gratefully in that farm house and saw her daily. I came to be as close to her as I was to Rex, closer in many ways, for Lucy had an understanding and a shrewdness about people that made communication extraordinarily simple. She was a bit like my mother, if my mother can be imagined as an unworldly woman.

Rex suffered a long nervous depression after the Congressional hearing. For a period of almost half a year he did not go to his office. His silence and his abstraction made our curious triangle a simpler one to live in. Lucy and I both ministered to him, and in doing so we almost forgot the brief time when our relationships had been so different. When Evadne and George had their first little boy, we were drawn even closer together. He was a grandson, after all, of all three of us.

Rex emerged from his depression a gentler, kinder man. He was less irascible with those of whom he disapproved, less impatient with those whose efficiency did not match his own. He lost some of his severity, some of his awesome, magisterial quality. What he and I had been to each other the reader knows. But now we became friends, deep friends, in a friendship that revolved around Lucy. In the last years of her life, despite increasing pain, I think that the three of us achieved something like peace, something even like happiness.

When Lucy died, nobody, even Evadne, with all her Prime sense of propriety, thought that Rex and I had to wait a year before marrying. It was so indicated, so obvious, so precisely what Lucy herself had wanted. I was sixty, Rex was sixty-two. Whom, in any event, should we have consulted but ourselves?

We have been married now fourteen years. I do not know if either of us would go quite so far as Rabbi Ben Ezra, because there are a lot of nasty physical things about old age, but they have been good years, and I am grateful to my Rex for them. I am also grateful to my God. Mother always said that my Catholic faith would become stronger towards the end, and she was right. Therefore, because Rex and I have agreed to read each other's memoranda, I will close with a request to him. Now that Guy's death has removed the impediment, I want him to marry me in the church.